SPIES LIKE ME

Also by Doug Solter

Skid

Rivals

Legends

My Girlfriend Bites

SPIES LIKE ME

BOOK 1 OF THE GEMS SPY SERIES

Doug Solter

First Trade Paperback Edition

ISBN-10: 0-9981466-0-9

ISBN-13: 978-0-9981466-0-7

Cover Art Design by Travis Miles

Website: www.probookcovers.com

To my mom, who taught me just how strong a woman can be.

SPIES LIKE ME

CHAPTER 1

The school's auditorium stage was bathed in colors. White for the actors. Orange for the wooden set representing the faraway pyramids of Egypt. Blue to emphasize the painted sky backdrop above it all. It was the opening night performance of *The Spy Who Loathed Me*.

Emma Rothchild strutted across the stage in a gorgeous floor-length silk dress, her costume for this scene. Tonight, she craved the eyes of the audience and knew this dress guaranteed their full attention.

Emma was deep into character. She was Russian spy Olga Tetrovich. Emma had studied online videos of Russians speaking candidly and mimicked their accents as best she could. Her drama teacher had complimented Emma on her dedication to the craft.

The MI6 spy George Bond followed Olga on stage, but hid behind a fake tree. The actor's rich brown skin might be a shock to the 007 spy traditionalists in the audience, but Emma hoped that his performance would win them over. Bond was following her in this scene, thinking she would lead the English spy straight to the microfilm that was stolen from him by a Brazilian dwarf named Tatu.

From a souvenir stand, Emma picked up a clay model of the pyramids, something a tourist would buy at a market. She smashed the stage prop against the table in dramatic fashion and held up the roll of microfilm hidden inside so the audience could see it.

George Bond made his move. He crept up behind Emma without detection while she slipped the microfilm into her small hand purse. Emma's hand came out holding a cap-gun revolver.

She pivoted on her heels, making her dress swoosh around her ankles, and aimed the gun at Bond. The move looked great in rehearsals.

"I don't think so, Mr. Bond," Emma said, with her gentle Russian accent. "Our brief partnership is at an end. I have what my government wants. Now I will take my revenge. Do you remember that man you killed in Vienna?"

"Yes, I do," George Bond said.

"He was my lover."

Emma waited for Bond's next line.

But the actor hesitated.

Emma was about to lose it. Did Lewis forget again? They'd rehearsed this scene, like, twenty times.

"What do you have to say about that, Mr. Bond?"

The line was an ad-lib, something to draw the next line out of the boy's mouth.

Lewis's face was a river of sweat as his eyes glazed over, the actor turning himself into just another tree on stage.

"Your silence is a good enough confession for me. Any last words before I fire?" Emma went off script, but Lewis could pick his line up there. She was trying to help him.

But the boy shook his head. Lewis wasn't taking the hint.

Emma pulled the trigger and the gun hammer snapped forward. She squeezed the trigger numerous times in a series of loud snaps. Emma dropped the weapon. "You planted that empty gun in my handbag, didn't you?"

Lewis nodded. Okay, he'd reacted to that ad-lib.

It was a sliver of hope, so Emma went with it. "Then I'll have to kill you with my bare hands." Emma approached Lewis with her arms raised in a karate-looking stance. The boy blinked, still trapped inside his scary place. What could Emma do now? Physically attack him? Bond was supposed to seduce the Russian agent, not have her attack him.

Then a breath of inspiration hit her.

Emma grabbed Lewis's shoulders. She guided him over to a bench on the set and made him lie down. Emma plopped her body on top of Lewis and pretended to struggle with him. Emma whispered into his ear, "Now get up and glare at me, Lewis."

His eyes blinked again. Lewis rolled out from under her and

stood on stage. Emma pressed her back against the seat of the bench and stayed there while Lewis glared.

Emma labored her breathing, as if she were being seduced. "Oh, why can I not kill you, Mr. Bond? What power do you hold over me?"

Lewis didn't move, his glare frozen on his petrified face.

Emma knew this would work better if Lewis helped sell it, but...she lifted herself from the bench like a graceful ballerina, trying to act seduced by Bond's man-powers. "Why can I not kill you, Mr. Bond?" she repeated.

Emma went for his lips, kissing Lewis with passion, as if the male spy had successfully messed with her brain. As Emma eased her lips away from his...life came back into Lewis's eyes. He gripped Emma and pulled her towards him and they kissed again.

Finally, the boy was acting.

It was a great kiss...until Lewis inserted his tongue into Emma's mouth.

She pushed him. "Mr. Bond...I can't resist you." She rushed the line out so fast she forgot to include her accent.

"Give me that microfilm, Miss Tetrovich," Lewis said, finally picking up his line.

Now it was Emma who was knocked off her game. That kiss completely took her out of character. The heck with it.

Emma tossed the microfilm down on the stage near Lewis without protest. The quicker they got out of this disastrous scene, the better.

* * *

The rock-climbing wall loomed above one end of the track-and-field oval. Emma wondered why her new school had a rock-climbing wall. Even at Van Dorn Hall they didn't have one, and it wasn't from lack of money. But Emma was learning that Berkeley...and California itself...was *so different* from New York.

Inside her parked car, Emma glanced at the plastic cap gun sitting on the passenger's seat. She'd used her own purse during the play and had forgotten to take the prop gun out before she left Friday night. Maybe Emma could sneak into the backstage storage room during lunch period and slip the gun back into the props box before someone saw her. She unzipped her backpack and slipped the gun inside a pocket.

Stepping out of her Mercedes, Emma slung the backpack over her shoulder and pressed on the key fob, making the car chirp as it locked its doors. A group of kids huddled around their ten-year-old Chevy gave her a look. Most of the cars in the student parking lot were much older than Emma's. And none of them were as nice.

Emma avoided their stares as she headed into school.

The commons area was crowded with students. Each circular wood table represented some collection of friends. It was ten minutes until first period and Emma already had her books, so she picked a quiet corner and sat on the floor with her back against the wall.

She checked the status updates of her friends in New York. They were on Eastern time, so it was lunch period there.

Emma found a post by Hayley. It featured a group selfie of five girls crowded around a booth at Horowitz's Deli down on Forthy-Ninth Street. That deli was their usual hangout since it was a football throw away from Van Dorn Hall. Her friends were smiling in their school uniforms, having an awesome time being together. As if they'd forgotten all about that missing sixth girl.

"Yo," a male voice called.

Emma lifted her eyes and saw Lewis standing there, holding a breakfast bar with an open pint of chocolate milk. His George Bond tuxedo had been replaced by shorts and a Manchester United soccer jersey.

"Thanks for the assist Friday. Meant to say something after but…forgot."

"The show must go on. So I made it go on." Emma didn't know what that was supposed to mean, but she let it go.

Lewis drank out of his tiny milk carton and took a moment to swallow. "Why'd you throw the microfilm down on the stage? That's not cool. Ruined the scene. A professional actor wouldn't lose it like that."

Emma wanted to say a professional actor wouldn't freeze on stage and blow half his lines in a live performance. Where did

Lewis get off telling her how to act?

"I was frustrated with the situation."

"You need to hide it better on stage." Lewis drank his milk again.

Emma couldn't help herself. "We went over that scene ten times. You should have nailed your lines, not leave me alone on stage, trying to save the entire production."

"I blew one line. You didn't have to 'save the entire production.' Get over yourself. Lucky you even got the part. How long you've been in our class? Five months?"

"I got that part because I'm good, unlike you. It's obscene how much you charm Mrs. Tuttle in class. Of course she put you in the lead role. It's just a shame you can't act." Emma's emotions were boiling over and she couldn't stop. "And while we're talking about being a professional? What's with that tongue diving you did on stage? George Bond seduces Olga with a kiss, not treat the roof of her mouth like a Popsicle."

Lewis scoffed. "You seemed to like it."

Emma glared as he walked with pride over to the table full of theater students. They listened as Lewis talked about Emma. She could tell because during the conversation they all flashed her dirty looks.

The final bell rang and Emma headed outside with the other students. The afternoon skies were dark and Emma could smell rain in the air. Emma pressed her key fob and the Mercedes chirped to welcome her. Emma reached her door and stopped. She moved over and touched the fender. There was a deep scratch that ran over the fender, across the driver-side door, over the rear wheel and dipped down under the brake lights. What kind of prick went around keying beautiful cars?

She knew her grandma would be pissed when she saw it. The Mercedes was Emma's welcome gift to California.

Emma drove over the Oakland Bay Bridge into San Francisco, the opposite direction of home. She went down Market Street and turned into the San Francisco Centre parking lot. Emma bypassed the open spaces and dropped the Mercedes off with the mall valet.

Today, Emma wanted to be pampered.

San Francisco Centre was built by the same man who built

the Caesar's Palace Forum shops in Las Vegas. The mall boasted five indoor floors of shopping bliss with some of the best upscale stores in the city. The fancy dome allowed sunlight to fall through the atrium with all its spiral escalators.

Emma squeezed the rubber guide rail as the escalator guided her up to the fifth floor. Emma would start there and work her way down for today's retail therapy session.

Emma shopped for some new shoes and picked out a new skirt with matching cosmetics before going into the Apple Store to look at the new phones. She found a Belgian waffle maker for Grandma, hoping to soften the blow about the scratch on the Mercedes. Emma also considered changing her look at school, thinking if she dressed more like a Californian, maybe the other kids would treat her better.

It took a while, but Emma made her way down to the ground floor, where the food court and adjoining restaurants were. The mall was busy here as the dinner crowd arrived.

Emma's phone chirped as Grandma sent her a text.

When will you come home for dinner?

Emma replied and asked Grandma if she wanted coffee from the Kaffee Cadre since Emma was standing right next to it.

Yes. Decapitated with two sugars, please.

Emma smiled. Auto-correct got Grandma again. Interpreting a decaf with two sugars, Emma ordered that along with a mocha swirl with extra whip. It was then Emma noticed a man watching her.

The stranger averted his eyes at that last second, but Emma was sure she caught him. The man was bald, with a chest the size of a refrigerator. His eyes were neutral. Neither sad nor happy. Just there.

The large bald man left his chair and dumped the contents of his dinner in the trash. The man didn't look in Emma's direction again as he left the food court and disappeared into a sea of shoppers.

Emma left the mall as soon as she could.

She drove down Market Street and made a right turn, allowing the leather-stitched wheel to slide through her fingers as the front wheels of the Mercedes corrected themselves for a new heading.

Something flashed in her rearview mirror. It drew Emma's attention to a blue sedan in back. Emma noted the driver. The bald man from the food court.

Emma braked at the next light and took a closer look. There was a large truck behind her now. Was the bald man behind it? Did he turn off? Was Emma too paranoid?

The light turned green.

Emma followed the traffic through the intersection. The truck turned off, leaving nothing behind her. The Mercedes climbed a hill and Emma braked for the next red light on top of it. She glanced at her side mirror.

There was the blue sedan again. He had switched lanes and dropped further back. Emma could still identify the bald man through the windshield.

Green light. Emma flicked her turn signal and made a right.

The blue sedan followed traffic across the intersection.

Emma relaxed and loosened her grip on the steering wheel. She traveled one whole block before the blue sedan scrambled out of a blind alley behind her. The car continued to follow, but from a distance.

Emma's heart thumped. Why did he make such a huge effort to backtrack? Why was he following her? Was he some psychopath hoping to kidnap a helpless teen girl and do awful things to her?

Emma stomped on the gas. The Mercedes answered as it raced down a steep hill. She didn't have much confidence in her driving. Emma avoided speeding in general, along with turning left at intersections. Right turns were safer and didn't go against traffic. Emma loved right turns.

The traffic light at the bottom of the hill turned yellow.

Emma hated yellow lights. Red was stop and green was go. Those signals made sense. But if you watched the adults, the yellow light was open for interpretation. One thing was certain to Emma. This creepy bald man was chasing her, and if Emma stopped...

She gripped the leather wheel and floored the pedal. The Mercedes roared toward the intersection—

Right when this huge panel truck rolled in, blocking her path.

Emma shrieked. Only one safe maneuver she could do now.

Her driver's safety blanket.

Right turn!

Emma yanked the wheel hard. The Mercedes squealed as its weight transferred to the left side wheels. Emma caught herself screaming as the Mercedes skidded sideways into the intersection towards the panel truck with its side mirrors gleaming in the sun.

With Emma's foot still glued to the gas, the Mercedes burned rubber as it changed direction, pushing itself hard into the right turn. The car scrambled away from the intersection.

Emma couldn't believe it. That was the best right turn she'd ever done. Emma accelerated up the next hill, trying to put more distance between her and the pervert.

At the next light, Emma took another hard fast right. Not as crazy as the last one, but the move still made her tires squeal. She checked her rearview mirror.

There was no sign of the blue sedan.

A sense of pride lifted Emma's mood. She wasn't a bad driver after all.

When Emma's attention fell back down to the road...a dog stood in her way.

Emma hit the brakes. The car shook. The tires squealed again.

But this time, a sickening thud was added.

The car finally stopped, tossing Emma against her seat. She hesitated a moment as reality settled. Emma popped open her door and scrambled out to the front of the car.

Sprawled across the pavement was a small terrier, his fur dirty and mangled. He had no collar. No identification of any kind.

The animal didn't move.

Sadness swelled inside Emma. Did she kill this poor dog?

Emma knelt beside him. The dog's stomach swelled and collapsed like a bag. He was breathing. He was alive! Emma stroked the top of his head. His fur was so light to the touch. The dog's eyes drifted open and took her in like a friend. His tail twitched as if he were trying to wag it.

Emma's heart melted all over her blouse. She had to save him.

CHAPTER 2

Emma gently scooped up the small terrier into her arms. His fur was wet and sticky. Her nose detected an awful smell coming from the dog as he shivered in her arms. Emma carried him over to the Mercedes. She managed to pry open the passenger door before placing her precious cargo on the leather seat.

Emma ran over to the driver-side door and jumped behind the wheel. She did a quick search on her phone for the nearest animal hospital. She pressed for directions and peeled out, flying around one of the famous cable cars as it crawled up a steep hill.

When she reached the animal hospital, Emma came in way too fast. She braked hard and late, causing her Mercedes to jump over the curb of the parking space and scrape the crap out of the car's bottom. As if the gigantic scratch across the side wasn't enough.

Emma ignored the damage and scooped up the terrier. It moaned and shivered again as she carried the poor creature through the sliding glass doors. Inside the small waiting area, Emma noted a girl at the marble-topped desk.

"I hit him with my car! He's bleeding and needs help." Emma said it over and over again, her voice cracking. Her emotions flooded her brain with craziness. The stench of death still lingered on her clothes.

Hearing the commotion, the vet's assistant came in and checked the dog. She took it from Emma and rushed the animal inside one of the treatment rooms. Emma was about to follow when the girl at the desk insisted she had to wait outside. So Emma put all her crazy energy into pacing back and forth across the waiting area, trying to ignore the framed pictures of happy animals not in pain.

Her grandma called ten minutes later.

Emma told her what happened and it took Grandma a half hour to find the place, but she did. The old woman entered the animal hospital through the swishing front doors. She wore a tie-dyed shirt with flowers and jeans dirt-stained on the knees. Her skin was whiter than Emma's, with her hair braided into two white ponytails.

The moment Grandma saw Emma, her mouth dropped. "Please don't tell me that's your blood."

For the first time, Emma examined her bloodstained arms. She also noticed her three-hundred-dollar blouse was ruined. "Oh…those are just stains."

Grandma came closer and her nose twitched. "You stink like the inside of a sweat lodge. Follow me, young one."

She escorted Emma into the single bathroom and hit the lights. Emma almost jumped back from her image in the mirrored glass. Not only was her blouse ruined, the cute matching skirt was stained so bad it looked like it was originally crimson not cream. Emma's face was a mess too. Streams of mascara had run down her cheeks and turned them black. She must have cried a lot on her way here.

Grandma opened the faucet and tested the temperature with her shaky fingers. Dipping into her rope-woven handbag, Grandma pulled out an old hand towel and some of her goat milk soap. She dipped the towel into the sink and washed Emma's face and arms.

Grandma rinsed blood out of the towel. "Any clue on who owns the dog?"

"I don't know. He didn't have a collar." Emma hesitated, still trying to calm herself down. "I couldn't stop in time. I was distracted and…"

Grandma hugged her from behind. "It was an accident. I know you brake for animals. You have a good heart."

Emma knew she wasn't that great, but Grandma believed it for some reason.

Next Grandma had Emma take off her blouse and skirt so she could scrub them in the sink.

"The car's a little banged up too," Emma said. "I'm sorry."

"Were you speeding?"

Emma wanted to be honest. But also didn't want to worry her grandma about some creepy bald man who might or might not be after her.

"Maybe a little."

"I wanted to buy you a hybrid or that new electric car. Even that small Fiat would be okay. But you wanted that gas-guzzling German sled."

"You said I could pick whatever I wanted. Hayley's dad drove one and I liked it. It was comfy."

Grandma scrubbed Emma's skirt in the sink. "Bet he worked on Wall Street."

"Yeah, I think he's like an investment banker."

"Capitalist swine. Of course he would have one."

Grandma cleaned Emma up and convinced the animal hospital to give up one of the free T-shirts their volunteers wore. The yellow shirt didn't match Emma's stained skirt, but at least it didn't smell.

An hour later, the vet came into the waiting area. "The dog was in rough shape. I have him stabilized for now. His spine was injured and the dog is in a lot of pain. There is a way I can attempt to repair his spine, but it will cost a considerable amount of money."

"I don't care," Emma said. "Whatever it costs."

The vet cleared her throat. "This dog is a stray. From what I can tell, he's been malnourished and abused."

"Abused?" Grandma asked.

"I found older injuries that would indicate abuse. Yes."

Emma closed her eyes. Not only did she hit a poor stray dog, she hit a poor abused dog probably searching for food. And maybe some love. She opened her eyes. "I want you to save him."

The vet hesitated. "It's a fifteen-hundred-dollar procedure and I can't guarantee he would survive. This poor dog has been through a lot in his life. I hate to say it, but…it might be best to let him pass. I can make it comfortable so he won't suffer."

Tears dribbled down Emma's cheek. She wiped them away as Grandma squeezed her hand.

"I admire your heart," the vet continued. "It takes someone special who's willing to sacrifice so much for an animal. Believe me, I understand where you're coming from. But sometimes, it's better for them if we let them go."

Emma could see it in his eyes. That dog didn't want to die. He wanted someone to give him another chance. He wanted Emma to give him that chance. She turned to her grandma. "We have to help him. Whatever it costs. I'll sell my car. I don't care, but we need to save him."

Grandma searched her granddaughter's eyes. "You'll have to take care of him. If you're giving him life, you must take on the responsibility of giving him a happy one."

"I will. I so promise."

"Then we need to name him. A good dog should have a good name. How about…Snoopy? He's not a beagle, but still."

Emma liked that name.

"Snoopy it is."

* * *

Mrs. Bracket's office was painted with dark oranges and browns with medical degrees dotting the walls. Emma wondered if she needed to remind people how overqualified she was to be a high school counselor. Mrs. Bracket made Emma turn off her phone so they would have zero distractions during today's after-school session. This drove Emma crazy because that prevented her from getting updates on Snoopy's condition.

"How's everything going with you and your grandma?" Mrs. Bracket asked.

"Great. We're like two best friends," Emma said.

Mrs. Bracket wrote something down. "How's the adjustment been going?"

"People are different here. More sensitive. Back in New York, you say what's on your mind because if you don't speak up, the city will run you right over, you know? And I'm used to that. But the people here…it ruffles their Birkenstocks when you stand up for yourself."

"Do you still miss your friends?"

Emma wasn't missing them anymore because her friends didn't seem to be missing her anymore. What Emma missed was her life there. She missed going to the deli and taking a number.

Folding a slice of pizza and licking the oozing cheese. Hopping on the subway and going to a Broadway show. Or a museum. Or to Central Park. Emma could go anywhere she wanted to, really. Emma didn't need a car. And who needed friends when you had one of the world's greatest cities to explore?

Mrs. Bracket crossed her legs. She always did that when she changed subjects. "Your grandmother emailed me about your car. Did someone key it?"

Emma opened the mini-fridge full of free soda bottles that Mrs. Bracket allowed each one of her "patients" to have. Emma popped open the bottle and sipped. She couldn't believe Grandma told her. "Yes, but it's not a big thing."

"Were you angry?"

Emma shrugged.

"Who do you think did it?"

"No clue. Probably a girl in one of my classes."

Mrs. Bracket leaned forward, resting her chin on her fist. Judging Emma's answers. "Why do you say that?"

"I just know."

"Do these girls bother you in class? Do they bully you?"

Emma didn't want to get into this. "They don't bully me, really. It's more…they don't like me."

"Why do you think they don't like you?"

Emma sipped her soda again and took inventory of the room. Mrs. Bracket sighed. "I'm here to help you."

"I don't live inside their heads. I have no clue."

"That's not what I asked. I asked you what reasons do you think would make those girls not like you?"

Emma rubbed her thumb over the glass ripples of the bottle of Coke as she rotated it in her hands. "I don't know. Jealousy? I drive a nicer car than they do. I'm a good student. I'm a great actor. I stand up for myself. I wear nice clothes. I'm pretty."

Mrs. Bracket leaned back, as if she was about to roll her eyes at the conceited teenage girl.

"Hey, I'm not vain. But I'm not stupid either. I grew up around adults for most of my life with all their grand balls and other social events. I noticed how they all looked at me. I was blessed. Seriously, blessed. But I've never looked down on those girls or said a bad thing about them. Yet they treat me like I've

slept with all their boyfriends or something. I don't understand."
Emma didn't want to say that much, but Mrs. Bracket had a
sneaky way of bringing the truth out of her. "Can we talk about
something else?"

"Sure." Mrs. Bracket sat back. "Let's talk about your father."

Emma scoffed. She couldn't win.

"Do you still think he was murdered?"

Emma crossed her arms.

Mrs. Bracket pressed her lips together and interlaced her
fingers on both hands. She acted so calm Emma wanted to
strangle her. "Why do you not believe the French aviation
authorities? Why would they lie about your father? What motive
would they have to do such a thing?"

"I don't know why. But I do know that my dad was a careful
pilot. He always did his preflight checks and never took chances
in the air. My dad would have noticed the tape."

"It was night. Some of his employees were with him. He
could have been distracted and—"

"Not my dad. He would have seen it. Someone put on that
tape after he did his checks."

Mrs. Bracket paused. "And yet, what if it was an accident?
Didn't witnesses testify that the plane was washed hours before
and they had to tape over the static ports to prevent water from
getting inside?"

"The ground crew also testified that they took off that tape,"
Emma said.

"Mistakes happen. People think they did something when
they actually didn't. The French still came to the conclusion that
your father missed it. Now, if the pilot wasn't your father, would
you accept the possibility that the accident might have happened
as they say it did?"

Emma had never thought about it like that. The only evidence
she had was her dad. She knew what type of man he was and
they didn't. But was that enough? Could her dad have made that
one mistake that killed him?

"I'm concerned you're holding on to this murder conspiracy
as an attempt to hold on to your father. To not let him go," Mrs.
Bracket said. "What are your thoughts about that?"

Emma's brain still swirled with thoughts as she left Mrs.

Bracket's office. Was she still holding on to Dad? Maybe the ground crew did forget to take off the tape. Maybe Dad did forget to do his normal preflight check. His trip to Europe was a last minute thing.

Something tripped up Emma's walk and she stumbled forward. Her backpack somersaulted to the pavement. That was when Emma realized she was outside. She had walked across most of the school's staff parking lot without even noticing. Her right toe ached from the parking curb she'd tripped over. Emma found her way to the student parking lot and her car. She tossed in her backpack and slid behind the wheel.

If Emma went straight home, Grandma would want a full report about her session with Mrs. Bracket as soon as possible. So Emma drove back across the bridge to San Francisco instead. Once again, she handed her keys over to the valet and pushed open the doors to the San Francisco Centre. The smells from the food court reminded Emma's stomach that she only had a piece of fish for lunch. At Salad Island, there was a tasty mandarin orange salad that would be good for her. But Emma gave into her sadness and bought a small Blizzard with gobs of cookie-dough chunks and vanilla ice cream.

Emma found a nice empty booth and nibbled on her treat as her thoughts and feelings drifted back to her father.

She zoned out for a while.

Until the bald man sat down next to her.

Emma tensed up immediately.

The man surveyed the food court with an eerie calmness that made Emma want to bolt and scream her head off.

He said nothing.

Emma's muscles tightened as she prepared herself to dash off like a rabbit.

"May I join you?" a kind, but firm woman's voice asked in a British accent.

Emma noted an old white woman leaning on her cane. She wore a modern, yet age-appropriate dress with a certain flare. Emma tossed another look at the bald man.

"Don't mind him. He's with me. May I sit?"

Emma nodded.

"Thank you." The old woman eased into her chair with

confidence and grace. "Good afternoon. May I introduce myself? My name is Mrs. B."

Emma was at a loss for words. What was going on here?

The woman continued. "Your name is Emma. Am I correct?"

"Yes," Emma whispered.

"Let us see here." The woman put on her reading glasses and licked her thumb before opening a pad of paper. "Emma Rothchild. Now living in Berkeley, California, but a recent transfer from New York City. You are sixteen years old. You drive a white Mercedes AMG Coupe. You dropped out of ballet class when you were twelve because you told your father that dancing hurt your feet. You were a straight A student at Van Dorn Hall, taking the usual college preparatory curriculum. However, you did take multiple electives in theater and performed smaller parts in off-Broadway productions. Very interesting."

The old woman took off her glasses.

"I watched your performance in the Van Dorn Hall's production of *Romeo and Juliet* on YouTube. You played Juliet a bit over the top I must say. And I did detect some nuances you stole from Miss Natalie Potter's Oscar-winning performance in that interesting film *Black Water*. If your drama teacher knew anything about acting, she would have spotted these errors and corrected you during the rehearsals. But I digress."

"I wasn't copying Natalie Potter. She inspires my acting. And what do you mean by…over-the-top performance?"

Mrs. B addressed the bald man. "I'm feeling a bit dry. Do purchase me some root beer, if you please."

The large bald man nodded and left.

"I would like to compliment you on rescuing and paying for the treatment of that injured dog. A very selfless act. Dr. Leslie Vanders does good work. Her record as a veterinarian is impeccable."

How did she know about the dog? Emma was sure she'd lost her bald friend at that traffic light. Or had she?

"Did you follow me yesterday?" Emma asked.

"My associate did."

"Why? Why was he following me?"

Mrs. B put on her glasses again and went through her

notebook. "Your father's name was Kenneth Rothchild, owner of Rothchild Industries, a conglomerate composed of numerous companies. A few tech firms in Silicon Valley, a prestigious New York law firm, two professional sports teams, a German toy company, and the crown jewel of the conglomerate—AirTech— a company specializing in climate control systems for commercial buildings worldwide."

"What's going on here?"

Mrs. B ignored Emma. "The French concluded their investigation into your father's crash. Based on their report, they believe it was a ground crew error complicated by pilot error."

The bald man placed a drink in front of Mrs. B, who pulled out the straw and removed the top before sipping. "Thank you," she said to the man before continuing. "Have the French told you anything else?"

Emma shook her head.

"Would it interest you to know that when they examined the wreckage of your father's jet, the French discovered a few other disturbing facts? Facts that are being kept classified?"

"Classified? What? Like, CIA classified?"

"All I can say here is…it wasn't pilot error."

"So what happened?"

Mrs. B didn't answer. She removed a phone from her small purse and pressed a few buttons.

Emma's phone chirped with a new message.

"Be at that address tonight at eight o'clock. I'll answer all your questions then." In one fluid motion, Mrs. B moved off her seat and used her cane to head away from the table. The bald man followed.

Emma stood up. "Hey, wait a second. You can't leave me hanging like that."

Mrs. B walked briskly through the crowd as Emma ran up to her.

The bald man stepped right in front of Emma, causing her to crash into him. She now got a full look at the man. He was much taller than Emma first thought. And much bigger. His black eyes looked down at Emma as if she were a bug about to be crushed under his shoe. Emma also noticed a deep scar running vertically down the man's throat. As if someone tried to open him up like a

Thanksgiving Day turkey.

Emma retreated back into the food court and left the mall.

CHAPTER 3

The address Mrs. B gave her was located inside an aging housing addition. Old streetlamps stood on the corners with their dim, yellow circles of light barely illuminating the crumbling streets below them. Emma guided the Mercedes over a few rough potholes until she stopped opposite a small and sad-looking house with a For Sale sign in front. The lights were on inside, but the shades were drawn.

Emma noticed her hands quivering on the steering wheel. Her guts begged her to drive away. But she knew she couldn't. If Emma didn't find out what really happened to her dad, she'd go crazy thinking about it. Especially if there was something she could do to clear his name. There were six people on that jet. Six families who trusted her dad to bring their loved ones home. He was responsible not only as the pilot, but as their employer too. Emma didn't want those families to think her dad was negligent. Or worse, incompetent.

Maybe this old lady held the answers she needed?

Emma opened the car door and stepped onto the pavement. She held the key fob to the Mercedes in her left hand with her thumb resting on the panic button. If she had to, Emma would make as much noise as possible, hoping this was the type of neighborhood where a teen girl running down the street and screaming for help would still make people call the police. Emma knocked on the front door.

No one answered.

She pushed the doorbell.

Nothing.

She tried the door. It opened with a loud creak that sent a chill up her back. The living room appeared empty with its bare walls and dusty wood floor. In the middle of that floor were two folding chairs that sat opposite each other. A cheap light fixture hung from the ceiling with a lazy fan rotating around it. The light was dim. The kitchen was dark. The hallway beyond the living room probably led to some dark bedrooms.

Emma didn't like this.

She took a few steps inside. "Hello?" Her voice echoed.

Nothing.

Emma stopped. This was as far inside as she was willing to go. Emma pivoted towards the front door just as a shadow approached her from a dark corner.

"You're late." Mrs. B's shadow faded as the light revealed her face. The woman had placed herself in a corner parallel to the door. Walking in, there was no way Emma could have seen her. "Please stand perfectly still. Before we proceed, my associate must search you."

Emma took a step back as the bald man appeared from the shadows.

"This is for your own safety as well as ours," Mrs. B said. "We must frisk you for weapons."

Weapons? Emma wondered if the woman was serious.

The bald man circled around to Emma's back and pointed at her left hand.

"Yes, I see," Mrs. B said. "Please lift your thumb off the panic button. We wouldn't want your car to accidentally disturb our precious time together."

Emma hesitated before lifting her thumb. The bald man smoothly removed the key fob from her hand.

"We will return it, of course."

Emma wondered if the bald man could speak. Maybe that scar of his went deeper than she thought.

The bald man rested his cold hands on Emma's hips.

She tensed up.

The man hesitated, as if he had second thoughts.

Emma's heart beat faster and faster. Her body prepared for an escape. Emma didn't want this strange man to touch her. She would lunge for the door and—

"On second thought." Mrs. B leaned on her cane. "This assignment isn't appropriate for you. I will search Emma myself."

The bald man withdrew his hands and stepped away. He held Mrs. B's cane as she frisked every square inch of the girl's body. Emma found the inspection most uncomfortable and unnecessary. But she was convinced the alternative would have been worse.

"Would you be so kind as to scan her?"

The bald man nodded and took out his phone. He clicked on a few buttons and waved the device all over Emma's body. Was he taking video of her?

Mrs. B smiled, as if reading her mind. "Do relax, Emma. We are searching for electronic devices."

The man waved his phone over Emma's back, legs, and her shoes before turning back to Mrs. B with a nod.

"Excellent. We can start." Mrs. B sat on one of the folding chairs and gestured Emma towards the other.

She hesitated, but sat down also.

Mrs. B crossed her legs at the ankles and studied Emma, who waited for the old woman to say something.

The woman kept quiet for a few minutes, as if she had all the time in the world.

After a while, Emma couldn't take it.

"You had some information about my dad?"

"Oh yes. Forgive me. The French aviation authorities were able to salvage and examine the pieces from your father's jet. The static ports were not covered with tape and the jet wasn't washed by the ground crew. Someone sabotaged the ports, causing them to malfunction and give out false data to the aircraft's instruments. Over the moonless Atlantic Ocean—it would be difficult for a pilot to fly such a crippled aircraft. Your father wouldn't have known up from down since he could not trust his instruments. And he had no visual horizon to help him."

"Why would they lie about the tape and the ground crew washing the plane?" Emma asked.

"Because it was necessary to cover up your father's murder."

Emma knew it. She was right. Her father was innocent.

Mrs. B leaned back. "You have sent forty emails and placed fifteen phone calls about your father to the French Embassy in Washington. Twenty-eight emails and twenty-one phone calls to

21

the U.S. State Department. Ten emails sent to your local US senator. And one to the president of the United States." She paused. "You are very persistent, Emma." Mrs. B reached into her purse and took out a gun.

Emma stared at it. This wasn't some plastic cap-gun that a high school actress used in a play. It was metal. It was black. It was real.

Mrs. B took out a long tube from her purse and twisted the end to the muzzle of the gun. Next from her purse came out a full magazine of ammo with shiny new bullets stacked inside it. Mrs. B clicked the magazine in place and pulled back the end of the chamber.

"Do you know what type of weapon this is?"

"No." Emma could hear her voice waver. Was this it? Did this woman set this all up...just to kill her? Was this Mrs. B responsible for her dad's murder?

"This weapon is a Walther P22 with silencer." Mrs. B placed the gun on her lap. "If you proceed deeper into your investigation about what happened to your father, then I fear there will be a man who will follow you to your school. Follow you home. Follow you to the mall you enjoy shopping at. That man will have a gun exactly like this one. And he will use it to end your curiosity forever."

Her words turned Emma's blood cold. The old woman's eyes were not joking.

Emma knew she was about to die.

But a quick flash of hope came to the woman's face. "Or you could help me help you."

Emma swallowed. "How?"

"You could join the organization. You fit the criteria. You are a loner who does not need the support from her peers to boost her self-esteem. Selfless when it comes to helping others who need your help. You are tenacious when it comes to finding out the truth. You are calm under pressure."

"How do you know that?" Emma asked.

"I surprised you at the door and you did not scream. I pulled out a weapon and you did not run for the door. My male associate touched you under the assumption of conducting a full-body search and you didn't flinch. Even now your mind analyzes every morsel of information I just gave you about your father, instead of letting your emotions distract your focus. Unlike most girls your age, there is a level of maturity inside you. And the biggest attribute I see? You do not trust people. You are still not too sure about me. Which is a wise approach for any intelligence operative to take."

Emma stared at Mrs. B. "Intelligence operative? Sounds like you're talking about being a spy."

"That is the alternative term. Yes."

Emma paused. "Who do you work for?"

"An organization."

"The FBI? No, wait. The CIA?"

"I am not at liberty to discuss that. But if you joined, that would be a different kettle of fish."

"Why would I join anything without knowing what it was first?"

"Why? So you can play an active role in bringing down those who betrayed and murdered your father. Or you could wait at home. Send out your emails. Make your phone calls. Mail your letters. Yet I assure you that none of it will bring you the answers you seek."

Emma knew she was right. The more she tried to push people for answers about her dad, the more she was met with silence. "Why do you need me? What do I add to all this?"

"I can answer that and all your questions…if you agree to join. Otherwise, that answer is classified." Mrs. B unscrewed the barrel of the silencer and slipped it back into her purse. "Think about my proposal. If you are keen to join, message me back on the number I sent to your phone." She put away her gun. "If I do not receive a message, then you'll never hear from me again."

Mrs. B stood up using her cane. She nodded to the bald man, who reached into his pocket and tossed Emma her car keys back. The bald man offered his arm to Mrs. B and she took it before disappearing into the dark hallway. Emma heard a door open and shut in a faraway room.

The lazy fan twirled above Emma as she pieced together what had just happened. Was Mrs. B for real? Could she make her into a spy? Did she even want to become a spy? Was she dreaming all this?

Emma pinched her arm and flinched in pain.

CHAPTER 4

Emma used her back to hold open the front door as she dragged the large wooden doggie cage inside the house. Emma hesitated. She didn't want to scratch up Grandma's polished wood floors, so Emma lugged the cage over to the Persian rug near the living room. Inside the cage, Snoopy wagged his tail as he struggled to stand with the plastic brace now hugging his midsection. His eyes focused on Emma as the dog's nose pressed against the tiny metal bars of the cage. Emma went to her knees and Snoopy's pink tongue poked through the bars, searching for a cheek to lick. Emma leaned forward to indulge his wishes. She couldn't believe Snoopy was still happy to lick the face of the girl who did such an awful thing to him.

Emma pulled up on the latch that released the cage door, allowing Snoopy to waddle out of his cage and go for a tour around the old house. The dog did a circle around the dining room table with all its tall wooden chair backs. He paused at the French doors that led out into Grandma's huge backyard garden, then continued through the strings of blue beads that hung over the door frame that separated the dining and living rooms. Snoopy found the kitchen and another set of French doors, where he paused to take another peek outside at the large garden. Satisfied with the first floor, Snoopy headed for the stairs.

Emma stepped in front of him, ready to intercept.

Grandma gently squeezed Emma's arm. "Don't baby the poor thing. If the stairs are too painful, he'll let us know."

Emma reluctantly stepped to the side.

The dog climbed the first step and paused.

Emma drifted closer. She couldn't help herself.

But Snoopy resumed his climb. He took it slow and steady on

each step, making his way up to the second floor. Emma followed and showed the dog around her bedroom. Next she headed for the other two rooms, but found Snoopy had ditched her.

Emma looked back down the hallway. Grandma smiled at something going on inside Emma's bedroom. Emma came over and peeked.

Snoopy had snuggled up to a pillow on top of Emma's bed. His eyes were closed as he took a nap.

"Smart dog." Grandma chuckled. "Knows a good place to snooze when he sees it."

"He must be exhausted. Stuck in a cage with a bunch of noisy cats and dogs and having all those humans poking him with medical procedures." Emma smiled at Grandma. "Thanks for letting him stay here. I know you don't approve of the pet thing..."

"Humans have no right to make animals into their servants. However, this dog is a victim of our society and deserves better treatment. I'm happy you're willing to make amends for your actions and give this dog a better life. So in his particular case, I'll make an exception. Hungry yet?"

Grandma made some homemade vegetable beef soup and baked bread. The hearty honey-wheat bread with crispy crust went so well with the soup that Emma enjoyed two pieces.

"You see? This is what you should be eating," Grandma said. "Fresh vegetables and natural grains. Good for the mind and body."

Emma didn't want to hear another lecture. "I don't eat that bad."

"Tell that to the package of chocolate mini-donuts I tossed in the trash. Oh, and that receipt for a cookie-dough Blizzard at the mall? Do all New Yorkers eat that much junk?"

"Are you searching my pockets, now?"

"When I have to wash your clothes, yes. You wouldn't have to worry about it if you did them yourself."

Grandma didn't understand Emma's life. She had to go to school. Chill out from all the stress of everyone treating her like a dead fish. Do her homework. And now she had a dog to take care of. *Plus some strange old lady wanted her to become a spy.*

That reminded Emma. "Something has come up and I need to talk to you about it."

Grandma carved out a slice of apple with her knife and took a bite. "Say your piece, little one."

Emma wondered how she'd do this. Tell Grandma the truth? That some old woman with a gun claimed to be a spy and wanted her to become one too? Grandma wouldn't go for that. Emma needed to come up with a good lie, something plausible that allowed her an excuse to leave the country. Spies always traveled to faraway places, right? In the movies they always went to Europe.

Emma stopped herself. That was it!

"There's this agency that runs...an exchange program for international students...and they have openings for American students who want to spend a semester in Europe. What do you think?"

Grandma cut another chunk. "You've only been here a few months. Do you hate California that much?"

"It's not that. I just think it would be fun. I've never been to France before and I've taken two years of French."

Grandma chewed on her apple slice.

"And while I'm in France...I could see if there's anything new I could learn about Dad."

Grandma laughed. "Just because I'm an old freethinker, don't assume I can't still think." She put her half-eaten apple down on the plate. "You want to use this excuse to snoop around France and cause more trouble. It won't work. The French are tired of you harassing them about the investigation and showing up at their front door will just provoke them. They might even toss you in jail." Grandma sighed. "Young one, your father is..."

Her voice faded. A sadness erased the glow from her face. The memories of her son were no doubt still sharp and painful.

Emma stopped eating and reached out for Grandma's hand, gripping the beads around her wrist.

Grandma recovered a little. "It was an accident and we have to accept the truth. No matter how it paints your dad."

A response pushed its way up Emma's throat and she couldn't hold back. "It's not the truth. It wasn't pilot error. Someone killed him, Grandma! And Dad's killer is still running free. We have to do something about it. We have to keep trying. Seriously, how can you give up on your son like that?"

Grandma stared at the plate with a half-eaten apple core and skin on it. Tears formed in her eyes. "This doesn't help either of us, you know."

Emma instantly regretted pressing the issue. Her grandma didn't deserve that. None of this was her fault. She didn't cause this catastrophe in Emma's life. Dad was her son and Emma knew this must hurt Grandma just as bad.

She cleared her throat. "Grandma, I'm sorry that I—"

Grandma left the table and opened the French doors into the garden. She shut them behind her as she disappeared into the foliage.

Emma knew things couldn't continue like this. Both her and Grandma needed answers. They needed this to end. Emma only saw one option available. She pulled out her phone and clicked out a quick text addressed to Mrs. B with only one word.

Yes.

* * *

On Saturday, the afternoon sun baked Emma as she lay out in the backyard, tanning her bod like a good California girl. It was only seventy-one degrees out, but the warm sun made it just comfortable enough to stay outside in her bikini. Emma was listening to the new Screaming Kelp album she'd downloaded last week. So far she was into it. Emma combed her long blond hair back and noticed Snoopy nosing his way through the herb garden. The dog quivered with energy as he sniffed each and every plant. His tail was wagging with constant approval. Snoopy was doing much better. He still needed the little brace for his back, but the little dog carried on with his new life with an enthusiasm Emma wish she had.

Grandma sat on one of the lawn chairs reading Ray Bradbury as she burned some sage in a clay pot. Grandma said the practice gave her wisdom and clarity while purifying the space. Emma thought the smell was pleasant, but she didn't believe the smoke itself was good for anything besides developing lung cancer.

Grandma flipped over a page. Emma wondered if Grandma

was still angry with her. Maybe she should make her a peace offering.

"Do you want to go to a movie tonight?" Emma asked.

Grandma didn't lift her nose out of the book. "I'm always up for a good documentary."

Emma forgot. Grandma's favorite movie theater was the art house one in San Francisco. That was not what Emma had in mind. "How about something with romance?"

Grandma slipped in a bookmark and placed her book on her lap. "Something animated. Even if it's a kids' movie, I don't..." Something distracted Grandma from finishing.

Emma turned her head and saw Mrs. B standing on the pebble-stone ring that surrounded the fire pit. The bald man from the mall was with her.

"Good afternoon, Emma," Mrs. B said. "I hope you don't mind the intrusion. Your gate was unlocked."

Grandma boosted herself from the chair and glared.

Emma wasn't expecting Mrs. B to drop by like this. She thought maybe a new message would pop up on her phone with another strange address. How would Emma explain this?

"Get out of here or I'll call the police!" Grandma said.

Emma had never heard this level of hostility from her. "No... it's okay, Grandma. This is...Mrs. Baker...the assistant principal at school." Emma jumped to her feet. "What a surprise. What are you doing here on a Saturday?"

"Such deception will not be necessary. Your grandmother knows who I am."

"Really? How do you know my grandmother?"

"I told you never to come here, Laura." Grandma's eyes betrayed a familiar disgust. "Ken told you to leave Emma alone."

"Yes, but wouldn't you agree the circumstances have changed?"

Grandma placed her book on the table and crossed her arms like a concrete block. "Emma? Head inside please."

"Why? What's going on?"

"Please do as I ask. This doesn't concern you."

Emma drifted towards the house. Curiosity weighed down her feet.

Mrs. B leaned on her cane. "This most certainly *does* concern

Emma."

"No, it doesn't. If you have something new to talk about, then discuss it with me, her legal guardian." Grandma's head snapped to Emma still lingering on the patio. "In the house. Now!"

Her voice scared Emma enough to reach for the French door handle quickly.

"This is not what Angela wanted," Mrs. B said.

Emma's hand froze on the handle. Angela was her mother's name.

"Emma!" Grandma yelled.

But she couldn't leave. Something strange was going on, and not only did it involve her father but her mother as well?

Emma spun around and walked to the fire pit. "What's going on? How do you know this woman, and how does she know my mother?"

The air felt thick.

No one spoke.

Snoopy ran up to see what all the commotion was about. He barked at Mrs. B, who stiffened.

Emma was determined to stand there in her bikini all night if necessary until she got answers.

Grandma closed her eyes. Breathed in. Opened them again to address Mrs. B. "Ken wanted you to leave her alone."

"And I honored his wishes. Until he was killed."

"It was an accident."

Mrs. B revealed a heartsick look towards Grandma. "We found out it wasn't."

"Fine. Then do whatever your fascist organization does, Laura. Why does Emma need to be involved?"

"Because she's been inquiring through official diplomatic channels about Ken's death for some time now. And since Emma is the heiress to the Rothchild estate, it gives her the perfect cover to investigate her father's—"

"You're disgusting. Using Ken's death as an excuse to recruit his daughter?"

Mrs. B scoffed. "I honored your son's wish for twelve years. However, I have an obligation to Emma's mother as well. Angela didn't want her daughter kept in the dark like this."

"I won't let my granddaughter be a pawn for a fascist

organization secretly supported by capitalists."

Mrs. B stood taller on her cane. "Once again, your information is based on paranoid conspiracy theories."

"My son saw the light and wisely left," Grandma said. "But I'll be damned if you steal his daughter."

"That's not why Ken left us."

"Horse shit, Laura...I don't believe anything coming from your scheming mouth."

"Let's be clear. I'm not here to steal Emma or to give her any more grief than she's already been through. I only want her to know the truth."

"Why is everyone acting like I'm not here! I want to know what the hell is going on with my mom and dad. Will someone please tell me the truth?" Emma wiped her watering eyes. "Please?"

Grandma and Mrs. B faced off again, each of them standing their ground.

"She'll find out sooner or later," Mrs. B said. "It's illogical to keep it from her."

Grandma blinked as if trying to extinguish a fire in her heart. "Fine. Make it quick."

Using her cane, Mrs. B approached Emma. She took a moment before speaking. "At one time, both your parents were members of a secret organization called The Authority. This secret group was formed after the carnage of World War I by a group of well-to-do families in Europe and North America."

"Well to do capitalist families," Grandma added.

Mrs. B lifted her chin. "These well-to-do families blamed the destructive world war on politics, nationalism, and greed on both sides. So they decided to form an organization that defended humanity. A secret organization immune to political, religious, and national agendas. These well-to-do families independently supported the organization as it grew in size and sophistication."

"Isn't supporting capitalism an agenda?"

Mrs. B pivoted to Grandma. "May I continue? Uninterrupted if possible?"

Grandma took her book into the house and slammed the French door shut.

Mrs. B went on. "Today, those well-to-do families span the

seven continents. The Authority answers to no government. No national or religious leaders. We pursue those who hurt the innocent for the sake of their own greed or twisted agenda. Emma, your family was one of the first to sponsor the Authority. Your grandfather and great-grandfather were pillars of our organization. Your father was the New York station chief for years. That's where he met Angela, your mother. They fell in love, married, and had you."

Emma digested the information. "My mother didn't die in a car accident, did she?"

Mrs. B steadied herself with the cane. Her eyes betrayed a hint of pain. "Angela was killed during an operation in South Africa. We were all devastated. Losing a daughter is—pardon me—your father took it quite hard, which was understandable. He wasn't quite the same man afterward. Your father stayed on the executive committee for less than a year after her death before he left the Authority."

Emma was only four at the time so she couldn't remember much...only that Dad told her that Mommy had gone to heaven and how sad her dad was.

Grandma watched both of them through the windows of the closed French doors.

Emma excused herself and slipped inside the house. Grandma held the edge of the kitchen island with an iron grip, as if it were the only thing keeping her from falling.

"Is what she said true?" Emma asked.

Grandma swallowed. "I'm afraid so."

"Were you ever going to tell me?"

"You deserve freedom from the family's legacy. A new path to discover yourself. There's so much good in you, young one. Your heart is pure and loving. You'll grow into a wonderful human being...if you turn your back on this woman right now. Tell her to never bother you again. If it comes from you, Laura will respect your wishes. Trust me. The Authority doesn't need to soil your life with their misguided patriotism. Besides all that, your father didn't want this life for you."

"But my mother did."

"Believe me. If your mother saw what it did to your father, she would have changed her mind."

"How is Mrs. B related to my mom?"

"She's Angela's mother, unfortunately."

"What? Then that makes her my—when were you going to tell me my other grandmother was alive?"

"The Authority doesn't need you. This is all Laura's doing. She wants you to fulfill the family's destiny, something your parents have already paid the price for." Grandma touched her chin. "Young one, their burden is not yours to carry. You have a choice."

"Then why keep me from making it?"

"I've always believed in free will. You should choose which path to walk upon. I don't like Laura or the organization she represents. But I won't stop you if that's the path you wish to choose."

"Good. Because I want to see what this Authority is all about," Emma said. "I want to get all the facts."

"I understand. I hate it…but I understand."

Emma hesitated before stepping back outside to the garden. "I want to know more before I make a decision. Can you show me your secret base…or whatever you wanna call it?"

Mrs. B tilted her head. "I'm pleased to hear that." She lifted her cane and pointed it at Emma. "Please forgive me, but it's necessary."

"What is necess—?"

A whiff of cold air blew up her nose and the world around Emma faded into blackness.

CHAPTER 5

Emma woke up in a fully reclined chair that was cushy and hugged her body. So comfortable. The room she was in featured black walls and floors with a single row of lights running along the ceiling. A series of fish tanks glowed inside rectangular slots along one wall, their reflected light creating a soothing place to relax. Chairs like Emma's were lined up along the center of the room. A few were occupied.

Mrs. B watched a big yellow fish swimming up and down the tank. She noted Emma's reflection moving against the glass. "Welcome to The Authority."

Emma tried to focus her eyes. Did she fall asleep?

No...Mrs. B had sprayed something in her face and poof, she was out. As her eyes finally cooperated, Emma's first impression of The Authority was that the place looked like some new-age aquarium.

"Sorry for putting you under sedation. But our location is a secret. I hope you understand."

Once the grogginess had worn off, Emma followed Mrs. B out of the fish-tank area and into a sprawling, open-office area with two levels. Glass walls separated most of the offices and meeting rooms. Everyone could see everyone else. It was bright, using yellow, white, and light brown as primary colors. A second area was designed like a jungle, using fake or real trees. There were these large, green pods scattered throughout the jungle. Inside these pods were comfy chairs in a semicircle.

"We moved into this facility a few years ago. You won't find this type of office at the CIA or MI6, for that matter. We keep secrets, yes. But not from each other. We need to see each other through the walls. Feel we are a part of one team, which is important when we're working alone on our assignments," Mrs. B said. "Most of these people are involved with risk assessment. They analyze data and make recommendations for future operations. Our eyes and ears in the world."

Emma followed Mrs. B into a different section of the vast complex.

"And this is what we call the labyrinth."

They entered a maze of dark blue walls, floors, and ceilings. The only light source was a series of white strips running along the top and bottom of each wall, their glow providing an ominous vibe to the area. Glowing white letters pressed into the walls identified different destinations…

CAC Division

EQ Division.

IT Division.

TR Division.

FO Division.

SH Division.

"The labyrinth always reminds me of a starship set from one of those science fiction movies," Mrs. B said. "I'm afraid I can't take you deeper into the labyrinth without the proper clearances. It's our most sensitive area."

They emerged from the labyrinth and headed back to the fake jungle area. Mrs. B picked a green pod and sat inside it. Emma followed. Mrs. B rested her hand on a pad, which came alive with options to select. Mrs. B touched a selection and the door to the pod slid into place and sealed. She touched another button and the pod emitted a slight hum.

"What did you just do?" Emma asked.

"I engaged the cone of silence mode. Have you ever seen the 1960s TV show *Get Smart?*"

Emma shook her head.

"Never mind. Inside joke. The cone of silence mode scrambles any device trying to capture audio or video within fifty feet of the pod. It also gives false readings to any thermal-imaging device. What we say in here will be private. So what do you think?"

"This place is amazing."

"And I didn't show you the truly amazing things inside the

labyrinth. But I'd like to."

Emma detected the hard-court press from Mrs. B that Grandma had warned her about. How eager Mrs. B was to sign up her granddaughter. But what Grandma didn't understand was that Emma had to do something. Even if The Authority never existed, Emma needed to find out what had really happened to her dad. The lack of answers created this dark chasm inside Emma and her life couldn't go on without finding a way over it. Maybe these people could help her find that bridge.

"What plan were you talking about?" Emma asked. "The one to use me as cover."

Mrs. B placed her hand over the pad again and a menu appeared. Her fingers flicked through some choices before a 3-D projected image of Europe hovered inside the pod.

"Basically, you'll be playing yourself. A representative of your father's conglomerate, visiting Europe to do your own investigation into your father's accident. In secret, you'll be providing my field operatives cover identities as part of your entourage. This will allow them to investigate the people and places your father visited in Europe right before his death." Mrs. B paused. "I have something else I'd like to show you."

She selected something else off the menu, then removed a tablet from a charger slot in the wall.

"Take a look at this."

Emma took the tablet and touched her finger to the screen. Only two folders were on the desktop.

The Authority Information Guide.
The Gems Project.

"The Gems are a special group of young ladies under my command. Each girl possesses different skills that make the team diverse and flexible as an intelligence unit, especially in places where adults can draw too much attention. I need a fourth girl to balance the group and I think you would be perfect." Mrs. B leaned forward. "Despite my enthusiasm…please don't feel pressured. I don't want you to rush into any decision. Take that pad with you and read about the organization and about the Gems. Walk around the place and look around. The only area you don't have access to is the labyrinth. Do you understand?"

"Yes. Of course."

Mrs. B smiled and opened the green pod, leaving Emma alone inside it.

Emma leaned against the cushions and processed everything she had seen so far. The tablet went into screen-saving mode as it waited for her. Emma touched the screen and it flashed back to life. She tapped on the first folder.

It gave a general overview of The Authority. There were no names used. Managers and controllers were assigned random letters and addressed in person as Mr. or Mrs., depending on gender identity. Station chiefs, agents and other field assets were assigned an animal. Some examples given were *Great Dane, Cricket, Lemur, Salamander,* and so on. The only exceptions were members of the Gems and Stars projects. Emma wondered what the Stars Project was about.

Next she clicked on *The Gems Project* folder. Three girls were listed as members; their real names and pictures were not shown.

The first Gem was code-named Emerald. She was seventeen years old. Half English and half Jamaican. Her skills took up two pages of her bio. Leadership. Marksmanship. Surveillance. Emerald was even a trained pilot in single-engine aircraft and helicopters. Emma was impressed. She just got her driver's license a few months ago and this girl could fly a helicopter.

The second Gem was code-named Sapphire. She was sixteen, the same age as Emma, but that was where the similarities ended. Sapphire was a computer whiz and science nerd from Saudi Arabia. At thirteen, Sapphire had created a science fair project about zero-g agriculture that got her invites from NASA and the European Space Agency, plus a waiting scholarship to MIT. Emma couldn't believe this girl. Sapphire would take one look at Emma and know instantly how stupid she was.

The last Gem was code-named Ruby. She was sixteen and her family lived in Okinawa, Japan. Ruby was trained in four different fighting styles: kickboxing, jiu jitsu, judo, and kendo. Ruby's skills also included scuba diving, gymnastics, and jungle survival training. But unlike the two previous girls, there was a new section under Ruby's bio labeled reprimands...

Failed to follow procedures.
Disregarded controller's orders.
Used unauthorized RPG rocket to destroy ex-boyfriend's motorcycle.

Emma read that last sentence again. She used a rocket to destroy a motorcycle? Ruby sounded like a psychopath.

How could Emma seriously work with these girls? She was a nobody. These girls flew helicopters, survived in jungles, got scholarships to MIT, created science projects about zero-g agriculture…that was insane. All Emma did was eat, read, and go to school. These three girls would take one look at her and laugh their butts off.

Her? She's part of our team? What a loser. She can't even drive a car without hitting a dog.

Emma put down the tablet and decided to have a look around like Mrs. B had suggested. She entered the large open area and climbed up the circular staircase to the second floor. Rows of people were at their computers. Glass walls surrounded them. Two men were having a conversation, but stopped when they saw Emma near them. Their eyes fell to her chest and Emma was disgusted. But then, the men completely ignored her. Emma touched the plastic badge pinned to her chest and realized they were only checking her badge.

She tilted it upward to read it…

CAC Guest Level 1

Emma wondered what CAC meant and why she was guest level one. No one said anything to her so Emma kept looking around the office. Numerous dry-erase boards hung on the walls. Some had titles such as—

Casualties of MOSSAD Operation Condor
North Korean Intelligence Operations in Hawaii
Uganda Army Coop Probabilities
Russian President Assassination Plot and Conspirators
CIA Space Drones

Emma caught one group watching a large monitor with satellite images of shoppers on a street. The corner of the frame had letters in Chinese. She had no idea why they were watching that street.

Emma went back down to the lower level and explored another portion of the complex that was adjacent to the labyrinth. She found a cafeteria with dark, solid-rock walls. The individual tables were thick and luxurious looking, the chairs big and comfy. Clean plastic trays were stacked to the side and waiting to be used on the buffet. Some dishes were steaming under the lamps. Salad was in another section. Desert in the other. Kitchen workers grinned and kept the island serviced.

Emma glanced at a hanging menu listing special drinks. Special food requests. And homemade shakes?

She had a horrible weakness for sugar.

"How much for a shake?" Emma asked one of the men.

He glanced at her badge. "It's a free service. What shake would you like?"

In five minutes, Emma sat at a table, enjoying the best chocolate shake she'd ever tasted.

Mrs. B's cane clipped against the tiled floor as she made her way to Emma and sat down. The large bald man followed and stopped a few feet behind her.

"I see you've discovered the shakes. That does look scrumptious. Do you mind if we share?"

Emma shook her head.

"Aardvark? If you would, do find me a spoon."

The large bald man nodded without a word and left.

Emma couldn't help herself. "Did you just call him... Aardvark?"

"Of course, dear. That's his name. Didn't you read the pad I gave you? The code names?" Mrs. B lowered her voice. "Aardvark is sensitive about his name. Don't make fun of it. The last man who did...well, he can only eat soft food for the rest of his life."

Aardvark arrived with her spoon. Mrs. B took it from him. Aardvark bowed and said nothing.

Mrs. B tasted Emma's shake. "What do you think of the

place? Does it interest you?"

Emma would be lying if she said it wasn't interesting. "How old was my mom when she joined The Authority?"

"Angela was eighteen. That's when I told her about what I really did during the day when she was at school."

"She didn't know until she was eighteen?"

"Being a part of this organization is a serious decision. One for a mature mind. You have a good head on your shoulders, dear. I believe that you can make that decision wisely." Mrs. B brushed back Emma's hair. "You look a lot like your mother. Same eyes. Same cheekbones. She was beautiful too."

Emma concentrated on her shake. "From what I remember, Mom was much prettier than me."

"You're both quite beautiful."

Now Mrs. B had stopped sounding like a woman in a position of power at a spy agency and more like...her grandmother.

But Emma had a grandmother. One that didn't want her anywhere near this place or this woman.

"My grandmother didn't act very happy to see you. Why is that?"

Mrs. B folded her hands on the table. "Your grandmother thinks the world would be a safe place if we destroyed all our weapons and just loved one another. Then, every human being would be happy and the earth would be this peaceful blue jewel tucked into the fabric of the Milky Way. Don't misunderstand. It's a pleasant dream. But it's still only a dream. What she doesn't realize is people like her need people like us to protect them. The artists. The visionaries. Those who elevate our societies. Those who fight for justice and equality. Those who fight against tyranny. They need people like us who are prepared to do whatever is necessary to protect them."

Emma and Mrs. B finished up the delicious chocolate shake. The bald man named Aardvark removed the glass and spoons.

"The day is fading. We should get you back home," Mrs. B said. "Aardvark will take you."

"Will I have to be knocked out again?"

"I'm afraid so, dear."

"What if...I joined The Authority?"

"Are you absolutely sure? This is not the same as signing up for a raffle. This would be a major commitment. Your life will never be the same." Mrs. B pressed her lips together. "No, perhaps you should sleep on it. Yes. That would be best. Tell me your answer tomorrow. Aardvark? Be so good as to escort Emma back to the relaxation room and prepare the girl for her trip back home."

Aardvark bowed and held his hand out for Emma.

Emma didn't move. "If I join, would you help me punish those who murdered my dad?"

"We will bring them to justice. That's all I can promise you," Mrs. B said. "I don't want you to join for revenge. I want you to join because you want to make a better world for all of us."

Aardvark waited for her hand.

"Okay, then. I don't need to sleep on it. I want to do it."

Mrs. B turned in her chair, a serious note on her face. "Your father's dead. Avenging him won't make the pain inside you disappear. You'll have to live with it for a long time. But I'm offering you a way to direct that anger and frustration into something positive. Do you understand what I'm proposing to you?"

Emma crossed her fingers. "I do."

"As a field operative, you could become injured. You could become crippled. You could lose your life. Again, do you understand what you are stepping into, Emma?"

Emma hesitated at the word crippled. She glanced at the deep scar on Aardvark's throat. She thought about her dad and what had happened to her mom. The world wasn't safe. No one was totally safe. But if joining The Authority would give her the confidence she needed to hunt down her dad's killers...then that was what she wanted.

"Where do I sign up?"

Mrs. B released a smile. "Report back here tomorrow after school to begin your training. Due to the time constraints of the mission, I'm afraid you won't go through the standard six-month TR program. However, we will focus on giving you the skills for the mission itself. Aardvark? Miss Emma can take the scenic route home now."

Aardvark nodded and again offered his meaty hand. This time Emma rested her palm on his. They walked over to the elevator landing and stepped inside the middle elevator. Aardvark pushed a button and they went up.

"Is this complex underground?" Emma asked.

Aardvark shrugged.

The elevator opened and they were in some sort of room. But the floor was curved and made of polished oak. In fact, the entire room curved like they were inside some sort of ball made of wood. There was a metal ladder in the center. Aardvark climbed up and opened the hatch. They popped through the hatch and Emma realized they were inside a gigantic barrel. A row of such gigantic wooden barrels lined each side of a massive warehouse. Were they inside a winery? Emma had seen pictures of one before, but had never been inside one.

Aardvark held open a door and gestured for Emma to go first. She went through and found herself inside a wine-tasting area filled with tourists, many of whom were nibbling on free pieces of cheese with their glasses of Chardonnay and Cabernet Sauvignon. Emma couldn't believe this. No one had a clue what was buried just under their feet.

They headed through the gift shop and out into the parking lot. A large sign hung from the main building—

Welcome to the Burlington Winery. Napa Valley.

* * *

After her morning shower, Emma picked out her clothes and got dressed for school. She discovered Snoopy waiting patiently by her door, ready to greet her for the new day. Emma rubbed his head and Snoopy followed her downstairs into the kitchen, where Grandma was finishing up cooking breakfast.

"It's a beautiful morning. I thought we'd have our breakfast in the garden." Grandma nuked a plate of turkey bacon in the microwave, then turned off the heat to the skillet of fresh scrambled eggs.

Emma poured herself some juice and felt the glass chill under her fingers. She still hadn't told Grandma about her decision to join The Authority. And it was odd that Grandma hadn't mentioned it since Emma had come back.

Emma wasn't looking forward to telling her.

Grandma topped Emma's plate of white cage-free eggs with gouda cheese. Then added the nuked turkey bacon. Next, a fresh biscuit from the dozen Grandma had baked this morning. The fruit was pineapple this time. Emma's favorite. Grandma and Emma went outside to the garden, parking themselves at the birch table under the lattice covering the deck. Grandma split her biscuit in half and coated one side with a locally produced jam. "What's wrong, young one? You're not eating."

Emma cracked off a piece of bacon and chewed.

Grandma observed her like an owl. "Is the bacon overcooked?"

"No. I like it this way." Emma shifted her eyes to her plate, cracked off more bacon and used her fork to spear a slice of pineapple.

She sneaked a look at Grandma. Who caught her.

Emma dug into the juicy slice of pineapple and washed it down with juice.

"Something on your mind?" Grandma asked.

Emma knew there was, and it was hard for her to say.

"You better come out with it." Grandma sipped her coffee.

Emma wiped her mouth with a napkin and sat back in her chair. "Mrs. B asked me to join."

Grandma hesitated before sipping more of her coffee. "And what did you say?"

Emma hesitated.

Grandma put down her coffee. "You told her yes."

"There was no pressure and she gave me plenty of time to think about it. But yeah, I have to do this."

"You don't have to do anything. You can walk away and be a normal kid. Your future is here in Berkeley, with me. The college is only a few miles away. You can be a vet or whatever you want to be."

"That's for after high school. I'm talking about right now. I have to find out who killed—"

"Captain Ahab died as he hunted down the white whale. Revenge consumed him. You're sixteen. Your future is clear. Filled with possibility. Why soil your heart? Your father wouldn't want you to do this for him."

"If something happened to me...Dad would spend all the money he had in the world to find the people responsible, wouldn't he?"

"Of course."

"So I love him just as much. And until I can find the people who killed him, I don't have a future to look forward to."

"Don't talk like that."

"For the longest time I didn't know what to do. Writing all those emails and calling all those officials and it didn't do anything. I felt helpless and depressed because I knew I was letting Dad down." Emma stroked the end of the fork with her thumb. "But now Grandma Laura gives me this chance to finally do something about it. Maybe she's taking advantage of me...but so what? I'm using her too because I don't want to stay in the dark anymore, wondering why. Why did my dad have to die?"

Grandma took another sip of coffee. The steam from the cup surrounded her. "Sounds like your mind is made up."

"It is."

"And nothing I say can persuade you from destroying yourself?"

Emma crossed her arms. "Nothing."

"I don't enjoy the idea of burying my granddaughter next to her mother and father. If you make me do that, Emma...I'll never forgive you."

CHAPTER 6

After school, Emma drove up I-80 northbound out of Berkeley and up through Vallejo until she could jump on California State Highway 29 to enter Napa Valley. Emma parked in the Burlington Winery lot and headed for the gift shop entrance. A small bell rang when she opened the wooden door. Emma kept her head down through the wine-tasting area, which was for twenty-one and over only, until she slipped through the *Employees Only* door that Aardvark had let her through the other day. Emma searched the vast collection of gigantic wine barrels and realized she didn't remember which one they had come out of.

"Can I help you?" A man with a beard approached. "You're not supposed to be in here."

"I know. I'm lost. I'm looking for The A—" Emma stopped herself. Maybe she wasn't supposed to say the name. Maybe this guy was a normal employee and didn't know about all the secret spy stuff. "Do you know where I can find a hollow barrel? One that has a ladder inside it?"

The man cocked his head. "This area is only for employees. I'm afraid you'll have to leave."

"Can I call someone quick? It'll just take a moment."

"I insist that you leave, miss."

Emma turned on her phone. "Seriously, it'll take like two seconds."

The man with a beard pulled his smock back to reveal a gun.

Emma froze as the man snatched her phone.

"Back the way you came, miss. Nice and easy. I'll give your phone back when we reach the parking lot." The man turned over his wrist and spoke into his watchband. "Echo six. UV detected. Escorting to PA. Transportation required."

"Hey, wait a second. I'm on the same side. I'm—"

"Stop talking and walk."

"But I know about everything. Give me a sec—"

"Move," the man grunted in a voice that would not tolerate another word.

Emma bit her lip and headed for the door while the man followed.

When they reached the *Employees Only* door, it swung open to reveal a long-haired hippie with round glasses. He shut the door and looked over Emma. "Is this your UV?"

The bearded man confirmed.

"I saw this girl with Aardvark yesterday," the hippie said.

Emma jumped on it. "Aardvark! Yes, he's my friend. He drove me home yesterday. Can I speak with him? Okay…crap… I know I can't literally speak with him, but if you could just go get him, please? I'm supposed to be here for training."

The bearded man put away his gun. "You're supposed to tell me a code word."

"I am? Nobody said anything to me about a code word."

"Take her to the gift shop while I call CAC," the hippie said.

It took twenty minutes before Aardvark came up to collect Emma and take her back down to the offices. Typing on his own tablet, Aardvark conveyed his apologies for not telling Emma about the official secret entrance near the Burlington Winery Mansion.

After providing Emma with her credentials for getting in and out of the facility, Aardvark led her down into the labyrinth. They followed the glowing signs pointing the way to the TR division and stopped at a sealed door. Aardvark had Emma swipe her new card to make sure it worked. A seal popped and air escaped as the door opened automatically. Aardvark didn't move, only gestured for her to go through. Emma did and the door sealed back into place.

Emma was on her own.

The TR division was a massive area carved out like a giant cave. There was a full gym, an indoor gun range and an area of mats where some men were wrestling each other as an instructor shouted at them. Another section had three large cubes balanced on heavy-duty metal pistons. One of these cubes moved and swayed as the large pistons hissed. Emma looked closer at the lettering on the cubes.

Flight simulator.
Evasive-driving simulator.
Submarine simulator.

Also, there was a rock-climbing wall from hell. Bigger and badder than anything Emma's school had.

A large woman with blond hair noticed her presence. "You look pretty. Are you here to pick up boys?"

Emma balked at her comment. The woman had a thick accent so maybe she'd just misunderstood her English. "Hi, I'm here for my training?"

"Name?"

"Emma."

"*Nyet,* we don't use real names here. What is your code name?"

"I…uh…I don't think I have one yet."

"Everyone have code name." The large woman sighed and pointed her phone at Emma. She snapped a picture and touched a few buttons. The woman waited and her phone dinged. She looked over the result. "Black Opal. That's what it says here… ah…you are part of the Gems Project, interesting."

"Black Opal is my code name?"

"According to your bio, *da.*"

"I don't like it."

"Tough cookies."

"Is there somewhere I could go to, like, get it changed?"

"You can't change it."

"It has to be a precious gem, right? So why can't I be like… Turquoise? Pearl? Diamond? Oh, Diamond would be sweet."

"Don't care if you want to change it to Pig Dung. It says Black Opal, so that is what I call you in training."

"What's your code name?" Emma asked.

The woman swelled. "Lioness."

* * *

The first two weeks of training with Lioness were intense. She made Emma run two miles every morning before school. On weekends Emma did four. Mondays and Wednesdays after school Lioness had her do upper-body weight training. Tuesday and Thursday afternoons were lower body. Every night they ran through self-defense moves at half speed. On weekends they went at full speed on the cushions inside the training, or TR division. (Emma wondered why they always said TR instead of the word.) Between running, weight training, and self-defense training, Emma somehow had to find time to keep up with school. She picked up the habit of bringing her backpack with her to headquarters so she could sneak in homework during breaks and meals.

On the Monday of week three, they skipped the weights. Lioness and Emma stepped inside another elevator which deposited them inside a shoddy-looking woodshed above ground. Lioness opened the door and they were outside in a field near one of the vineyards. The sun hung low over the horizon as Emma followed her instructor up a grassy hill that overlooked the Burlington Mansion, which was another part of the gigantic estate and winery.

Lioness pointed at the ground. Her way of saying *stand here*.

Emma complied.

Lioness faced her, backtracking several paces. "Today, show me all you have learned. Do not hold back. I expect you to commit fully to each move, regardless of consequences. Understand?"

Emma nodded.

"I have a surprise for you." Lioness glanced up into a nearby tree. Something rustled in the branches before dropping down to the ground with a thud.

It was Aardvark. He grinned and bowed his head towards the two ladies.

Emma waved at him like a best friend.

"Today," Lioness said, "Aardvark will be your attacker."

"What?"

"Silence."

Despite his scary looks, Emma knew Aardvark was a kind man and she didn't want to fight him.

"Wrist sweep. Go," Lioness barked.

The grin left Aardvark's lips. His eyes concentrated as he grabbed Emma's shoulders and forced her backwards.

Emma tried planting her feet, but couldn't.

Aardvark threw her to the ground, where her teenage body buckled under his heavy weight.

"Wrong! Wrong!" Lioness yelled. "Your hands were inside his arms. You could have attacked. Why didn't you?"

Aardvark released Emma.

"I...I didn't want to hurt him."

"A man attacks you and you don't want to scratch out his eyes?"

"But I can't hurt someone who—" Emma couldn't help but gawk at the scar running along Aardvark's neck.

"Someone you pity?" Lioness asked.

"I didn't say that."

"You didn't have to." Lioness faced Aardvark. "Do you want her to pity you?"

A shyness came over the large man as he pointed his eyes to the ground.

Lioness got into Emma's face. "I teach you self-defense. Not love your enemy. Here, you are expected to either neutralize or incapacitate your opponent." She shoved Emma forward. "Do you get angry?" She shoved Emma again. "Huh? Is there a point you're willing to strike back to save yourself?" Lioness spun Emma around and threw her to the ground.

Emma's body tensed. A flash of anger bubbled up her neck.

"Pretty little blond girl. Daddy's little pet poodle. Do you have an edge? Where is it? Can you fight back? Do you have the will to fight back? Do you need a prince to come save you? Reality check. There will be times when there's no boy around to save you, and with this training, you won't need one." Lioness pulled Emma up to her feet. The woman gently raised the girl's chin. "Focus on the goal and take the necessary actions. Repeat them if necessary. Strike as hard as necessary. Do what it takes to make your opponent retreat. If he doesn't retreat, neutralize him. It's either him or you. Understand?"

Emma nodded as Lioness withdrew to the side.

"Again."

Aardvark grabbed Emma's shoulders and pushed her back once again. This time, Emma shoved his face to the side. But Aardvark was strong and he forced his neck forward even though Emma pushed against it with all her might. Emma's feet dangled from the ground. Aardvark held her up so high Emma couldn't touch the ground.

Emma kicked his knees, but Aardvark still wouldn't let go.

This was hopeless. Emma was like a dog's chew toy.

Emma then realized her hands were still inside Aardvark's arms, which meant—she stabbed his eyes with her thumbs, pressing in as hard as she could.

Aardvark grimaced in pain and stopped.

Emma used the hesitation to plant her feet and break away from him.

"Again," Lioness said.

Aardvark came forward. This time Emma locked her arms with his and kicked his shin over and over again. Emma didn't stop until he broke off the attack. Aardvark hobbled to the side like an old man, Emma's kicks having done damage to his legs. The bald man dropped his butt on the ground and relaxed.

"Are you okay?" Emma asked.

Tears streamed down from his eyes. The pain must have been horrible. But Aardvark nodded and gave her a thumbs-up.

"You made a man cry. Excellent," Lioness said. "Now I teach you how to make all men run away from you in terror."

During week three Lioness taught Emma basic karate strikes. They drilled every afternoon and night until Emma could do her punches fast and aim them. Lioness went over some leg strikes, which Emma was much stronger at.

On week four, they went over everything again. The self-defense moves were honed to perfection. Every karate move was judged until Lioness was satisfied with the results.

"Tomorrow will be your final exam," she said to Emma. "You will face attackers positioned at three corners of the fighting area. Each attacker is a black belt with years of practical experience in hand-to-hand combat. Your goal is to prevent yourself from being either knocked out or dragged out of the ring. Good luck."

CHAPTER 7

Emma was back inside the giant cave area of TR division. Her blond hair was pulled back with a fabric scrunchie and her face absent of makeup. Today, Emma was all business. She stood in the middle of the cushioned mats that composed the square combat area. Emma's heart banged against her chest. Her palms were sweaty and she had to constantly wipe them against her karate smock. Emma had never liked violence. The sight of blood always made her want to throw up. Hurting people gave her no pleasure whatsoever, and despite Lioness's praises, Emma saw her new skills to hurt and cripple other human beings as a power she never wanted to use unless it was absolutely necessary.

Unfortunately, today it was necessary.

No one else was training in the simulators or on the rock climbing wall or even in the gym area. Every person with a training uniform stood outside the combat area, watching Emma with great interest. Mrs. B and Aardvark were there, along with a handful of men and women in business suits who would lean over to ask Mrs. B discreet questions. The spotlight was on Emma and the actress inside her swelled up to accept Emma's new role as Buffy the Vampire Slayer.

"Ready, Black Opal?" Lioness asked.

Emma paused before realizing that question was for her. She closed her eyes to prepare herself. "Yes."

"Bring them out."

From behind the spectators, three opponents walked in a solid line. Each was dressed in a black karate smock with large hoods that hid their faces. One by one each opponent broke off from the group and positioned themselves at three corners of the combat area. They took off their hoods and revealed themselves. Just as Lioness had taught her, Emma analyzed each potential threat.

Man number one: Long black hair with a full beard. Emma guessed that he was Latino, but from what country she wasn't too sure. His body looked athletic and swift.

Man number two: Military-cut blond hair and a square jaw. His chest was a boulder. His arms like tree trunks. Maybe not swift, but could knock Emma into space with one well-placed hit. He looked like Ivan Drago, the blockhead Russian that Rocky fought in that 80s boxing movie. For some reason, Grandma thought Sylvester Stallone was hot and insisted on watching his movies with Emma whenever they came on TV.

Man number three: Long dark hair that was tied into one long braid that disappeared behind his—Emma was wrong. Opponent number three wasn't a man.

It was a girl.

She was young. Almost Emma's age, but shorter. Her long dark hair shone under the lights. She was light-skinned with cool, pink undertones and quite beautiful. Her body was thin, yet athletic. Emma could tell by her features she was of Asian descent, but that was all. The butterflies intensified inside Emma's stomach. She didn't want to fight another girl. Injuring a man trying to hurt her felt more justified.

"Prepare to defend yourself," Lioness yelled. "Number one, attack."

The bearded man bowed in a respectful manner, then charged at Emma. He threw a series of karate shots towards her and she blocked each one. Emma then punched his face. The man countered by sweeping his leg under Emma, dropping her to the ground.

The bearded man stepped over Emma to pin her. But Emma kicked him hard in the gut, shoving him back. She jumped to her feet, just as the man came in with his own leg kick.

Emma ducked, twisted her body on instinct and swung her foot out, catching the man in the back of his knees. He stumbled back to regain his balance.

She planted her feet, waiting for the next attack.

The bearded man aimed a strike at her chest. Emma brushed

it off.

But it was a fake.

The bearded man struck her in the jaw. Emma recoiled a few steps back, tasting copper in her mouth. Tears formed in her eyes and she tried to blink them dry.

The bearded man grabbed Emma from behind and pulled her towards the edge of the ring. If he succeeded, Emma would fail the test.

She gathered herself, stepped inside the bearded man's leg and threw him headfirst into the cushions. Her training kicked in as Emma jumped into the air. She used gravity and her elbow to come down hard on the square of the man's back. He gasped and stayed down on the mat.

Emma withdrew and put herself in the middle of the fighting area again.

"Number one, can you continue with the exercise?" Lioness asked.

The bearded man got up slowly, wheezing. He held up his hand for a moment as he struggled to breathe. Emma must have knocked the wind out of his lungs.

He finally shook off the discomfort and prepared himself.

"Continue," Lioness said.

Emma braced.

The bearded man threw himself at her. Emma ducked a leg strike, but caught a punch to the back part of her shoulder. The bearded man followed up with a punch aimed at her face.

But Emma reacted quickly and the punch skipped off her cheek. Still...it hurt like burning your finger in the oven and it made Emma stumble back. She knew her punches couldn't take him out, but there was one move she could do. The move Lioness had made her practice over and over again.

Emma prepared herself.

Now.

Emma ran at the bearded man, jumped and twisted her waist like a coil as she used her momentum to swing her leg around. A bloodcurdling yell escaped her lips as her foot struck her attacker on the side of the head. The bearded man collapsed to the cushions with a massive thump and didn't move.

Emma had knocked him out cold.

"Remove him from the fighting area," Lioness said.

Two medics jumped into action. They checked the man's eyes before carrying him to the infirmary.

"Number two, attack," Lioness said.

Ivan Drago smiled as he bowed. The Russian mountain lumbered towards Emma.

What did she have to lose? Emma ran at him again, twisting her body around for another epic kick. She missed the side of his head, but did catch his mouth and nose with a strike that snapped the man's head to the side. Emma lost her balance and tumbled to the ground. She turned to watch Ivan drop to the ground.

But the Russian just stood there, staring her down as he spit out something white and grinned. One of his upper teeth were missing.

Ivan came at her.

Emma threw a side kick. He blocked it. She threw a punch. He swatted it away like her fist was a fly. She tried a front kick to his gut. But Ivan caught her foot and shoved her backwards, landing Emma on her butt.

Ivan lumbered over her.

Still on the floor, Emma kicked his stomach. Ivan only grunted as he grabbed both her legs and dragged Emma towards the edge of the fighting area. She felt like a giant bag being dragged across the floor. Emma struggled but couldn't break her legs free. But she did have access to Ivan's feet. She grabbed one in mid-step and pulled back with all her might. Ivan fell forward onto the mat, but recovered quickly and flopped onto his back. Emma felt her hair being pulled while Ivan's massive hand clamped down on her shoulder blade and pulled her up to him. He released her hair and put his hand against her throat and squeezed.

Emma coughed. The man was so strong it felt like her windpipe was in a vise. She grabbed his wrist, but it felt like iron. No way could she move it. Emma would have a broken larynx just like Aardvark. What could she do to him? Ivan was too strong.

Emma then remembered Ivan was still a guy. She released the man's wrist, cocked back her elbow, and punched his berries.

Ivan's grip loosened on her throat. It was working.

Emma punched and punched and punched with both fists. As long as he held her throat, Emma wasn't going to stop.

Finally, Ivan's hand fell from her throat. Emma rolled off the man and coughed as her lungs welcomed more air. She had to get back to her feet. She had to be ready for his next attack. No matter how bad Emma felt, she had to be ready.

Emma forced herself to stand as she locked herself into a fighting stance.

But Ivan stayed down, rolling back and forth. He said something in high-pitched Russian to Lioness, who then argued with him in Russian. Emma wished she knew what they were saying.

Ivan eventually got to his feet and limped out of the fighting area, but not before giving Emma a dirty look.

Emma tried to relax, but her body was in full rebellion. Her muscles ached. Her face hurt. Her neck still felt broken from the last attack. She didn't feel like a girl anymore. She felt like a used punching bag.

Her next opponent smiled when Emma met her eyes. She readied herself for whatever this new girl would bring.

"Number three, attack," Lioness said.

The girl ran forward, jumped to her hands and executed a series of somersaults that built up momentum as she closed in on Emma.

For a moment, Emma froze, unsure of what to do.

The girl broke out of the somersault and kicked Emma right in the chest, tossing her five feet back as Emma rolled end over end, catching herself just short of the boundary to the fighting area. Emma's chest screamed in pain. Where did that come from? Despite her chest, Emma pushed herself up and threw a kick at her opponent.

The girl ducked. As Emma's back was exposed, the girl struck and Emma tasted the cushions. The girl came up behind her. Emma tried a back kick and found air. She rolled and kicked upward again, hoping to catch her by surprise. But the girl dodged the kick perfectly.

Emma jumped to her feet and attacked with a series of punches. Her opponent jerked away, ducked, and twisted her body like a snake to avoid every strike. Emma couldn't hit her.

Unlike the men, this girl was agile and could react quicker. Emma tried an inside kick. The girl countered with her own kick that swept Emma off her feet and threw her down on the cushions again. The girl bowed and held out her hand. Was she for real?

Emma took her hand, and sure enough, the girl pulled Emma to her feet.

The girl readied herself, giving Emma the initiative. Emma tried some side punches combined with a few kicks. Her opponent avoided every move yet didn't counter with a hit of her own.

What was this girl doing?

Emma improvised and grabbed her in a wrestling move. But the girl tumbled forward and used her legs to push Emma into the air. Emma sailed a few feet before her butt landed on the cushions. Emma wasn't hurt, but she felt like an idiot. This girl wasn't even trying. She was having fun with Emma, making her look stupid in front of Mrs. B and Lioness. Like a little girl wrestling her teddy bear. How would anyone take Emma seriously as a spy if she couldn't even defend herself against another teenage girl?

Emma jumped to her feet and closed in on her opponent. Like before, the girl handed Emma the initiative to make the first move. Emma tossed a front punch and the girl sidestepped left. Emma repeated the same front punch and the girl repeated the sidestep. Emma repeated another punch with her right hand, then reached out with her left to grab the girl's dark hair. Emma pulled hard, throwing her surprised opponent off balance and making the girl shriek.

Instead of a karate strike, the girl pulled a handful of blond hair and Emma shrieked. Both girls spun around each other like a merry-go-round, each girl holding on tight with neither one letting go.

"Stop pulling my hair," the girl said in English with an unmistakable accent.

"You stop pulling first." Emma wasn't going to let any girl embarrass her like this.

The girls kept spinning inside their hair-tangled death grip while laughs echoed throughout the training facility.

"What are you two idiots doing?" Lioness asked.

"She's pulling my hair!" Emma shouted.

"You pulled my hair first!" the other girl shouted.

"Stop this immediately," Lioness said in a tone that sounded like thunder.

The girl let go and tried to separate herself, but Emma held on tight.

"Black Opal, you are not chimpanzee. Stop acting like one."

Emma released her grip and stood at attention with her frazzled hair covering her face like a cloud of blond cotton candy. Emma knew she would get chewed out and readied herself for it. But Lioness didn't march over to her. She faced Mrs. B instead.

"The test was satisfactory…up until the end." Mrs. B fired a look at the two girls.

Emma's opponent bowed lower and kept her eyes to the ground.

"I agree," Lioness said.

Mrs. B turned to a man watching. "Would you be so good as to give everyone in your division a fifteen-minute break and thank them for their patience?"

The man nodded to Mrs. B and flashed a look at Lioness.

"Of course," she said.

The people assembled streamed out of the training facility. Soon only Lioness, Mrs. B, and the two teen girls remained.

Emma braced herself for the storm about to hit. The girl next to Emma didn't move an inch, like she was made of ice.

Mrs. B leaned on her cane. "You do realize this girl would have beaten you, Black Opal, if you hadn't pulled her hair and disrupted her discipline. What have you to say about that?"

Emma calmed down and thought about it. "I knew I couldn't win honestly. She's too good. So I got frustrated and did it."

"You're right, she is too good," Lioness said. "And that was by design. Despite her age, Ruby is one of the most skilled hand-to-hand fighters we have."

It hit Emma like a rock. Ruby? The girl from Okinawa? The one who blew up a motorcycle with a rocket?

"Against your first two opponents, you did well and that's what I trained you for," Lioness said. "Yet Ruby was the real test. She's years beyond you in ability. However, I'm pleased you lasted against her, and even tossed in a surprise no one expected."

Mrs. B cleared her throat. "I might add that pulling someone's hair is useless against a Navy SEAL or a Russian paratrooper."

"With respect." Lioness paused. "When in a life-or-death struggle, one sometimes must improvise to survive. I think Black Opal responded well to the challenge."

Emma straightened. Maybe she wasn't in trouble after all.

"Very well." Mrs. B sighed. "It's a minor quibble and I will not languish in it. Black Opal, you've passed your self-defense test. We will continue your general training later. But for now, this will be adequate for the mission ahead of us." Mrs. B reached inside her purse and brought out a small gift card envelope. "This is for you." Mrs. B handed it to Emma. The word *congratulations* was written on the front.

Emma opened it. Sitting in the sleeve was a gift card for the San Francisco Centre Mall.

"Now be a good girl and take Ruby out to the mall. You two should get better acquainted."

CHAPTER 8

Emma led Ruby up the metal ladder inside the gigantic empty wine barrel. Both girls passed through the winery's gift shop and went outside to the parking lot. Emma unlocked the doors of her car and the two girls climbed inside it.

"Mercedes AMG," Rudy said. "How fast does it go?"

Emma pushed the start button. "I don't know. I just got it a few months ago."

"No speed?"

"I don't like to drive like that."

Ruby nodded. "Safety conscious."

Emma rolled out of the parking lot and took California Highway 29 south out of Napa Valley towards Vallejo. As the car settled on a speed, Emma flipped on the cruise control. She gripped the leather-stitched steering wheel and exchanged a few glances at Ruby, who grinned. Normally Emma welcomed uncomfortable quiet over uncomfortable conversation, but Mrs. B was quite insistent that Emma should get to know this girl, so…

"Can you tell me your real name?"

Ruby shook her head. "Top secret."

"Oh. Sorry. I'm new to all this spy stuff, so—"

Ruby covered her mouth as she laughed. "Only kidding. Messing with you. My real name is Miyuki."

"Miyuki?"

"Mi-yu-ki. Yes, it's Japanese for awesome girl from Okinawa." She laughed again. "What is your name, Black Opal?"

"Emma."

"What does Emma mean in English?"

"I have no idea." Emma thought about it. "It's English for normal girl who loves books and puppies, I guess. I'm boring."

"You forgot to add pulls hair like a mother-trucker." Miyuki laughed again. Her laugh was so rich and genuine. Something a person could get addicted to.

Miyuki talked all the way from Vallejo, through Berkeley, and over the bridge to San Francisco. She told Emma about the Gems and how they moved here from London, where they were stationed previously. About how much she looked forward to seeing America. About how Emma's habit of not looking before changing lanes was a tad dangerous.

"I know. I keep forgetting there might be a car over there." Emma checked her side mirror as they reached the end of the Golden Gate Bridge.

Miyuki's eyes lit up like a little girl. "So beautiful. San Francisco is so beautiful."

Emma focused on the traffic, which could get tricky heading into the city. Miyuki continued to point out every fascinating thing she saw out the window. There was no desperate need to be loved in Miyuki's voice. No compromising herself in some attempt to get Emma to like her more. Miyuki said whatever she was thinking at the top of her head, and Emma found it refreshing.

Emma led Miyuki into the San Francisco Centre Mall and the girl's eyes were dazzled by the five indoor floors of shopping.

Miyuki ran up to one of the spiral escalators and craned her neck up toward the domed skylight. "This place is gorgeous." She took Emma's hand. "Show me around. Which store is your favorite?"

"Favorite? I can't pick just one."

"Then show me all of them."

Emma loved this girl. They started on the fifth floor and worked their way down. The girls hit Emma's favorite stores, and Miyuki bought just as many clothes as Emma did. Dresses, skirts, blouses, T-shirts, pants, jeans…it was obscene. And so much fun.

Miyuki twisted her ankle and studied her footwear. "I need new shoes. Which is your favorite shoe store?"

"Oh, Bailey's on the second floor. The best," Emma said.

They took the spiral escalator down to floor number two. Bailey's greeted the girls with two sparkling display fronts as they plunged inside the heart of the store, where shoes, shoes, and more shoes were on display. Miyuki shook with glee as she attacked one display, picking out boxes and sizes to try.

Miyuki wobbled on some six-inch heels. "What do you think?"

"Those look great. But can you walk on—?"

Miyuki caught her heel on the carpet and fell backwards on top of a display, which collapsed to the floor in a crash that turned the heads of everyone inside the store.

Emma rushed to her. "Oh my God. Are you okay?"

Miyuki covered her mouth and giggled. "These shoes make me walk like a drunk giraffe." Miyuki slipped them off and apologized profusely to the Bailey's sales staff as they repaired the display Miyuki broke. Then she bought all the shoes off the display because she felt obligated.

Emma led Miyuki out of Bailey's with two large bags of shoes. "You do know some of those shoes won't fit you."

Miyuki shrugged. "I'll find good homes for them. Some girl would be happy to have them."

The girls took the bags down to the Mercedes and stuffed them in the trunk.

"Would you like to share tea with me?" Miyuki asked.

Next to the food court, Miyuki and Emma found a small coffee table inside the Kaffee Cadre. A handful of people worked on their laptops as a cappuccino machine gurgled as it steamed milk into a high froth. Miyuki enjoyed a cup of honeysuckle tea while Emma went for the espresso. After two straight lattes, the cappuccino machine fell silent.

"May we join you?" A girl with brown skin accented by cool, bronze undertones and an English accent approached their table. Behind the first girl trailed another. She wore a pink and green-flowered headscarf that covered her hair and neck. Her warm, orange-brown skin had a glow about it. She was beautiful. The girls didn't wait for an answer as they sat with Miyuki and Emma.

"You wear a size seven, don't you?" Miyuki asked the girl

with the head scarf. "The leopard pumps, white sandals, and the red heels should fit you."

"Thank you." The girl with the head scarf spoke in a quiet and polite way. "Is the black dress for me too?"

"Isn't it beautiful? Mrs. B will have a porpoise when she reads the credit card statement. But if it's for our mission—"

The English girl interrupted. "She'll have a cow...not a porpoise."

Miyuki lightly clapped her hands together. "That's right. Ha! I said porpoise."

The English girl leaned forward, her curly ribbons of golden-brown hair were way out of control. "The name's Olivia, love. Code name Emerald."

The girl with the headscarf showed Emma a polite smile. "My name is Nadia. Code name Sapphire. Very pleased to meet you."

"Mine is Emma. Oh, code name Black Opal. Do you know if there's a way I can get my code name changed?"

Olivia ignored Emma's question. "Did you notice we've been following you this entire time?"

"Emma would have noticed, but I distracted her." Miyuki sipped her tea and grinned politely.

No, Emma hadn't noticed the girls at all.

"We followed you the moment you entered the mall," Olivia said. "Observed what shops you favor. What things you bought. Your mannerisms. The way you interacted with Miyuki."

"Wouldn't it have been easier to just come up and say hi?" Emma asked.

"I like to observe my targets. You learn quite a bit about a girl when you watch her. Especially when she doesn't think she's being watched."

Emma didn't like how Olivia said target.

"And what did you learn about me?" Emma asked.

A smirk appeared on Olivia's face. She loved this. "Your family's wealthy. Appallingly wealthy. Your clothes, that Mercedes you drive, and your shopping habits reflect that to obscene levels. You're also a loner. More comfortable with yourself than around others."

"How do you know that? You can't know that by only

watching me."

"Inside California Limited Miyuki excused herself to find a ladies' room. Once she was gone, your body language changed immediately. You were putting up a front. A public face for her. And judging by how relaxed you became, acting nice around people exhausts you. But you're a good actress. Must give you points for that, love."

Emma's defenses went up. What was with this girl? How dare she call her out in front of Miyuki like that. Emma actually liked the girl. She wasn't being fake to her like Olivia implied. It wasn't a total act, but sometimes Emma couldn't help herself. It was a habit she'd developed in junior high to protect herself.

Miyuki squirmed in her seat. "Would you girls like some tea?"

"No one cares for you at school either," Olivia continued. "It's unnerving the way the girls fire eye-daggers in the hallways at you. Yet all the boys still drool when you pass by, for obvious reasons. It's a shame none of them are brave enough to pick through the layers of ice around you."

Olivia threw it all out on the table like it was no big deal. Peeling Emma back like an onion. Exposing every flaw. Every blemish. And Olivia had the added nerve to recite it all back like a stupid book report. Like she was trying to help Emma correct these "flaws."

Emma then realized something. "You spied on me at school?"

"When Mrs. B first thought about approaching you, I suggested we do a bit of reconnaissance first. Gather some intelligence. See what kind of girl we were dealing with."

"Right now you're dealing with a furious girl who doesn't like being treated like something's wrong with her."

Miyuki shifted in her chair. "Would you girls like to share a cookie with me?"

"I wasn't casting judgments on you. Merely stating my observations," Olivia said. "What's with that 2.5 grade point average anyway? Had a 4.0 in New York, didn't you? How does a girl get into a good medical school with a 2.5 grade point average? You still want to become a doctor, right?"

Emma wanted to throw her coffee in Olivia's face and burn

off that smug little grin of hers. But Emma did something worse. She opened her mouth.

"You're a rude bitch."

"Ouch. We're not acting now, are we?" Olivia asked. "This is the real kitten coming out with her claws, isn't it, love?"

Emma ran out of the coffee place and out into the mall as shoppers looked on with mild interest. The tears came on and Emma tried to fight them back. But they trickled down her cheeks anyway. Emma knew all her weaknesses. All her failures. Of course she pretended to be happy and pleasant to be around. She didn't want everyone in California to hate her.

Emma reached the indoor parking lot and found her car. She pushed the start button and the engine rumbled. Emma backed out of the parking space, automatically engaging the car's backup camera. Clearing the space, she touched her brakes and was about to shift the car into drive when she noted something on the backup camera screen. It was Miyuki running up to her car, with paper napkins in hand.

Emma hesitated.

Miyuki slowed behind the car, seeing the backup lights still shining.

Emma put the car into park.

Miyuki tried the passenger door, but it was locked. She flashed a warm smile through the glass.

Emma flipped the unlock switch. Miyuki eased into the passenger seat. She offered Emma one of her paper napkins with the Kaffee Cadre logo on them.

Emma took one and blew her nose.

"What Olivia did…" Miyuki sighed. "Mrs. B wanted her to observe. Not collect a psychiatric evaluation of you."

"I thought we're supposed to work together as a team?" Emma asked. "How can I trust someone who tears me down like that?"

"Olivia is paranoid about many things. She wants to take the mystery out of everything and everyone. And when she does, Olivia tends to focus on the negatives instead of the positives. Believe me, though, she'll risk her life to protect yours. The same as I or Nadia will. Nothing is more important than the team." Miyuki's face softened. Her beautiful green eyes released this genuine vibe that melted away Emma's hesitations. She didn't know if she fully trusted Olivia, but Miyuki had won her over. "Olivia just received a text from Mrs. B. She wants us back at headquarters. If you don't mind driving."

An hour and a half later, Mrs. B led the four girls through the glass-walled risk-assessment area and into the fake jungle. The woman gestured towards one of the green pods. Once the girls were inside, the pod made a sucking noise as it sealed itself from the outside. Mrs. B selected the cone of silence mode from the pad and a different hum radiated around the enclosure. The four girls watched as Mrs. B pointed her cane towards a 3-D picture of AirTech headquarters in San Jose.

"The operation will be a fact-finding mission," Mrs. B began. "First, you will investigate a company called AirTech and collect any information related to Ken Rothchild's business trip to France in August of this year. We are especially interested in any AirTech dealings with a company called AgEurope in France. They're a recent customer."

"Black Opal's father owned AirTech, yes?" Miyuki asked.

"It's a subsidiary company of Rothchild Industries," Emma said. "I actually know Ben. He's one of my dad's best friends."

"Who's Ben?" Olivia asked.

"Oh…he's the president of AirTech. When his family lived in New York, I used to babysit his kids."

"Good, then you shouldn't have any problems getting his cooperation," Mrs. B said. "That leads me to your covers. Black Opal will play herself. However, we need an excuse for you three girls to be with her also," Mrs. B touched her pad, sending the information to the girls' phones which all beeped.

Olivia made a face. "Her personal assistant?"

"More to the point…you'll be a corporate liaison from Rothchild Industries. Your job is to supply information and support Black Opal on her trip to tour her father's holdings in Europe, which is logical since Black Opal will be inheriting her father's corporation when she turns eighteen."

Nadia raised her hand. "I don't understand. It says here Ruby and I will be Black Opal's entourage? What exactly is an entourage?"

"We'll be her besties!" Miyuki said with too much enthusiasm. "We follow Black Opal everywhere and give her advice. Emotional support. And party with her every night. We'll be inseparable."

"Exactly," Mrs. B said. "I want you and Sapphire to stick close to Black Opal. If she stirs up trouble, I want you there to protect her. Be vigilant, yet act as if you're the most irresponsible girls on the planet."

Nadia touched her headscarf. "Party girls?"

"It'll be fun," Miyuki said. "I bought us different outfits for every night we go out to clubs. It'll be epic."

"Remember, this is a cover," Mrs. B said. "Only *act* irresponsible. Don't forget to protect Black Opal."

Olivia crossed her arms. "So they go out dancing every night while I have to be at a real job. That's not fair."

"Nothing is ever fair, Emerald. But we all still must carry on." Mrs. B put the pad on her lap. "Any questions?"

"What should I be doing?" Emma asked.

"I want you to go around and demand answers. I'm giving you permission to ask the questions about your father's death that you've been wanting to ask for months now. Be aggressive. Stir up the pot and let's see if we can flush out some answers."

CHAPTER 9

The spacious reception area inside AirTech company headquarters had the normal things. Pictures of happy employees on the wall, chairs with company reading material scattered around the tables like a doctor's office, and the commanding reception desk observing it all. But what made this reception area unique was the large display model of an ultramodern office building at its center. The model had clear, see-through walls exposing a complex but regimented system of air handlers, water pipes, and ducts running under the floors and over the model ceilings. The building's roof was molded with large sheets of thin solar panels. Digital displays explained the various features of the high-tech design.

Emma didn't have a clue about advanced climate control management systems. But she was proud that one of her family's companies made something so important to people who worked in such buildings. She checked in at the reception desk.

"I'll tell Mr. Gooden you're here." The receptionist picked up a phone.

Ten minutes later, a tall black man in his late thirties buttoned his blazer as he came down the wide central staircase behind reception. Ben Gooden's arms opened as he headed straight to Emma, who accepted the man's hug.

"Great to see you, young lady. How are you and your grandmother doing? You holding up okay?" the man asked.

"We're fine I guess. Still seems like it happened yesterday."

Ben's face softened as he touched Emma's arm. "Rosa and I would love to have you guys over for dinner. The kids would love to see you too."

"Right. Kids don't love their babysitters."

"Mine do. We haven't found a good replacement since you moved to California. They miss your magic tricks." Ben noticed Nadia examining the building model with great interest. "Isn't that a beautiful piece of engineering?"

Nadia appeared to shy away from the sudden attention, but she kept her eyes on the display model. "The statistics on energy efficiency are quite impressive. The way you designed the panels on the roof and molded the other solar panels down the corners of the building is also impressive. They supply energy to the building's climate control system during the night hours, isn't that correct?"

Ben joined Nadia near the model. "Yes, a very astute observation. This new system can keep the climate control system running without outside power for five days. On reduced power it can go as long as two weeks."

"Two weeks? That's amazing."

Emma introduced Ben to the other girls before he led them up the stairs. For being a president of a major company, Ben's office was cluttered with stuff. The white dry-erase boards were filled with scribbles and numbers. Piles of books and air-conditioning models sat on the floor. Ben had to clear off some files from his leather couch so the girls could sit. He offered them something to drink and finally asked what he could do for them.

Emma spoke first. "I'm doing my own investigation into Dad's death. It wasn't an accident. His plane was sabotaged."

Ben sat back. "Sabotage? The French investigation said it was pilot error."

"They're wrong. I can't tell you how I know. But I know. I swear to God. Someone killed my dad and your engineers. And I need your help to find out who."

Ben thought about that. "Why would someone kill your father?"

"That's what we need to find out, Mr. Gooden," Olivia said.

"Have you told the police?" Ben asked. "Isn't this something they should be investigating? I share your desire to get answers, Emma, but you don't know anything about conducting a criminal investigation."

"But I—"

"All four of us want to expose whoever did this," Olivia interrupted. "We'll turn over all the evidence to the proper authorities when the time comes. But all we're asking for is your cooperation, Mr. Gooden."

Emma fired a look at Olivia. Ben was her family friend and she wanted to do the talking.

"No offense to you, young ladies, but you're just a bunch of kids."

"Ben? I need to know why Dad was over there in the first place," Emma said. "Did he call you at all during his trip?"

Ben sat back in his chair, his mind digging. "We talked a lot. There was this pending agreement between one of Ken's tech firms and the Polish government. Your dad had been working on the deal for months."

"Was that normal for him to fly clear across the Atlantic in his private jet for a simple business agreement?" Olivia asked.

"Ken was very hands-on in all aspects of his business. If he thought he could help seal the deal, he would fly to Siberia if he had to."

"My dad was a workaholic to the extreme," Emma said.

"Ken loved it. He wasn't the type of owner who sat at home and let other people run his companies. Whenever he could find time to dip his toe into something, Ken would do it. Sometimes it made people frustrated."

"Frustrated enough to kill him?" Olivia asked.

Emma watched Ben for an answer.

"Despite Ken's idiosyncrasies, people loved working for him. Ken could have let one of his executives handle the Polish negotiations, but he wanted to do it. That's the way he was."

"Why were the AirTech engineers on his plane when it crashed, then?" Miyuki asked.

Ben folded his fingers together. "As I said, I talked with Ken a lot when he was in Poland. One night I mentioned some strange modifications my engineers had discovered on a follow-up to a job we did for a European customer."

"What kind of modifications?" Olivia asked.

"Well, one of my engineers found that our customer made unapproved modifications to the climate control systems we installed. I told my head engineer to document the changes and send them to me. When I told Ken about this, he was intrigued and wanted to get involved. Since he was in Europe anyway, he flew to France and met with them." Ben cocked his head. "Are you sure his plane was sabotaged? I wish you would tell me how you got this information."

Emma stood up and faced her new friends. "Do you mind leaving us alone for a minute?"

"Why?" Olivia asked.

"Please?"

"What will you tell him?" Nadia asked.

"Not what you think I'll say. Please?"

Nadia and Miyuki left the office. Olivia hesitated by the threshold of the door and studied Emma.

"Trust me."

Olivia didn't look convinced, but she left and shut the door anyway.

Emma came up to Ben's desk and eased into a chair. "Do you trust me?"

"I trusted you with my babies for years. Of course I trust you. But what you're telling me, Emma, doesn't add up."

"I've got powerful friends helping me with this investigation. They've got access to info other people can't get. I can't tell you who they are, so all I can say is...they want to help bring the people who killed Dad to justice. And that's the truth."

Ben frowned. "What have you gotten yourself into?"

"There's nothing to worry about. Grandma knows these people and she's fine with everything." Emma crossed her fingers under the table. "We really need your help because I don't think we'll get very far without it."

Ben sighed and shook his head. "I need to know more."

"Sorry. As much as I'd like to...I can't tell you more. You'll just have to trust me."

Ben left his chair and walked towards a dry-erase board, staring at the mess of blue and black scribbles.

"You've never let me or Dad down," Emma said. "Please don't start now."

Ben cooperated and gave the Gems an empty office and his master password to AirTech's internal computer network.

Flipping open a couple of notebook computers, the girls went right to work, searching the company's database for anything out of the ordinary. Emma didn't know what to do. She knew how to use a computer. *Duh, who didn't these days?* But the other girls were trained in cyber investigations and knew what things to look out for while Emma could only do a thorough search of her social media news feeds. To be useful, Emma brought up drinks and snacks for everyone from the company's break room on the second floor.

Nadia found the original AirTech climate control designs that were installed for a company named AgEurope, the one Mrs. B wanted them to flag. "Interesting." Nadia leaned closer to the screen. "AgEurope is a part of the Raymond Foods empire. And AirTech put in new systems for all the other Raymond Foods companies too."

"How many companies?" Olivia asked.

"According to AirTech's billing department," Miyuki added, "all of them."

"Hang on," Olivia said. "I'll look through the project files."

"Already there," Nadia said. "The installment dates all occurred within a three-year period."

"Sounds like a major project for AirTech," Olivia said. "So their engineers noticed something strange after they finished with the AgEurope install, right?"

"That's what Ben said," Emma replied with a mouthful of chocolate mini-donut.

Olivia scoffed at Emma's lack of manners. "Anything else, Nadia?"

Nadia pressed her lips together. "Earlier, I found a way into the Rothchild company servers in New York and hacked into Mr. Rothchild's personal email. Didn't find anything strange the last few months he was alive. No threatening emails. Arguments. That sort of thing."

Emma swallowed. "You hacked into my dad's email?"

"Only as a precaution. Our investigation must be thorough." Nadia glanced up at Emma and pointed at her own mouth. "You have some chocolate."

Emma wiped her mouth and glanced at her fingers. "Thanks."

Nadia hesitated. "You now have more between your…"

Emma broke out the compact and guided her tongue over her teeth while she double-checked.

"Find anything else, Miyuki?" Olivia asked.

She shook her head. "No Swiss bank accounts on file. No financial records look out of place. Read through some Chinese toy contracts that looked legit also."

Olivia leaned against the office wall, deep in thought. "And I checked the HR database. Think we can rule out disgruntled employees. No processed reprimands issued by your dad. No files on ex-employees suing your dad or making threats."

"This is a dead end," Miyuki said.

"It still brings us back to AirTech's dealing with AgEurope," Nadia said.

"I could...told...that." Emma was munching on another mini-donut. "That's where...should..."

"Could you please not talk with your mouth full?" Olivia said. "I can't understand a flipping word you're saying."

Emma fired her a look and finished her donut. "I said...I could have told you that. That's where we should've started. No one working for my dad would have done this."

"How do you know that?" Olivia asked. "We can't take anything for granted."

"Because everyone loved my dad."

"Rothchild Industries has over one hundred thousand employees in all of its companies. It's illogical to assume that every single employee loved your dad. That's statistically impossible."

"Whatever," Emma said. "It's true."

"You girls argue statistics," Miyuki said. "Meanwhile, I'll go pack for Europe."

CHAPTER 10

Their flight landed at Charles De Gaulle Airport in Paris around seven that morning. Ben Gooden did offer Emma the corporate jet for the hop over the Atlantic, but after what happened to her dad, Emma wanted to go commercial. The Gems headed straight for the rental car area, where Olivia presented a special black credit card to the man at a special check-in desk. Normally a group of teenage girls couldn't rent a brand-new Renault sedan. But this was Paris, and special things always happened in Paris.

"Mademoiselle Emerald, your car will be waiting here, on the lower level." The man drew it out on a paper map with French and English labels. "Remember to return the car full of petrol or my employer will charge a fee and Mrs. B wouldn't like that. Enjoy your stay in Paris."

"*Merci,* Turtledove," Olivia replied with our contact's code name as she took the key fob from him.

They walked through the concourse and past a line of waiting taxis to reach the lower level of the parking garage. Olivia tossed the key fob to Nadia, who slipped into the driver's seat as they packed their bags in the trunk. Nadia took on the heavy traffic through Paris and Emma was impressed how calm the girl was behind the wheel. Inside the confusing French traffic roundabouts, huge trucks would try to cut Nadia off, but she weaved her way in and out of each problem without once freaking. By noon, she parked the Renault across the street from AgEurope headquarters.

Emma prepared herself to step inside the building. "How do I look?"

"Perfect."

The way Olivia said this told Emma it wasn't a compliment.

"Do we need to go over our parts again?" Emma asked. "Olivia is my assistant—"

"We know that already, love. We've done this spy thing before. The big question is are you ready? Do you know what you're going to say?" Olivia asked.

"Of course. I got this."

Emma's heels clicked along the tiles of the ground floor as she held her head high with confidence. She was the heiress to the Rothchild fortune. Her father's corporation was powerful and well respected around the world. She had to represent it well. Emma made sure she looked the part. Designer dress, shoes, sunglasses, jewelry, bag…it was the perfect costume.

Emma noted the reception desk and veered towards it. She crossed her arms and sighed at the receptionist, who finally acknowledged her.

"Please tell…" Emma drew a blank.

Olivia whispered in her ear, "Jacqueline Boyay."

"Yes, of course. Please tell Jacqueline Boyay that I'm ready to see her now."

The receptionist paused. "Mademoiselle Boyay is in a meeting. May I ask what this visit is regarding?"

"You may not," Emma said. "Her office is which floor?"

"The top floor. I'll need to clear your appointment with her assistant first, Mademoiselle…?"

"Rothchild. And I don't bother with appointments." Emma's method acting technique took full control of her senses. She now felt powerful. In control. A young woman not to be underestimated or messed with. "Tell Jacqueline I'll be waiting in her office." Emma pointed her shoes towards the elevators and walked on the first one that opened its doors. Olivia, Miyuki, and Nadia all exchanged worried looks before joining her. The doors closed. Emma pressed the button at the top and the elevator began its climb.

"What are you doing?" Olivia asked. "You're supposed to be playing yourself. Not some stuck-up princess spitting on the peons."

"I'm playing a more confident version of me. Hey, it got us on the elevator, didn't it? Just play along and everything will be fine."

"If you goof this up, I'll personally twist your perfect neck."

Emma threw her a look. "Try it and I'll straighten that broom you call a hairstyle."

Olivia gasped.

"Would you both please chill?" Miyuki asked.

"I agree," Nadia said. "Take it down a level."

The elevator stopped and revealed another large reception area with no windows. Small LED lamps emphasized pieces of modern artwork hanging on the dark walls. A well-fit man in a well-tailored suit stood up from the only desk in the room.

Emma knocked her head back and marched towards him. "I'm Emma Rothchild, daughter of Kenneth Rothchild. Jacqueline will want to see me. Is her office straight through those glass doors? Thank you, sir. Handsome suit, by the way." Emma headed for the outer office doors.

But the man's hand grabbed her arm.

"Mademoiselle Boyay cannot be disturbed," the man in the suit said, his eyes not in the mood to play along.

"Oh yes, I know she's in a meeting. Only wanted to cool my heels. Any harm in that? Of course not. Men don't understand how difficult it is to walk around in heels all day." Emma glared at his hand. "Could you please stop wrinkling my blouse? It's quite expensive."

Miyuki and Nadia glanced at each other.

"Mademoiselle Boyay cannot be disturbed," the man repeated with added annoyance.

Emma rolled her eyes. "You said that already. Are you sure we can't wait for her? How about inside this lovely reception area? That way you can make sure we don't steal your art collection."

The man didn't loosen his grip.

Olivia offered him a business card. "I work for Mr. Gooden, president of AirTech. The company that built the climate control system at your new office here? We have some unfinished business that Mr. Gooden would like to tidy up. What time does Miss Boyay have available on today's calendar, sir?"

The man released Emma and took Olivia's card, examining it.

Emma dug her fists against her waist. "You're a rude baboon.

I've never been treated with such disrespect in all my—"

Miyuki jumped in front of Emma. "You must see this amazing painting. It has cows!"

"What?"

Miyuki took Emma's hand and guided her away. Nadia came up from behind and shielded Emma from the man's line of sight. The three girls didn't stop until they reached one of the paintings near the elevator.

"What are you doing?" Emma asked.

"Let Olivia do her thing," Miyuki said.

"Yes, you were about to get us all thrown out," Nadia whispered. "Now, admire the pretty painting."

Emma scoffed and took in the massive picture of a wheat field near a Dutch windmill. Normal enough. But the sky wasn't blue. It was painted to look like, chocolate?

"You lied," Emma said. "This painting doesn't have any cows."

The girls watched as Olivia discussed something with the male assistant. Finally, the man returned to his desk. Olivia quietly joined the other girls. "Jacqueline's on her way."

All the girls were relieved.

"Emma, if you're going to act like...whatever it is you're doing...act nicer. We want people to help us, not piss them off so they won't talk."

"Sorry about that," Emma said. "But it felt good, so I went with it."

The girls each found a seat and waited.

A half hour later, the elevator opened and out stepped a woman with high cheekbones. She wore dark slacks, short spikey blond hair, and a business suit. Blood-red lipstick covered her lips. The woman sized up the four girls before heading inside her office without a word.

A phone rang and the man with the suit answered in a low, businesslike tone. The man finished and stood.

"Mademoiselle Boyay will see you now."

The four girls stood up in unison as they checked their clothes.

"She will only see Miss Rothchild and the AirTech representative." The man eyed Miyuki and Nadia. His cold stare forced them back down into their seats. The man opened the double glass doors, allowing Emma and Olivia to step inside before he closed them.

Jacqueline Boyay's office was modern and cold. Silver with black accents. Strange Gothic statues placed with the eye of a designer who loved bleakness. The only color was the sun coming from the window. It surprised Emma that this was a woman's office.

Jacqueline invited them to sit and offered them something to drink. Both girls declined. The woman then poured herself a scotch and sipped it while she slid behind her black desk. Jacqueline crossed her long legs and studied the girls.

She said nothing.

Emma summoned her courage. The stage was lit. The curtain was up. The people in the audience were watching and waiting. It was showtime. "My time is valuable, Jacqueline, so I don't appreciate it being wasted like this. However, I do need answers, so let's get to it, okay? Great. I—"

"Sorry to hear about your father," Jacqueline interrupted. "He was a great man and I admired him. It must be hard on you and your grandmother."

Emma froze, thinking about her dad took her right out of character. She swallowed. "Yes…um, thank you."

Jacqueline took a sip and peered out the window. "When I was six, there was a fire at our home. I remember the cries from our dog as the flames closed in on him while I cried and screamed for help. The firemen came in time to save me. But my parents burned to death. To this day, I still remember every detail." Jacqueline took a larger sip from her glass before glancing at Emma. "I understand."

Emma melted. "Oh my God. I'm so sorry."

Jacqueline swirled her glass of alcohol. "Believe it or not, it made me a stronger woman. I hope a similar transformation will happen to you. A phoenix from the ashes." The woman placed her drink on the desk and sat back in her leather chair. "May I ask the reason for your surprise visit?"

"I'm here to investigate my father's death."

"The investigators said it was an accident, if I remember correctly," Jacqueline said.

"I found evidence to the contrary, so I'm conducting my own investigation."

"What makes you think it wasn't an accident?" Jacqueline asked.

Emma's confidence flowed back into her veins. "I'm not at liberty to discuss what I know at this time. But I wanted to ask you a few questions about what AirTech did for your company."

Jacqueline's eyes flicked to Olivia. "Shouldn't you ask Mr. Gooden's assistant here first?"

Olivia didn't hesitate. "Mr. Gooden has offered the vast resources of Rothchild Industries to aid Miss Rothchild in her investigation. We've given her all the information about AirTech's climate control system. However, Miss Rothchild would like to see one of the newly installed systems herself."

"Why would you be interested in that?" Jacqueline said.

"Some AirTech engineers who were assigned to the project died in the same accident that claimed Mr. Rothchild," Olivia said.

"Do you suspect there's a connection? Intriguing." Jacqueline looked out the window again for a moment before swinging around on her chair and picking up the phone. "Pierre? Cancel my appointments this afternoon and bring my car to the front. I'm giving Miss Rothchild a tour of the growth labs."

CHAPTER 11

Nadia couldn't believe what she saw in the bathroom mirror. Her headscarf gone. Her long dark hair exposed to the world as it covered her shoulders over a low-cut blouse. The short designer skirt she wore that exposed her elephant-trunk thighs. Yet, this is what Allah blessed her with, so Nadia embraced it just like all His other gifts upon her life. Like a brain that could figure out complex problems with ease. Like a loving father who understood his daughter's wonderful gifts and encouraged Nadia to develop them, even if that meant being away from her home and family.

If her father saw Nadia dressed like this, he would wrap her in a blanket and forbid her from ever leaving the house. In the West, it was seen as a cute outfit for a young teenage girl. In Saudi Arabia, it would be judged obscene and Nadia would be questioned by the church police. Yet, for this stage of their operation, it was vital that Nadia keep her party-girl camouflage intact no matter how uncomfortable it made her feel.

Nadia knelt inside the bathroom and took the opportunity to do her noon prayers. This was the least suitable place and Nadia hoped Allah would feel the love that was in her heart and not judge her by the surroundings or for not having her prayer mat with her. Nadia finished and did one last minute appearance check before she emerged from the private bathroom and joined Miyuki on the couch in Mademoiselle Boyay's reception area.

Twenty minutes earlier, Miyuki had pitched a major fit about going to some boring food growth lab instead of shopping on Avenue Montigue. Emma argued and Nadia agreed with Miyuki. Frustrated, Emma told Nadia and Miyuki to wait in the office until they were done with Mademoiselle Boyay's tour.

It was all according to plan.

Nadia had tried hacking into AgEurope's mainframes. But for a food company, they had a formidable wall of cyber security. Even the Authority's best hackers could only penetrate a few sections. Now if Nadia could crack Mademoiselle Boyay's laptop, she was confident spies could get into all the sections of the company's mainframe. But first they needed to occupy Jacqueline's assistant, Pierre, who had stayed behind to watch them.

The man worked on his laptop, while monitoring the two girls like a hawk. His eyes reacted to any hint of movement. Miyuki also noted a bulge under the man's suit jacket. She was sure it was a gun. A strange item for an executive office assistant to carry.

"Any ideas?" Nadia asked.

"Fire alarm?" Miyuki asked.

"He would escort us downstairs."

"What about the air vent?" Miyuki's eyes pointed up to a vent located where the wall met the ceiling.

"Wouldn't balancing on a chair while crawling up a wall look suspicious?"

"Maybe we are making this too complicated," Miyuki said. "All I need is to distract him so you can slip under the woman's desk. Problem is he'll notice you've disappeared from the couch."

Nadia agreed that was a problem. She thought about it for a moment.

"I have an idea."

After Nadia returned from the bathroom a second time, Miyuki jumped from the couch and folded her hands behind her back as she examined a painting. Showing her boredom, Miyuki drifted past two more paintings before ending up in front of Pierre. "Excuse me. Do you have any snacks? I'm hungry."

Pierre stopped typing. "A café is next door."

Miyuki grimaced. "Then I must go all the way downstairs and back outside. Very inconvenient."

Pierre went back to typing.

Nadia sank to the floor and crawled like a dog over to

Pierre's desk unobserved. She tapped Miyuki's sandal.

"Does Miss Boyay have snacks in her office?" Miyuki stole a few steps past Pierre, who leaped off his chair and intercepted Miyuki.

"You're not allowed in there."

Nadia scrambled behind a file cabinet, trying to make herself small.

"Don't be a bully." Miyuki backed away from Jacqueline's office, drawing Pierre away from the door. "I'm just looking for snacks."

With Pierre's back turned, Nadia scrambled inside Jacqueline's office like a spider. She resisted the urge to look back until she tucked herself safely under the woman's desk.

Miyuki flopped down on the couch, acting mad.

Pierre stiffened. "Where's the other one?"

"The other what?"

"The other girl. The one that was sitting with you."

"Oh, her? She's in the toilet."

"She was just in the toilet." Pierre glanced at Jacqueline's office.

Nadia retreated back behind the desk. She heard footsteps coming towards her. That wasn't good. Nadia closed her eyes and hoped that Miyuki could think of something quick.

"She's been complaining of stomach problems since breakfast," Miyuki's voice rang out. "And poor girl is going through her period. Double whammy."

The footsteps stopped and reversed out of the room.

A perfect ad-lib by Miyuki. All men recoiled at the thought of anything dealing with a woman's...well, Nadia remembered her brothers' disgust when they accidentally discovered their twelve-year-old sister having her first period. It was the most embarrassing moment of her life.

Miyuki's voice chirped away and faded a little. Nadia peeked around the desk for a better look at the situation. Sure enough, Miyuki had led Pierre over to the bathroom door. Nadia pulled out her phone and opened up the app that activated the special iPod she'd left on the corner of the bathroom sink.

Pierre tried the door, but it was locked. He pounded on it.

Nadia pressed the transmit button. She touched her lips to the phone and moaned. "Oh…I feel so sick. I can't come out or I'll embarrass myself all over your floor." Her voice echoed through the bathroom door perfectly.

Pierre took a step back. Still unsure.

Miyuki leaned on the door. "Oh, girl…need me to come in and help you?"

Nadia smiled, thinking of something that should be the final straw. "No, thank you. But I will need a fresh tampon if you have one."

Pierre looked uncomfortable as he retreated back to his desk and resumed his work.

Nadia tried not to giggle too much. But she could tell Miyuki had even more trouble than her keeping a straight face as the girl sat back on the couch.

Nadia turned her attention to Jacqueline's computer. She didn't have enough time to pore through all the files and shared drives before its owner came back, but Nadia didn't need to thanks to Copy Cat, a little virus Nadia designed herself.

Once inside a computer, Copy Cat allowed Nadia's computer to mirror the infected one. It was as good as Nadia sitting inside this office while sipping a cup of tea as she read everything on the AgEurope network. But first Nadia had to hack into this computer.

She gently pulled out the cable for the main keyboard and plugged in her own mini keyboard. This was a special keyboard, every button cushioned from making the smallest click. Perfect for a time like this. It took Nadia longer than expected, but after ten minutes she was through the security protocols on the computer. Nadia plugged her thumb drive into the USB port and uploaded Copy Cat on to Jacqueline's hard drive. Then clicked execute.

CHAPTER 12

The sign read Growth Lab 12. The underground farm was composed of rows and rows of plants in various growth stages. Potatoes, tomatoes, carrots, squash, pumpkins…all kinds of edible crops. Jacqueline told Emma and Olivia about the growing process. How they used genetic engineering to produce drought-tolerant crops and to increase the yield each one produces. How her scientists meticulously studied and nourished the seeds until they developed into perfect specimens to be later introduced into their company farms all over Europe and Africa. She spoke about their advanced growth lighting system that gave plants the same amount of sunlight as the sun.

Emma's mind checked out right after the previous forty-five-minute tour of the massive underground seed storage area. Someone into farming and crop yields would be fascinated by this place. However, Emma was on the verge of scratching her eyes out. None of this was remotely interesting to her.

But when Jacqueline talked about the new AirTech climate control system, Emma paid closer attention.

"The new system regulates the environment at a precise temperature and moisture content, depending on which growth zone. You'll be pleased to know, Miss Rothchild, that your company's product has improved our energy costs by twenty percent. Our scientists are pleased with the accuracy of the new system. Our old climate system had difficulty keeping moisture and temperature at a consistent rate."

"It's great to hear about a happy customer," Emma said. "I'm sure Ben—Mr. Gooden—will be happy to hear how pleased you are. Won't he, Olivia?"

"My name's Lisa, Miss Rothchild." Olivia glared before

snapping a thermal picture of the ceiling and shutting off her phone. "Yes, he'll be pleased, I'm sure."

Emma bit her lip. Lisa was Olivia's cover name. "Of course...Lisa. How stupid of me. Olivia's the name of my ferret."

Olivia ignored the jab and stepped over to Jacqueline. "The temperature and moisture content must be critical since these underground vaults are all sealed and self-contained."

"*Oui.* Each vault requires different environmental settings. For instance, you don't want moisture in the seed storage rooms because it would create mold and damage the seeds."

"How many facilities like this does Raymond Foods own?" Emma asked, trying to keep herself focused on the conversation.

"I can only speak for AgEurope; our two growth labs are in Paris and Capetown. But our grain and seed storage facilities cover Europe and most of Africa. Fifty of them at least. Our largest storage facilities are located in Africa due to the high food demand." A unique buzzing sound came from Jacqueline's phone. She checked it with a slight frown on her lips. "A problem has come up at my office. Apologies, but I must stop our tour and see to it."

Emma sneaked a glance over at Olivia. They both were wondering the same thing.

Forty minutes later, Jacqueline's driver brought the Mercedes to a stop in front of AgEurope headquarters. Jacqueline led Emma and Olivia back into the building and up the elevator to the top floor. Jacqueline clopped her way into the reception area, where Miyuki and Nadia waited on the couch. Jacqueline gave them a long look when she passed.

Miyuki sprang up and hugged Emma. "Thank God you're back. We were sooooo bored."

Nadia held her stomach. "I'm not feeling too well."

"You're not? What's wrong?" Emma asked.

Nadia winked. "I think it was something I ate on the plane." She winked again.

"Why are you winking?" Emma asked.

Olivia pinched her arm. Emma flinched and shut her mouth.

"She's blinking because she lost her contacts in the toilet,"

Miyuki added.

Jacqueline stood over Pierre's desk with her arms crossed.

Pierre addressed her gaze. "*Oui?*"

Jacqueline asked him a question in French. Emma translated the words in her brain. *Has anyone been inside my office?*

"No one. I've watched it every minute you were gone, Mademoiselle," Pierre answered in French.

Jacqueline pivoted her body towards the girls.

Emma tried to keep her reaction low key and barely moved her lips to the Gems. "She's suspicious. Thinks someone was in her office."

"Alright then." Olivia flicked the girls a look. "It's time to give Jacqueline a show. Make it good."

Miyuki nodded. "We should go shopping now! Can we, Emma?" she asked in a loud voice.

"I want to go back to the hotel." Nadia complained as she held her stomach again.

"You're such a dork. We're in Paris! Who wants to stay in their stupid hotel rooms?" Emma asked, playing along.

"I'm not feeling well," Nadia said.

"*I'm not feeling well,*" Miyuki mimicked in a high voice. "Don't use that as an excuse to not go out tonight. I won't let you."

Nadia smirked. "Watching you get drunk and rubbing up against strange guys isn't my idea of fun."

Miyuki threw back her head. "What do you mean by that? Are you saying I'm a sloth?"

"A slut. I'm saying you're a drunk slut."

Miyuki pushed Nadia backwards on to the couch. The girl caught her back against the seat cushions without rolling off. Miyuki teared up. "Don't ever call me that again."

Nadia shot her a look. "Drunk slut. Drunk slut."

"You little…"

Olivia held Miyuki back. "Girls, behave yourselves, for God's sake. This is a business meeting."

Emma thought of something and went with it. "Hey, these are my friends and you don't give them orders."

Olivia acted shocked as she released Miyuki. "I'm sorry, Miss Rothchild I didn't mean any disrespect to your friends."

"Do you want me to call Mr. Gooden tonight and have you on the next plane to San Francisco? I can get him to fire you. Do you understand?"

Jacqueline watched with great interest as she approached the girls with her hands behind her back.

Emma separated herself from the girls. "I'm so sorry, Mademoiselle Boyay, my friends know better than to embarrass me like this."

Nadia and Miyuki dragged their eyes to the ground like naughty puppies.

"It's quite all right," Jacqueline said. "What are your plans tonight? Besides shopping and dancing, of course."

Emma glanced at Olivia, who looked at her tablet.

"There's nothing on your schedule, Miss Rothchild," she said.

"Excellent. Would you be my guest for dinner?" Jacqueline asked. "The restaurant Le Coq Rico. Shall we say eight?"

CHAPTER 13

Emma leaned over the iron rail of the small balcony that overlooked the Seine river. She enjoyed the late afternoon breeze tossing her hair around…and the moment to be alone. Emma could hear the girls inside the suite behind her, chattering away as they got ready for dinner with Jacqueline Boyay.

Emma had been with the girls for less than a week and already she felt overwhelmed by all the drama. Miyuki and Nadia had been nice, but the weird vibe coming from Olivia still bothered her. Olivia was no doubt the leader of the Gems, based on the way Mrs. B addressed her during the mission briefing and the way the other two girls followed Olivia's suggestions. Maybe Olivia was threatened by Emma joining the group. Whatever it was, Emma didn't care. Her priority was finding justice for her dad, not trying to please the queen bee.

In the meantime—Emma closed her eyes and enjoyed the peace and quiet.

"Emma, you getting ready?" Olivia asked.

She sighed and stepped back inside the suite. Miyuki was adjusting her earrings in front of a mirror. Her makeup was perfect. Olivia danced into her dress, forcing it to fit against her body. Nadia worked on her laptop, still wearing her *Girl Scientists Rock* T-shirt.

"Did you get in?" Emma asked her.

Nadia smiled. "My program worked perfectly. I've been scanning Jacqueline's emails and some other files on the company's servers. I found the schematics to the climate control system you saw on your tour. They've been modified."

Emma knelt. "How?"

Nadia brought up the plans on the screen. "Look at these new pipes that run through all the different buildings. They're connected to sprinklers that span over the farms and the seed storage bins."

"So what? Probably water pipes for putting out a fire, right?"

"Okay, but then why don't these pipes come out of the water system, which is here? These pipes span out from this large container here." Nadia clicked on a different folder that brought up more plans. "See? Those pipes and that container aren't in the original AirTech design plans. And think about it, why would you need to water seeds in long-term cold storage?"

Emma thought about it. "You know, Jacqueline mentioned they were always concerned with moisture getting into the seed storage areas. Weird. So why put in a sprinkler that's not hooked up to a water pipe?"

"Exactly," Nadia said. "And if Raymond Foods wanted the modifications done to all of their facilities around the world, why not have AirTech design them into the master plans since Raymond Foods was paying them millions to install it anyway? It doesn't make sense."

"I bet my dad's engineers were wondering the same thing. Maybe they brought this up to Jacqueline?"

"Didn't Mr. Gooden say that his engineers brought it to his attention first?"

"Right, and Ben told my dad, who then talked to the engineers. But then they all decided to fly back home instead of confronting Jacqueline about it. I wonder why?"

"Your dad needed proof," Olivia said, jumping into the conversation, her dress now on. "Think about it. Raymond Foods paid his company eighty-four million dollars to install these new systems. That's a lot of flipping money to lose if they piss them off by making baseless accusations against AgEurope. I'd wager your dad wanted his lawyers involved before approaching Jacqueline."

"We should send all this to Ben and see what he thinks," Emma said.

Olivia glanced at Emma's and Nadia's clothes. "We leave in a half hour. You both better hurry and get your pretty on."

Le Coq Rico sat on top of the Montmartre butte. The

restaurant had wood-paneled walls, plush seats and the scent of roasted chicken. Jacqueline reserved a private room in back, where the five ladies all sat together. The meal itself was in traditional French style. The first course was appetizers. The second, soup. The third, cheese. And the main course, grilled chicken with snails. As he delivered each course to their table, the young waiter complimented Emma in French. At first it was her lovely dress. Then her lovely earrings. Then her cute New York-accented French.

Emma was always cautious around boys. The problem wasn't getting them to pay attention to her. The problem was understanding what they expected from her. Emma tossed the problem around in her head once again when she found a note on the side of her main dish.

Le Café Oui Parle. Midnight. I'll be waiting.

The waiter was in his early twenties. Obviously confident. And cute. Maybe this guy was modest in his expectations. Could Emma hope for a guy like that? One that knew how to romance a girl? A guy patient and willing to go that extra length to win her heart instead of expecting quick gratification from a blond object?

Emma showed the note to Miyuki, who giggled and swiped it from Emma. She gave it to Nadia and her eyebrows lifted.

Miyuki leaned over and whispered, "Are you going?"

Emma referenced Jacqueline with her eyes. "Not now. We'll talk about it later."

Miyuki paused. "I think you should meet him. It's Paris! What do you think, Jacqueline? Should Emma go meet this young man at the café?" Miyuki offered the note to her. "Isn't it romantic?"

Jacqueline put down her wineglass and examined it. "From our waiter? He is handsome. But I thought you wanted to go dancing with your friends tonight?"

Olivia grabbed the note from the table and read it. Her mouth twisted down.

Nadia speared a small piece of chicken with her fork. "Didn't you swear off boys this month, Emma? You wanted nothing more to do with them, if I remember."

"Ha! That's before the French hottie served us cheese." Miyuki giggled.

"Can you tell us more about Raymond Foods?" Olivia asked, desperate to change the conversation. "AgEurope is a division, am I correct?"

Jacqueline sipped her glass of wine. "*Oui,* Mr. Raymond owns food companies all over the world. North America, Europe, Africa, the Middle East, Russia…his market share is astounding."

"And the company grows the food, processes it, and distributes it too?" Olivia dotted her lips with her napkin before returning it to her lap.

"From plants to pancakes." Jacqueline smiled. "The Raymond Foods company motto."

Jacqueline and the Gems worked on their meal and conducted more mindless small talk, crystal clicking as knives and forks touched plates. The young waiter did another check of the table. He held a long warm smile for Emma. She played it cool and concentrated on Jacqueline when she spoke.

Jacqueline savored more of her wine as she glanced at Olivia. "How long have you been working for Mr. Gooden? Pardon me, but you look…rather young to hold such an important position. You must be quite brilliant."

Olivia played it off. "I graduated early. Wasn't looking for a job straight out of school, but Mr. Gooden had this training program for new college graduates that I stumbled into. And I liked the company."

"You enjoy climate control systems for buildings?"

Olivia took her time chewing her food before answering. "To be honest, not really. I'm interested in football. Rothchild Industries owns the team in Chelsea. I'm hoping to transfer there and be in sports management one day."

Emma admired the save. Olivia knew how to think on her feet.

Olivia drank some water. "What's it like to work with Ron Raymond? From everything I've read about him, he's intense."

Jacqueline finished her wine. "He's a demanding boss, yet fair. People think the food industry is boring and lacks innovation. Ron Raymond sees it differently. The man is a visionary. Like a Steve Jobs or a Bill Gates. New crop-growing techniques. Genetic crossbreeding to build stronger seeds. Better animals that are healthier to consume. More humane slaughtering techniques."

Nadia and Emma stopped eating their roasted chicken.

"I admire the man," Jacqueline said. "He's a man of action. Says he'll do something and always follows it through to the end. He gets things done."

"A workaholic?" Emma asked.

Jacqueline grinned. "You're familiar with such men. Your father?"

"My dad so loved his work. The time we were together, he would be talking about this new project and that new project. What exciting new gizmo his tech firm designed. His hockey team getting into the Stanley Cup playoffs."

"Your father was proud of what he built. Ron and your father had a lot in common. I'm sure that's why he picked your father's company to do business with. Ron Raymond only works with men who see the world as he does."

Emma wondered if Ron Raymond had any children. And what those kids were like. Did they feel like runner-up in their parents' lives too?

Jacqueline and the girls wrapped up dinner and said their goodbyes. Miyuki and Nadia acted inpatient, wanting to go straight to the clubs that were Paris hot spots to see celebrities. Emma noted Pierre driving up to the curb in a dark sedan, replacing the driver she had seen earlier that day. Maybe Pierre was more than just Jacqueline's executive assistant? The woman in question climbed into the sedan and was whisked away to places unknown.

The Gems went back to their hotel, dropping their entourage cover for the night.

Emma slipped off her heels in the elevator as it took them up to their floor. Olivia took the pins out of her pulled-back hair and let the curly strands drop over her shoulders. Miyuki read a fashion advertisement on the wall in French. Or maybe she was looking at the pictures.

Nadia pulled at her skirt. "I hate my legs. They look like they came from a Muppet."

"You be quiet." Miyuki playfully draped her arm over Nadia's collar. "You don't look like a…what is Muppet?"

"A Muppet is like Kermit the Frog or Miss Piggy," Emma said.

Miyuki clapped her hands together. "Yes! Ha! I love Gonzo."

"Just call me Miss Piggy, then," Nadia said. "Short and fat legs."

"Don't be stupid. You have pretty legs," Miyuki said.

"Seriously, you're tripping over nothing," Emma said. "You won't let any guy see them anyway."

"What do you mean?" Nadia asked.

"Well, since you're a…" Emma stopped and changed course. "Hey, there's advantages to not showing your legs. You don't have to shave a lot." She threw up a smile.

Nadia frowned. "Since I'm a what?"

Emma bit her lip and didn't quite know what to say.

"That woman is dangerous," Olivia said out of the blue, not paying attention to the conversation. "The hairs on my neck wouldn't stop prickling. I'd wager Jacqueline's involved in whatever is going on here. Tonight she was fishing for answers. We better keep our guard up."

The gold elevator doors opened. No one moved.

Nadia was still waiting for Emma to answer her. Miyuki stared at the floor in an awkward kind of way.

Olivia tilted her head. "What's up with you lot?"

Nadia fired Emma a look before stepping off the elevator. Olivia shrugged and followed. Miyuki was next, leaving Emma alone. She caught her image in one of the elevator's shiny gold walls. Emma shook her head at herself before picking up her shoes and trailing the girls down the hallway.

A hotel employee stepped to the side to let them pass before continuing. Nadia slowed, her mind occupied with something. Emma passed her and reached their hotel suite just as Olivia swiped the room's card key. The red light turned green and she pushed the door open. Inside the room, all the drawers were pulled and dumped on to the floor. Articles of clothing were everywhere. Pillows sliced open and the contents scattered all over the beds like confetti. Sheets pulled off. Closets stood wide open. Hangers thrown to the ground. The bathroom was hit too. Drawers ripped out, as someone had rummaged through the cosmetic bags and cabinets too. It was a mess.

"Glad we had our purses with us," Miyuki said.

"And our phones," Emma added.

Olivia scoffed. "This is why Jacqueline invited us for dinner."

"What if it was a burglar?" Emma asked. "I'm sure they have crime in Paris."

"It's too convenient, love. How would the burglar know we'd be gone?"

Miyuki held up a diamond necklace. "And why would he not take this?"

Dad's sweet-sixteen gift to Emma. She held out her hand and Miyuki handed the necklace back.

"My laptop's gone," Nadia said. She hesitated a moment before rushing out of the room. The girls followed Nadia back into the hallway. She ran to the elevator landing. The hotel employee was still there, waiting on an elevator. He had dark hair and a trimmed goatee.

"Sir? Did you recently see anyone around suite 811?" Nadia asked.

The man acted confused. "I do not speak English."

Emma stepped in and repeated Nadia's question in French.

"*Non.* I saw no one," he said in French.

"May we see his messenger bag?" Nadia asked.

"Tell him we want to search it," Olivia added.

"Give us your bag. Please? We want to search it," Emma said in French.

The man shook his head.

"This bloke works at a premier five-star hotel in Paris and doesn't speak a syllable of English?" Olivia asked. "And where's his name tag? The hotel employees down in the lobby all had one."

The man with the goatee went very still…then shoved Nadia into Olivia. The girls smashed into each other and fell to the floor.

The man hauled ass down the hallway.

Miyuki charged after him. Emma followed her halfway down the hall before realizing the other girls were still at the elevator.

"Go! We'll head him off in the lobby," Olivia shouted.

Emma gave a thumbs-up and ran towards the end of the hallway. The door to the fire escape was drifting shut, so Emma threw it back open and plunged into the dark stairwell. Below her, loud steps echoed around the concrete. Emma bounced down the stairs as fast as she could. Round and round each flight of stairs she went, each floor descending in order...

Seventh floor.

Sixth.

Fifth.

Fourth.

Third.

Second.

Emma reached the ground floor. She shoved open the door and the crisp night air bit her skin. The wide street next to the hotel was dark. A handful of streetlamps were at a distance, but not any close enough to make a difference here. Miyuki stood a few feet away, scanning the quiet street.

Emma breathed hard. "Did you lose him?"

"He's here somewhere." Miyuki tried to catch her own breath. "Take this side of street. I'll take the other. Behind us is dead end, so I assume he went this way."

The two girls split up. Emma walked along the sidewalk, peeking around cars and in the windows to all the closed shops. Emma tried to remember her training. If the man tried to attack her, Emma wanted to throw a kick because if she could knock the man silly in the head, the girls could come and help when he recovered. But Emma hoped Miyuki would find him first.

A shadow moved.

Emma froze. *Leg kick*, she reminded herself. *Leg kick*.

She took a few more steps. Whatever it was, that shadow was hiding behind the corner of this cheese shop. Emma wondered if it was safe to call out to Miyuki. Her friend might not have enough time to come save Emma from getting her butt kicked.

Emma prepared herself. Time for the actress to get into character. "Whoever you are, come out from behind the building or...I'll kick you in the head." She hoped that sounded threatening enough.

It did. The man jumped into view and ran down the sidewalk.

"Miyuki!" Emma yelled as she ran after him.

Miyuki hauled ass from across the street and joined Emma as they chased the man around a few corners.

A luxury hotel stood proudly on the street. Above the main entrance, a large metal sign with black letters that glowed in the night spelled out **The Hotel Beau Barriere. Paris.** Waiting under the cloth awning were two valets dressed to impress.

A man with a goatee raced past them.

Then Miyuki and Emma bolted past, yelling at the top of their lungs.

The valets laughed.

"Two girlfriends. Very bad, *oui*?" the first valet said.

"Hey!" a girl yelled.

Olivia stormed out of the main entrance, with Nadia in pursuit as they ran after Miyuki and Emma.

"Four mad girlfriends?" the second valet asked.

"He's a dead man, *non*? Glad I'm not him," the first valet said with a laugh.

Emma watched the man with the goatee veer away from the hotel and out into the busy street. French drivers slammed on their brakes and honked as the man weaved through the vehicles. Emma slowed.

Miyuki didn't. She charged right into traffic, navigating the mess of angry drivers wondering what the hell was happening.

Emma pushed herself forward, tracing Miyuki's path through the maze of stopped cars.

Olivia and Nadia ran parallel to the street, looking for a less dangerous way across it.

The man stopped near a white Peugeot and climbed in back. The Peugeot's driver pointed a gun out the window.

Gunfire cracked the air as Miyuki hit the ground and rolled under the cover of a parked car.

Emma's heart pumped like a racehorse. This was real. Holy crap. People were *shooting* at them.

The driver aimed his gun at Emma.

She copied Miyuki and dropped to the ground.

Crack. Crack. Crack. Real bullets pinged into the cars above her.

The sound of tires squealing pushed Miyuki back to her feet. Emma took her cue and peeked over the Toyota she was hiding behind. The white Peugeot raced down the street. There was no way to catch the man now.

Miyuki rushed over to a young Frenchman unchaining his motorbike. "May I borrow this? I give back."

The Frenchman scoffed at the question.

"So very sorry." Miyuki lifted her leg and shoved the man off his motorbike before climbing on it.

Emma ran over to her. "What are you doing?"

"Chasing after them. Hop on."

Emma had never been on a motorbike before. Didn't they need helmets?

Miyuki jumped on the starter and the cycle roared to life. "You coming?"

Emma didn't want to, but Miyuki might need her help. She swallowed her fear and tossed her leg over the bike, settling in behind Miyuki.

"What are you two lunatics doing?" Olivia yelled from across the street. "Don't go after him. It's too flipping dangerous."

Miyuki gunned the throttle. The motorcycle's front tire lifted off as they flew down the street. Emma held on tight. Getting shot at was terrifying. But being on this motorcycle wasn't exactly calming her down either.

Up ahead, the white Peugeot made a left.

Miyuki's hand opened up the throttle and the bike accelerated. She weaved around cars and threw the bike around a city bus. They were so close to it that Emma could've reached out and touched the metal rivets. Miyuki leaned into the left turn and didn't slow. Emma glued herself to Miyuki and closed her eyes. She felt the motorcycle clear the left turn and shift its weight to the center.

Emma opened her eyes and saw a wall of traffic. All three lanes.

Miyuki braked hard and steered the bike up on the sidewalk, whipping around surprised pedestrians. But the girls were making better progress than the traffic snarled up beside them.

"Do you see them?" Miyuki asked.

"Not yet," Emma replied.

Miyuki guided the motorcycle off the sidewalk and in between two lines of traffic, using the seam in between the vehicles as a bike path.

A white Mercedes.

A white Honda.

A white Peugeot. Emma pointed. They were in the far left lane.

Miyuki maneuvered in front of a slow delivery truck. They were almost on top of the car when—

The white Peugeot gunned its engine and smashed into the back of the next car, shoving it out of the way. The driver swung a hard left and raced down an alley.

Emma's head jerked back as Miyuki launched the motorcycle in between the two remaining cars and scrambled into the alley.

The Peugeot picked up speed. So did Miyuki. Her bike was gaining. The girl's unrestrained hair whipped Emma's cheeks and eyes without mercy.

Without slowing, the white Peugeot flew through an intersection where the alley met another road. A truck barely missed them.

Miyuki raced through the same intersection as cars slammed on their brakes to avoid them.

Emma and Miyuki zoomed down another alley, still gaining on the Peugeot.

The car slammed on its brakes, creating a burning rubber smell inside the narrow alley.

Miyuki slowed the cycle. Emma wondered what the car was doing. Were they surrendering?

The Peugeot's white backup lights glowed. The engine raced, creating another smell of rubber as the car hurtled itself...at them.

Miyuki kicked the rear tire out and skidded the bike to a stop. The narrow alley was only big enough for the car. There was no way to drive around them.

The car picked up speed.

"Miyuki!" Emma said.

"Do you have your purse?"

Emma touched it. She almost forgot it was there. "Yes."

"Use your Forest Fire mascara."

"My what?" Emma was confused. "You want me to do your eyes right now?"

"No. Don't use on eyes. Use on *them*."

Emma thought Miyuki had lost it. But then it dawned on her. That gadget training guide Emma was given to read by Mrs. B and didn't. *Cosmetic Weapon Tactics.*

"Hurry." Miyuki planted her leg and spun the back wheel around, swinging the bike around to face the opposite direction.

The Peugeot closed on them.

Emma searched through her purse. Red-hot lipstick. Sleeping Beauty face cream. Raise the Roof rouge. Forest Fire mascara.

Miyuki accelerated. Emma hoped they could outrun the car and not have to rely on her to save them. But a loud crack and the whiz of a bullet reminded Emma that these men didn't need a car to kill them.

Emma took out the mascara and popped it open. It looked normal. How did she set it off? Oh, why didn't she read that stupid book!

"How do you use it?"

"Instead of pulling out brush, push down on the top three times," Miyuki yelled. "It should beep."

A bullet ricocheted off the handlebar, barely missing Miyuki's hand.

Emma pressed the top three times and it beeped.

"Now what?"

"Explodes in three seconds."

"Three?" Emma threw it behind her. The eyeliner popped like a firecracker. Emma glanced back and saw smoke pouring from the container as it filled the tunnel with a black cloud.

Miyuki went flat out down the alley until she reached another open crossroad. Miyuki skidded the bike to a stop.

The girls listened.

Smoke poured from the alley and obscured their vision, but there was the unmistakable sound of metal scraping against stone. The driver couldn't avoid hitting the narrow walls if he couldn't see them. Then a loud crunch of steel. The Peugeot's engine revved up and down in a strange manner.

Soon the sounds of metal being abused stopped.

"He's stuck in the alley," Miyuki said.

The engine died and a round of heavy coughing echoed from inside as men's shoes clattered against the stones.

Miyuki kicked the stand out with her foot and climbed off the motorbike. "Better get ready to kick some butt."

Emma caught herself breathing hard, the adrenaline percolating through her veins. But she was ready, especially with Miyuki by her side. Emma climbed off the bike and got into a fighting stance.

The girls waited.

The footsteps became distant.

Miyuki inched her way into the alley still hazy from the smoke. She coughed and Emma ran up behind her with a Kleenex covering her mouth. She gave one to Miyuki. They peered into the alley and could make out the outline of the Peugeot. It was slightly crooked with part of its left back bumper sandwiched against the wall of the alley. The opposite front right bumper was mashed against the other side of the wall.

There was no sign of the men.

"They ran out the other side," Miyuki said, disappointed.

CHAPTER 14

The morning sun lifted above the Seine as Paris woke up to a new day. Since Nadia's laptop had been stolen, the Gems tracked down a web café near their hotel. They huddled around a public computer with a web cam as Nadia inserted a thumb drive that contained an encrypted Authority program that scrambled their IP address and location. She told Emma that the program would also erase their digital footprint from the public-use computer. Emma didn't quite understand what the girl was saying, but trusted Nadia knew what she was doing.

The Gems first placed a video conference call with Ben in California. It was around midnight there. Olivia explained to him about what they'd found out and asked him about the decision not to confront AgEurope or Raymond Foods about the modifications.

"Yes, Emma's father offered to fly the engineers back to California so we could discuss those modified schematics with our lawyers. Those unauthorized modifications could have liability consequences for our company, not to mention ruin AirTech's reputation if they caused an accident or an explosion. Are you implying that Jacqueline Boyay and Raymond Foods are involved in some kind of conspiracy?"

"We only know she's involved somehow, Mr. Gooden," Olivia said. "Do you know why Raymond Foods would make these modifications? It doesn't make any sense to us, but we're not engineers."

Ben glanced to the side at another screen, looking over the schematics Nadia had sent him. He shook his head. "Part of this modification uses sprinklers in the seed storage area. Which doesn't make sense because those vaults are all airtight."

"What does that mean?" Emma asked.

"Air pumps remove all the oxygen from the vaults when there's no one inside. It's like a vacuum sealing a bag of frozen meat you want to store in the freezer for a long period of time. The vacuum inside the vault protects the seeds. The strange thing is...you can't have a fire without oxygen, so why put fire sprinklers in a place a fire can't exist?"

"Yes," Nadia said. "And why risk the sprinklers leaking water into a controlled environment designed to eliminate the chance for mold to grow?"

"Thanks for the info, Ben," Emma said. "We'll keep you in the loop if we find anything else."

"All right. You should call your grandma. She's worried."

Emma bet she was more than worried. "I will, Ben. Thanks!"

They closed down the video call and the connection. Olivia took her phone and walked outside to contact Mrs. B at her special number for further instructions. Emma, Miyuki, and Nadia bought some coffee, tea, and baguettes, then found a table. Emma's sleepy brain welcomed the caffeinated liquid. She'd barely slept last night due to hearing gunshots in her sleep.

"Last night, you upset Olivia." Nadia sipped her tea. "Taking off on that motorbike like that. So dangerous."

Miyuki scoffed. "We needed more answers. Capturing that man would help."

"Those answers aren't worth sacrificing your life. Or Emma's."

"She jumped on the bike to help me. Wouldn't you do the same?"

"Of course. But—it was too reckless. You're always so reckless." Nadia drank her tea.

Miyuki nibbled on her baguette, her face sad.

"Where did you learn to ride a bike like that?" Emma asked.

Miyuki cheered up instantly. "I do motocross in Japan. Competed in events. When I was a little girl, I used to ride my bicycle everywhere in town. Then I discovered motorcycles. They go much faster than bicycles."

"Did you really blow up your boyfriend's motorbike?"

Miyuki grinned at her baguette. "Maybe."

"Maybe? What's the story behind that?"

"He cheated on me with girl from another school. He wasn't on his motorcycle when I did it," Miyuki said, "but it did make him pee-pee in his pants."

Even Nadia smiled at that one.

Olivia entered the café and found their table. She paused at the food. "Did no one get anything for me? I could've been a bit peckish, you know."

"Sorry," Nadia said.

Olivia joined them. "I spoke with Mrs. B and she wants us to go back to America and pay Mr. Ron Raymond a visit."

Nadia sliced her own baguette in half and placed one half on a paper napkin next to Olivia. "Does Mrs. B suspect he knows what Jacqueline's plans are?"

"Either that or could give us a clue as to why." Olivia took the gift baguette and smeared it with some butter before taking a bite. "I'll book us a private jet tonight, courtesy of Mr. Gooden. That way we can fly straight to Kansas City."

"No," Emma said. "I want to fly commercial again."

"It wastes so much time. We'd have to change planes and wait for hours at airports. Quicker if we fly direct."

"I know. But I'd feel safer."

"I'll check the plane myself after the pilot does, love."

"She's a registered pilot, Emma," Nadia added.

"No, I'd feel better on a commercial plane."

Olivia scoffed. "You're a young American heiress traveling abroad. They always take private jets. It's part of your cover."

"We can fly commercial," Miyuki said. "No biggie."

Olivia stared at Miyuki, but the Japanese girl didn't flinch.

"Perhaps we should," Nadia said, her eyes reaching out for Olivia's approval. "If it would make Emma more comfortable."

Olivia threw up her hands. "Fine. We'll leave in the morning and waste hours getting there, then."

* * *

The Airbus 380 aircraft boasted two passenger decks and seats for up to 538 passengers. It amazed Emma that something so big could fly way above the clouds. The Air Global first-class section of seats were divided into a one-two-one layout. Olivia booked two rows of middle seats together, picking Nadia as her seatmate while leaving Miyuki with Emma. The chairs were huge and comfy with plenty of private space in front to put up one's legs and relax. The chair itself even reclined to form a nice bed. Before takeoff, the first-class steward came by with complimentary wine. But the girls were offered orange juice.

Miyuki removed the privacy screen between their two seats, and for once, Emma didn't mind.

"Look. Complimentary slippers." Miyuki giggled and showed them off on her feet. "I feel like English princess."

"I can see you in this beautiful pink dress," Emma said. "Wearing your hair up in a tiara...as you sit on top of a motorcycle."

Miyuki covered her mouth and laughed. "You're so funny." The girl let her laugh fade before gazing at Emma with her gentle eyes.

"What?"

"I'm happy you joined the Gems. We needed a girl like you."

"What kind of girl am I?"

"The kind of girl that jumps on the back of a motorcycle with me. Please don't misunderstand, if I needed them, Olivia and Nadia would be there for me. We've been through a lot together in a short amount of time, but Nadia and Olivia are close and... they don't get me sometimes," Miyuki said. "I like to have fun. I don't like sitting around and worrying about things. What's the point? Every new day is a gift and I want to bathe myself in it like sunlight and have it warm me up inside."

Emma wished she saw life like that. It must be amazing. She hoped some of Miyuki's attitude would rub off on her.

"A gift, huh? That's an interesting way of looking at it."

"You disagree?"

"Seeing my grandma at breakfast every day is a gift," Emma said. "She's healthy now, but she's old. I worry that...someday I'll wake up and not see her there making breakfast. Bad enough my dad..."

A wave of sadness crashed against Emma, choking off her words.

"I understand," Miyuki said.

Emma swallowed back the tears. "I keep...I keep losing the

people that I love. My mom. My dad. Grandma might be next. I want it to stop."

"I'm afraid you can't stop death."

"But why me? What did I do? Everyone else gets to have their parents around, but I feel like I'm being punished for some horrible sin." Emma lay back in her chair, letting her head sink into the leather. She didn't want to dump her problems all over her new friend. Emma feared she would push Miyuki away like she did everyone else in her life.

Miyuki softened and took off her seat belt. "Would you like a hug before takeoff?"

Emma wiped her cheek and nodded.

The four jet engines spooled up before the tractor pushed their aircraft from the gate. In fifteen minutes, the large plane soared into the air and headed west towards the Atlantic Ocean.

Emma thought about listening to music, but chose to read for a while. She'd just bought *A Howl in Space*, the second book in the thrilling *Star Wolf* sci-fi werewolf series, and couldn't wait to get started. Miyuki selected a street racer video game from the plane's entertainment system menu. She wore headphones, but still squealed with delight every time her car did a wicked slide or huge jump.

After a while, Emma felt the orange juice and bottle of water she'd drunk at the airport collecting down in her basement. She placed her bookmark and unfastened her seat belt.

Miyuki slipped off her headphones. "Am I bothering you?"

"No, just going for a walk." Emma flashed a smile as she stood in the aisle. Emma waved as she walked past Olivia and Nadia, who were curled up in their seats having a deep conversation. Most likely about her.

Emma reached the first-class lounge. A tasteful display of donuts, muffins, cheeses, and breads were set up on the counter. Another steward prepared bottles of liquor for the bar. One older passenger sat on the couch, enjoying his French newspaper.

Emma took care of business in the lavatory. She washed her hands and checked her face in the mirror. The morning disaster look she'd worn at the hotel was gone. Her face looked okay, but those strands of blond hair went every which way but straight.

Emma had left her purse in the seat, so she tried to tame the rebellious strands with her fingers. It wasn't working. Emma remembered the hair scrunchie she still had in her pocket. She pulled back her unruly hair into a large ponytail and tied it off. Emma was satisfied and stepped out of the lavatory. She stopped by the display of cheese and took a nibble. Then another little nibble. It was good cheese.

"They're both out cold," a hushed yet tense voice said.

"What do you mean? Both pilots?" a louder voice asked.

Emma stopped chewing. She approached the forward passageway the crew used to access the cockpit. Two flight attendants were there and looked scared.

"I went up to the cockpit and the door was open. The copilot is on the floor near the door as if he struggled to unlock it before he passed out."

"And Captain Ashcroft? She's out too?"

The other nodded. "I think the plane is on autopilot, but…do you know if anyone on the crew has flying experience?"

Emma's heart was beating so fast she couldn't breathe. Was this how her dad had felt when he knew it was hopeless? When her dad had known he was going to die? Emma felt her legs giving out, so she dropped into a chair. Her brain replayed her father's accident as if she'd been there. The screams. The terror. Her father fighting for control of the aircraft…and losing. The images were fast and furious, beating her up inside.

"Don't tell the passengers," the older flight attendant said with renewed professionalism, her years of training coming out in full force. "Go to each member of the crew and tell them the situation. See if we can find someone with flying experience. Meanwhile, I'll get on the radio and declare an emergency."

The younger attendant walked into the lounge without seeing Emma. She whispered to the steward setting up the bar. His face turned white as he shook his head. The attendant left and the steward ran off too.

They were scared, Emma thought. Just like she was.

"No wonder you didn't come back." Miyuki bounced into the lounge, eying the food. "Mmm, blueberry muffins. Look fresh too." Miyuki saw Emma's face and knelt. "Are you okay?"

Emma laid her hands on Miyuki's shoulders to brace her for

the news. "Both pilots have passed out. The flight attendants were just talking about it. They need someone to fly the plane."

Miyuki absorbed the news.

Emma shook her. "Don't you understand, Miyuki? I'll never make it to my seventeenth birthday because we're all going to die horrible deaths."

Miyuki grinned.

Emma couldn't believe it. The end was coming and this girl thought it was funny?

"Don't be silly," Miyuki said. "We know a pilot. Olivia! She can fly this plane."

Emma's mind recycled the info. Yes! It was in Olivia's bio. She could fly planes. And even helicopters!

"C'mon." Miyuki grabbed Emma and ran down the aisle to where Olivia and Nadia were.

Miyuki stood there shaking with excitement.

Olivia caught her eyes. "What are you all giddy about, love?"

"Ha!" Miyuki clapped her hands together. "Guess what *you* get to do today."

CHAPTER 15

Olivia couldn't believe what Miyuki told her about the pilots. It sounded like her friend was explaining the plot to a Hollywood movie, not real life. Certainly not her life. Olivia turned and glanced back into the cabin. She could see the crowded business and economy sections. A mother and a little girl were playing a card game. There must be a lot of families on this plane.

Olivia took note of Emma's face, the color drained from her skin. No doubt this situation created a major panic inside her due to her father's accident. Now it created a major panic within Olivia too.

"You two are bonkers. Totally flipping bonkers. I can't fly a 380, for God's sake."

"Why not? It's a plane, yes?" Miyuki said.

"You daft cow, this isn't some small plane with an engine and four seats. The 380 has four giant jet engines. It's a huge flying boat that needs at least two pilots to fly the bugger. I can't do it all by myself."

Nadia touched Olivia's arm. "You have us. We'll help you."

"You're a good pilot. You can land anything," Miyuki said with this boundless optimism that made Olivia want to scream.

A good pilot? Olivia was used to flying alone. The pressure of doing everything correctly was easier to manage when it was just her and the airplane. That way she didn't have to worry about killing innocent people if things went wrong. There was no way she could handle this.

"I can't. I've never flown anything this big. I'll kill everyone," Olivia said.

"You should at least tell the crew you have experience," Nadia said.

Her friend was right.

"I—I could help them with the radio calls. I'm sure they'll find someone else with more flying experience. It's a huge plane."

"Of course they will," Nadia said.

"What if they can't?" Emma asked.

"Then we're doomed," Olivia said.

Inside the forward lounge, the Gems presented themselves to the senior flight attendant. The woman was surprised the girls already knew about the situation and begged them not to say anything to the other passengers. The senior flight attendant had Olivia sit down while the crew completed their discreet inquiry of the passengers. The question was phrased by the crew into a plea for someone to help the captain with the radio because the copilot felt ill.

Olivia prayed they would find someone else. She knew a 380 was far too big for her to handle.

Twenty minutes later the crew gathered in the lounge and closed the curtains from the cabin.

A steward began. "I found an aircraft mechanic that works out of JFK, but he doesn't know how to fly. That's all."

The senior flight attendant frowned. "Anyone else?"

Everyone shook their heads.

The senior flight attendant crossed her arms and considered her options.

Olivia's stomach burned as her nerves cut through her patience. "You can't revive the pilots at all? Did you try smelling salts?"

"We did," the senior attendant said. "Whatever drug they're on, it's knocked them out for good."

"They were drugged?"

"Someone gave them coffee before we sealed up the cabin and pushed back from the gate. He wasn't someone from our crew. Yet he wore an Air Global uniform." The senior flight attendant walked closer to Olivia. "Do you have ATP flight experience?"

"Not right now," Olivia answered. "I only hold a private license, yet I'm rated for multiengine aircraft."

"How old are you?" a steward asked.

When adults asked a question like that, they were already judging you as a child. Olivia thought about lying, but didn't. "Seventeen years old."

All hope evaporated from the adults. Even they knew Olivia couldn't do a task like this.

Nadia squeezed her friend's hand. "I've seen this girl land a plane in a raging thunderstorm." Nadia raised her chin. "I know she can do this."

Olivia's spirit lifted. It was a wonderful thing for Nadia to say. But they had almost died in that thunderstorm and Olivia knew it had been a mistake trying to land in a mess like that.

"She'll have to do it or we're all dead," the steward said, losing his cool.

"Juan, I'll tie you up in a seat right now if you can't control yourself," the senior attendant snapped. "We need to focus, people. We must keep the passengers calm so that means we need to be calm. If anyone asks, tell them we have someone assisting the pilot with the radio and we'll be heading back to Paris. Loren and Samuel? I'll need your help carrying the pilots to the crew bunk. We must keep them out of sight and comfortable. Is that understood?"

The crew broke up and left the lounge, keeping the curtains shut.

The senior attendant pivoted to Olivia. "What do you need from us? I can sit in the cockpit to assist you if that would be helpful."

"No, thank you, I've got my copilots right here." Olivia looked at the girls behind her. Nadia and Miyuki nodded.

Emma was distracted, her eyes dancing around the cabin, her arms held close to her body. She was barely holding it together. Olivia wrote her off as useless in the coming crisis.

The girls made room as the two male stewards gently lifted the unconscious pilots off the floor of the cockpit. Olivia came in first and slipped into the pilot's seat. Her eyes scanned the instruments and the controls. This was the nerve center of the aircraft. The joystick to her left controlled the lives of over five hundred people.

Olivia stopped herself. She couldn't think like that. *Just fly the flipping airplane, love.*

Out the windshield, the crisp blue sky was rich with color, with a layer of cotton-candy clouds below them. A gorgeous day for flying.

The weather gave Olivia back some confidence as she slipped the captain's seat belt straps snugly over her chest and settled in to her new environment. Olivia closed her eyes for a moment and settled her stomach. She opened them. "Right…flight level 320. Heading 314. We're level. All four engines good. Plenty of fuel, I think. I see the autopilot is engaged. All right, then. Let's do this flipping thing."

Olivia twisted in her seat. "Nadia, you're my copilot. You'll do radio calls and help me with the instruments. Miyuki? Behind me there should be an operator's handbook for the Airbus 380. It might be buried under there, but find it. I'll need you to refer to the diagrams inside to help me find the cockpit switches and displays that I'll need to land this bird. Emma, you'll go through the landing checklist and call it out to me when the time comes."

Emma swallowed. "Landing checklist? Where's that?"

Olivia rifled through the side pocket next to her seat, found one, and gave it to Emma. Nadia climbed into the copilot's seat and put on the seatbelt straps. She pulled back her hair and slipped on the headphones. Nadia activated the radio and called out exactly what Olivia told her to say to air traffic control.

The radio crackled back. *"Roger, Global 614. We have an Air France 380 captain en route to assist you. Do nothing at this time. We have traffic above and below you clear. Please tell me the name of the pilot and what is her flight experience. Over?"*

Nadia hesitated. "Do you want to give out your real name?"

Olivia watched the artificial horizon on the digital panel in front of her. "I can't. Make up one for me."

"Amelia," Emma said.

Nadia shrugged and used the name in her call back to the ATC.

"Why Amelia?" Miyuki asked as she rummaged through all the flight books.

"Amelia Earhart," Emma said. "That girl who flew around the world."

"Oh thanks. That was the girl who died, wasn't it?" Olivia

knew the story well. In the 1930s Amelia Earhart flew around the world in a two-engine prop-job with only radio beacons and mathematics to navigate by. She was on the last leg of the round-the-world trip when her plane disappeared over the Pacific and was never heard from again. Olivia hoped they'd have better luck.

It took a while, but Miyuki found the Airbus 380's operator's handbook. It was thick. Miyuki opened it up and tried to find the section on cockpit controls. Meanwhile, the French Airbus captain came on the radio and wanted more details on "Amelia" and her flying experience before proceeding. Olivia answered his questions. The French pilot's voice helped calm Olivia down even more.

"Compared to the previous aircraft you've flown, the 380 will respond slower to your inputs," the French pilot said over the radio. *"Remember to be gentle on the controls. Take your time and be deliberate in each action. Remember to think in terms of where you want the plane to be. Stand by for a turn."*

Olivia gripped the joystick and concentrated.

"We'll begin with a turn to the right. Your new heading will be 014. You will not need to use the flight controls for this. We'll use the autopilot instead." The French captain explained where the heading selector was on the auto pilot and Miyuki agreed as she checked it with the manual.

Olivia turned the selector knob to 014 and pressed the execute button. The plane made a gentle turn to the right, doing a complete 180 before stopping when it reached its new heading.

"Good. You're on course back to the airport. Now we need the plane to descend." The French captain then gave Olivia step-by-step instructions on how to tell the plane to descend. Soon the computer smoothly guided the large aircraft down to its new altitude. *"The system in the 380 is very sophisticated. We'll use the autopilot to make your approach to the glide slope. Once your plane makes contact with the ILS, the aircraft should guide itself to within fifty feet of the runway. Then you'll land as you would in a normal aircraft."*

Olivia relaxed. Fifty feet from the runway? Easy landing. It would be just like landing a Cessna. She could do this. Why was she getting herself so worked up?

"Yet remember, Amelia, the 380 is a much larger aircraft. Once you've touched down, the aircraft will use a large amount of runway. But that's all right. Paris has some of the longest runways built for the 380. Still, you will need to use maximum reverse thrust and brakes when you touch down."

The captain made more adjustments to their heading, altitude, and speed. So far the plane's computer was handling it well.

"Ten miles out," the French captain said over the radio. *"Your aircraft should be picking up the ILS now."* He then went on to explain how to check that in the cockpit.

Thanks to Miyuki, Olivia knew which screen to check. But an ominous message glowed in red…

AUTOLAND FAULT
MODE N/A

Olivia's stomach dropped. She knew her job was about to get much harder. She activated her radio. "The aircraft is giving me a warning message." Olivia repeated the warning to the pilot on the ground.

There was silence for a couple of minutes.

Olivia shot Nadia a worried look.

"Global 614 to Paris ATC. Did you copy our last transmission?" Nadia asked.

The radio crackled. *"We downloaded your aircraft's maintenance log…apparently the auto-landing feature does not work."*

"Oh, that's brilliant," Olivia said. "Flipping brilliant."

"You must use the visual approach slope indicator to make your approach. Prepare to take control of the aircraft."

Using her shorts, Olivia rubbed off the sweat from her left hand before grabbing the joystick. She placed her right hand on the four throttle levers. Her feet on the rudder pedals. Her heart pounded like a jackhammer. She now gave herself a fifty-fifty chance of dying.

Olivia swallowed and breathed through her nose, trying to calm herself. She switched off the autopilot and the plane released control to her hand. Olivia carefully nudged the stick right and left, keeping the wings level. She nudged the stick forward to keep the aircraft descending. But she watched her pitch angle to keep the massive plane from stalling. If she stalled the plane, they would most certainly die.

Olivia reduced the throttles and the aircraft slowed.

"You're doing great," Miyuki said.

"We'll make it," Nadia said with confidence.

Sweat trickled down Olivia's neck. She didn't dare take her hands off the controls to wipe it off.

The captain came back on the radio. *"Seven miles from touchdown. 1900 feet. Speed 230 knots. Your approach is a bit high."*

Olivia nudged the joystick forward, bringing the nose down a little.

"Well done. Six miles from touchdown."

"We need to go through the checklist for landing," Olivia said. "Emma? You ready?"

"I guess. What do I do exactly?" Emma asked, her voice cracking.

"It's easy," Olivia said. "Start from the top and call out each item, loud. When I say check, push the tab on the list to the right and that marks it as completed. When we get to the end, tell me, okay?"

"Okay, let me know when you're ready."

"Go ahead."

"De-icing system?"

"Check."

"Um…speed brake?"

"Wait…ah…where is that?"

"Second lever from your right," Miyuki said, her nose buried in the 380 manual.

"Thanks." Olivia pulled it. "Got it…I mean check."

"Spoilers?"

"Where are those bloody…ah. There. Spoilers are armed."

"Flaps?"

"Flaps…not sure. Let's put them down to twenty." She moved the flap lever down. "I'll ask the captain about that one. Check."

"What the hell's that sound?" Emma shrieked.

"It's the flaps coming down, love. Don't panic. That's a good sound. What's next?"

Emma didn't answer.

"C'mon, Emma. Focus."

"Sorry." Emma flipped the tab over for the flaps, marking it complete. "Um…landing gear?"

Olivia leaned over and pulled down the gear level. Another heavy rumbling sound.

"Please tell me that's the landing gear," Emma said.

"Are those the little wheels on the bottom of the plane?" Miyuki asked.

"Little wheels are down with four green lights," Olivia said.

Emma flipped over the last tab. "That's it. Checklist is done."

"Okay. Landing checklist completed." Olivia watched her airspeed. They were going much slower now.

Nadia keyed the radio. "Global 614 to Paris ATC. Landing checklist completed. Flaps set to twenty. Is that okay?"

"Thanks for reminding me about the flaps, love."

"Twenty should be fine. Do you see the visual approach slope indicator?"

Olivia could see a series of ultrabright lights just to the left of the large runway ahead of them. She now felt more confident as she keyed her headset. "I see them." Olivia adjusted her height and pulled back on the throttles.

"Three miles to touchdown. You're too slow. Apply more power. We don't want to stall the aircraft."

"What happens if we do that?" Emma asked.

"At this altitude? Basically, we're dead." Olivia nudged the joystick forward and increased the thrust levers.

"Two miles. Speed good. Altitude good. Your heading is—"

Silence.

"My heading is what? Where the hell did he go?" Olivia yelled.

Emma noticed the large 380 operator's manual sitting on the lower console. She pulled it off.

"Monkey balls! I bumped the radio." Miyuki grabbed the book from Emma and raced through it to find the radio section.

"You must have changed the frequency," Nadia said.

"What was the old frequency?" Olivia yelled.

Nadia balked. "I don't know. It was already set when I sat

down." She looked around the cockpit. "Is there a chart I can look for?"

"There must be one," Emma said.

"It's too flipping late," Olivia grumbled. "I'm one mile from the runway. Just have to go in." Olivia blinked and leaned forward. With new determination she hurtled the large aircraft toward the crest of the runway. "Better strap yourselves in, girls. Nadia? Get on the intercom and tell the cabin to prepare for landing."

Emma pulled the seat belt tight across her waist. Miyuki did the same in the jump seat behind the captain. She took Emma's hand and squeezed. Emma placed her other hand on Nadia's shoulder. The girl tried to smile and placed her hand on top of Emma's.

*One hundred…*a computer voice called out inside the cockpit.

Olivia knew she was one hundred feet above the runway. The aircraft drifted to the right. Olivia cursed and gave the aircraft more left rudder. The aircraft centered up. The threshold of the runway filled the windshield.

"You're straight. Looking good," Nadia said.

Fifty…

Forty…

Thirty…

Twenty…

Ten…

The aircraft then floated a bit above the runway.

"Get down there, you beast." Olivia pushed the joystick forward.

The aircraft dropped to the runway hard. The nose gear rumbled against the ground. The aircraft shook. Olivia pulled the reverse thrusters to full, and the engines whined. She punched the brakes. "Nadia! Can you help with the brakes? The pedals on the top rudders, press them both."

With Nadia's help the jet shuttered as the engines and brakes struggled to bring the large plane under control.

The ground passed under them fast. Much faster than it seemed from the air.

Orange lights glared ominously across the end of the runway. The plane still rushed towards them.

"Olivia?" Emma asked, scared out of her mind.

"I've got the flipping brakes and the reverser going full. C'mon, stop, you stupid plane."

The orange approach lights grew in size.

They weren't going to make it.

"Hang on!" Olivia stepped on the left rudder and the large aircraft veered hard to the left as it entered a taxiway adjacent to the runway.

Finally, the 380 slowed to a crawl. Olivia put the thrusters back to idle and the engines went down to a slight purr.

The aircraft stopped.

Olivia's head collapsed against the headrest, her curly hair drenched with sweat. The tension released from her body.

"You did it!" Miyuki launched herself over the pilot's seat for a hug. Nadia reached in too. Emma came in from the opposite side.

The group hug felt good to Olivia. She needed it. "I was so flipping scared. Oh my God."

"You were brilliant," Nadia said.

"Thank you!" Emma said.

The back door of the cockpit opened. The senior flight attendant looked relieved, but still anxious. "Could you please kill the engines so we can evacuate the aircraft?"

"Damn, I forgot." Olivia broke up the hug and found the necessary switches, flicking them off. Soon the engine noise died.

The senior flight attendant paused. "That was a hell of a thing you just did. I'll make sure everyone in the world knows your name. What is your name, by the way?"

Olivia straightened. "Amelia."

"Well done, Amelia." The woman left. The PA system came to life, ordering the passengers to evacuate the aircraft in an orderly manner using the emergency exits.

Olivia started to worry again. Tell the world about her?

"Bullocks, we need to sneak out of here quick."

"Why? You need a rest," Miyuki said.

"We're spies, you knob. They can't know who any of us are, and you heard the flight attendant, the media will want to interview me."

Nadia's eyes went wide. "And the authorities too."

Olivia climbed out of the pilot seat. "We need to hide among the passengers and look for a way to slip out of the airport. It'll be better if we go individually. Emma? You first."

"Wait. Where do I go? Shouldn't we have a meeting place somewhere?"

Olivia's phone rang. She checked the number. It was Mrs. B. "Hello?"

"A helicopter is en route to your location," Mrs. B said over the phone, her voice all business. "Go to the north end of the airport and wait for extraction."

Olivia was impressed. The woman was always ahead of the game. "How did you know?"

"The plight of Air Global flight 614 has been live on the news for the past two hours. When they mentioned the teen girl pilot—the conclusion was fairly obvious to draw, my dear. Now get your team to that helicopter before the French authorities get wise."

Olivia briefed the girls and led them out of the cockpit. The nearest cabin door was open, letting in sunshine as passengers jumped out and slid down the inflatable slide. The plane was half empty now. Most of the exits over the wings were popped open. The Gems avoided the line of passengers waiting for the slide.

Olivia bent down to look out one of the windows. "Emergency vehicles are collecting people on this side so—" she pointed to the opposite side—"we go on that side."

"Here!" Miyuki found an unopened wing exit.

Olivia helped Miyuki take the emergency wing door panel off and laid it on a chair. The girls followed Olivia out the window exit, each girl helping the other down on to the wing. The Gems slid down the extended wing flap and landed on the tarmac feet first.

There was confusion all around them.

Five hundred passengers were scattered in all directions as French rescuers struggled to herd them into one area. Firefighters pulled out their hoses and checked for any possible fires.

The Gems broke into a run as they left their plane. They ran up one of the taxiways.

"The north end should be down near...there. Where those

hangars are," Olivia said before sprinting across the runway that separated the girls from the hangars.

The other three girls stopped.

At the end of the runway, a passenger jet spooled up its engines as it prepared for takeoff.

"Come on!" Olivia shouted. "Quickly!"

Nadia ran for it.

The engines screamed as the jet rolled forward.

Miyuki tried to run, but Emma didn't move. The girl shook her head.

The jet closed in on them fast.

Miyuki went behind Emma and pushed her forward. The two girls broke into a run.

The jet's nose lifted off the ground, exposing the belly and undercarriage heavy enough to crush a teenager's bones. The Gems dropped to the ground as the aircraft swished past them, the wash from the jet's engines acting like a mini tornado, tossing the girls' hair and the grass around them in a most violent fashion.

Soon they reached the north end and the hangars. A couple of private jets were parked in a row. Nadia got the girls' attention and pointed over at the runway they'd just crossed. An airport police car raced towards them with its blue lights flashing. The Gems searched the sky. No sign of the helicopter.

"What do we do now?" Emma asked.

"Sit tight. It'll be here in a minute," Olivia said.

"We might not have that minute," Nadia replied.

"Can you fly one of those?" Miyuki gestured toward the private jets on the tarmac.

"It's too late," Olivia said. "Besides, I doubt they would let me take off."

The police car closed the distance. It was hopeless. The helicopter wasn't coming.

"All right," Olivia said. "We'll just have to shut up. Don't say anything to the police. No matter—"

A distant roar crept over her last sentence. Whatever it was... it was coming in fast.

The girls turned just as a slick-looking helicopter flew into view. It was low off the ground and hauling butt. The pilot spotted them and whipped his craft around to slow down, then hovered ahead of them before landing. Whoever the pilot was, Olivia could tell he knew how to handle a chopper.

The girls lowered their heads as they opened the helicopter doors and climbed inside. Olivia patted the pilot's shoulder and gave him a thumbs-up. The pilot put the chopper back into the air and raced it just inches above the trees, leaving behind two French police officers wondering what just happened.

CHAPTER 16

As soon as their private jet landed in San Francisco at 4 a.m. local time, the four sleepy girls were whisked away to The Authority headquarters in Napa Valley where Mrs. B had each girl placed in a comfy recliner inside the dark relaxation area to sleep with the fishes. She also posted Aardvark to make sure the girls were not disturbed.

Emma stirred around noon. The other girls were still sleeping, but Aardvark nodded to her as he sat patiently nearby. He showed Emma to a private bathroom where she could shower and change clothes. (The Authority had managed to "steal" their bags from their Air Global flight.) Once all the Gems were up, showered, and changed, Aardvark escorted them to the cafeteria, where Mrs. B brought in a special lunch just for them. A pizza from Tony's Pizza Napoletana in San Francisco. The girls had woken up hungry and devoured it.

After lunch, Aardvark escorted them inside the labyrinth with its dark blue walls, floors, and ceilings. They followed the glowing white-lettered signs leading them to the CAC Division. They entered a black room with a large black table. Aardvark nodded to the Gems and left them alone. The metal door closed and sucked in air as it sealed back into place. The Gems sat around the table and waited.

Ten minutes later, the door seal popped as air escaped. The door opened automatically, revealing Mrs. B and four other members, who entered the black room. Mrs. B did not introduce them as they took seats around the table.

Mrs. B remained standing as she leaned on her cane. "May I begin by saying…well done. This international organization was founded on the principles of protecting all human beings. We pride ourselves on doing whatever it takes to achieve those goals. Yesterday, Emerald here exhibited bravery in the most gallant way possible. Her efforts and those of her fellow team members resulted in the saving of over five hundred innocent lives."

Mrs. B moved to the other side of the room. "Officially, we do not give out medals. We do not give out prizes or certificates of achievement to hang on your wall. Our world is a secret one where there is no audience clap when the final curtain drops. However, we can tell you…well done, Emerald. You are a credit to our organization."

Mrs. B clapped and the rest of the room joined her. Olivia lowered her chin, a touch of humility on her face. Nadia hugged her. Miyuki gave a whoop and pumped her fist in the air. Emma even caught herself whooping too. Maybe she still had issues with this girl, but Olivia did save her life. She'd saved everyone's life on that plane.

As the clapping died down, Mrs. B spoke again. "The flagrant attempt on your lives concerns us. I'm afraid we're dealing with a cunning and ruthless enemy. One we've dealt with in the past."

"Venomous?" Olivia asked.

"That's what we've come up with. It reeks of desperation, yet I think it signals you ladies were too close to something. Something important enough to kill Black Opal's father, his engineers, and our agent."

"One of our agents died?" Nadia asked.

"We didn't tell you about that part of the operation. However —yes, we had an operative working at an AgEurope facility in Germany. He was killed in a forklift 'accident' yesterday. Strange this accident occurred just hours after your doomed flight left Paris. It's no coincidence."

"I still don't understand what this is all about," Emma said. "What's so important about food and seed storage facilities?"

"Raymond Foods and its worldwide divisions produce seventy-two percent of the world's food." Mrs. B walked around the room. "If Ron Raymond is involved in some scheme with Venomous, then we are facing a real threat, indeed."

"What's Venomous?" Emma asked. "Is that like a terrorist group?"

"The brief explanation? Terrorists are motivated by ideology, while Venomous is motivated by money. Murder for hire, extortion, kidnapping, blackmail, their criminal organization is well financed. Their organization is so secret the world's intelligence services have just as much trouble penetrating their network as we do. Basically, they're a thorn in the side of the world. And we think it was one of their operatives who not only poisoned your pilots…but also sabotaged your father's plane."

Emma sat up.

"Observe the video screen." Mrs. B clicked a remote and a giant HDTV lowered and flickered to life. "We acquired this video through the airport's security cameras."

It was the interior of an air bridge docked to their airliner. A man dressed in an Air Global flight stewards uniform walked down the length of the bridge and turned slightly towards the camera as the image froze. The hi-def camera zoomed in on the man's ID.

"We processed his ID through the airport's log-in records and found this same ID was used to access hangar seventeen located in the public aviation section." Mrs. B glanced at Emma. "Hangar seventeen was where your father's plane was stored right before the crash."

Emma's blood went cold. She studied the high-def image of the man on the screen. He had a puff of facial hair on his chin and ratlike eyes. A sudden feeling of déjà-vu took over her.

"That's the man who ran off with my computer," Nadia said.

Emma knew she was right. That was the man she and Miyuki had chased through the streets of Paris.

"May I add another wrinkle?" Mrs. B asked. "This man you see has been identified as Bertrand Petit. Three years ago, Mr. Petit moved from France to San Jose, California, to work for AirTech as a building environmental engineer. Then died in a plane crash."

"Wait, what?" Emma asked.

"Bertrand Petit was a passenger on your father's jet. The French authorities have him listed as dead." Mrs. B glanced up at the screen. "Obviously Mr. Petit made a miraculous recovery."

"So if Bertrand works for Venomous," Olivia said. "I'd say there's a good chance Jacqueline Boyay does too."

"A strong possibility, but we still don't know the entire picture." Mrs. B leaned on her cane. "I've discussed this with the other controllers and we feel this operation deserves top priority. We need to find out the objective of this Venomous operation. Who's involved. And how we can destroy it. All our resources in Europe will be looking for Bertrand. We think he's the key to exposing this new operation."

"How can we help?" Emma asked.

Mrs. B eased her way around the room, her cane supporting every step as the woman's mind worked on the problem. She stopped. "We need to find out how deep Ron Raymond is involved in all this. We need you girls to get close to Mr. Raymond and his immediate family and see what they know. Mr. Raymond is either working with Venomous...or he's clueless about what's happening inside his own company. We need to know which."

Emma stared at the man on the screen. Bertrand Petit. A funny name for a murderer. She hoped she would have a chance to capture him. One round kick to his face would make her feel good.

"Are you listening, Black Opal?" Mrs. B leaned on her cane, waiting for a reaction.

Emma snapped out of her thoughts. "Sorry...could you repeat that?"

Mrs. B flashed her a disapproving look. "I said...you'll continue your role as your father's crusader of justice, but with a small adjustment. I want you to get close to Mr. Raymond's son, Ryan. His girlfriend broke up with him last month. Perhaps you could exploit that. Get Ryan to talk to you and he might give you better access to his father."

Emma bit her lip. Did Mrs. B want her to seduce a boy for information? How would she do that?

* * *

Since the Gems wouldn't be leaving until tomorrow morning, Mrs B suggested that Emma should spend the night at home with her grandmother. The idea of sleeping in her own bed sounded great to Emma.

The moment Emma stepped inside the house, Snoopy waddled across the wood floor, his tail wagging like crazy. Emma received some licks to the face and she gave him a kiss in return. Grandma ran up to Emma and gave her a tight hug. Tighter than she had ever hugged her before. The two of them stayed up and watched a movie together on the couch. Some romantic comedy that was dumb enough to laugh at. Emma welcomed the stupidity and the escape from her recent reality. The two of them didn't talk about The Authority, and Grandma didn't ask what Emma had been doing for the past few days. That night, Emma slept in her room with Snoopy laid out near her feet. The dog's back brace still prevented him from curling up. Still, he didn't move from her side the whole night.

In the morning, Grandma made breakfast again, as if it were just another normal day. Fresh strawberries. Scrambled egg whites. Turkey sausage. Whole-wheat rolls with goat cheese. She even made some fried potatoes with herbs from her garden. Grandma opened the French doors, and the crisp morning air filled the house with promise. They both slipped on sweaters and had breakfast in the garden once again. Emma broke off a piece of turkey sausage and dropped her hand below the table for Snoopy. The dog ate from her fingers and licked them with appreciation.

"Laura called me yesterday. She said you'd only be staying for one night." Grandma sipped her steaming herbal tea. "How will you make up all these missed school days?"

"You could tell them I have the flu," Emma said.

Grandma fiddled with the end of one of her long white braids. "How many cases of *flu* can one girl have in a school year?"

"Mrs. B...I mean Grandma Laura mentioned something about finding me a professional tutor. Someone who'd be more flexible with my schedule than a school. Like some of those child actors have in Hollywood."

Grandma straightened in her chair. "No. You're going to a normal school with normal kids. Despite this insanity."

Emma stopped eating. "I don't see how I can do that now."

"I'm still your legal guardian. You're still sixteen. I could pull the plug on all this."

"Pull the plug? What do you mean?"

"Order Laura to leave you alone or I'll bring in the police or the FBI. You're still a minor."

"You told me I had free will to choose my path, remember? Well, I'm choosing this life. It's what I want."

Grandma shifted her pose, maybe regretting what she'd said.

"I know who killed dad. It wasn't an accident," Emma said. "And I can't walk away now. Not when he's still out there free as a bird."

"If Laura can find the killer, let her take care of it."

"I want to do it. I want to kill him."

Grandma's mouth drifted open, shock on the old woman's face. "Good God…don't say things like that."

"Why not? I could do it. After what that man did to Dad and all those men who worked for him? Not to mention trying to kill me and five hundred innocent…" Emma stopped herself. She'd better not mention the almost air disaster. "I won't give a monster like that any forgiveness."

A cloud of sadness overtook Grandma's eyes. "Killing only turns you into a killer, one no higher or mightier than the one you kill."

"No, it doesn't. The good guys right the wrongs of evil people. And this man and others like him are evil. I know you mean well, Grandma. And I would do anything for you. But I owe it to Dad to find him."

Grandma raised her voice. "Your father never wanted you to collect some gruesome debt that would turn his daughter into some weapon of death." She was breathing hard, her emotions rising to a fevered pitch.

Her words unnerved Emma. The raw emotion coming from a person she loved.

"It's too late. I'm all the way in this. By choice." Emma collected her plate and orange juice and walked through the open French doors into the kitchen.

Emma placed her items on the counter and leaned against it. Even from inside the house, she could hear Grandma sobbing in the garden.

A tear traced Emma's cheek. Maybe she was losing her soul to evil. But it was her life and she wanted control of it.

CHAPTER 17

Tonight, Raymond Foods planned to celebrate the completion of their new world headquarters with a giant gala in downtown Kansas City, Missouri—home of numerous regional federal government offices, good barbecue, and the people who made greeting cards. Raymond Foods was putting on a show for the world, and Ron Raymond himself would deliver the keynote speech. Securing an invitation proved easy since Emma was still heiress to the Rothchild fortune and the large corporation that went along with it. As Mrs. B had said before they left San Francisco...

"Wealthy people love to show off to their equals."

With Miyuki's help, Emma dressed to impress. A sleeveless, long red dress that opened up just over her chest. A slit to the side exposed the side of her legs in a peek-a-boo style that shaped her long form quite nicely. The outfit suggested quite a lot of things for wondering eyes. It wasn't a dress for nice girls. It was a dress for a young woman who wanted to conquer the room.

Still posing as her entourage, Miyuki and Nadia wore nicer, more classic dresses for the gala since Emma was the one who needed to stand out. Olivia didn't want to squeeze into another dress, so she wore dark business slacks and a white blouse. Nothing dressy, but she felt more comfortable, and it went along with her cover as Emma's assistant.

The taxi released the Gems in front of the new Raymond Foods world headquarters skyscraper. There was excitement in the evening air. A large RF symbol made of steel and glass rotated on a motorized platform. As the emblem rotated, it glinted from the spotlights placed at the far corners of the street.

Various elegant couples in full formal dress made their way inside the new building. The sounds of music and people having a good time escaped from its doors.

Emma was nervous. Her mission was to seduce a boy and she didn't know how she would do that. Would she have to pretend to like this son of a billionaire? What if he looked like a toad? What if he smelled like garlic? Or Cheetos? When she was on stage, Emma pretended to love her leading man, but that was a play. All she needed were a few good lines that someone else wrote for her and boom, he was in love with her. But this was real life. How could she seduce a guy without a script?

She would have to improvise. It wouldn't be easy. Most likely Emma would have to charm a nerdy rich boy who had never talked to a girl a day in his life and pretend to like him. And of course this boy would have no clue it was all fake, making Emma feel bad when she had to burst the guy's heart wide open after they used him. Or worse, his money could have made him into a total jerk, making him expect Emma to give him all the attention he thought he deserved, and Emma would have to go along with it while inside hating herself.

Emma pushed her thoughts away and prepared the actress inside for tonight's performance.

The Gems stepped into a giant lobby area that was three stories high at least. Glittering crystal chandeliers hung from the ceiling. The light they produced bounced off the large silk curtains of white draped over sections of new walls that still lacked decorations. Well-dressed people were everywhere, soaking up the celebratory vibe.

Olivia touched Emma's shoulder. "I want you to circle around the party and—"

"I've got this," Emma interrupted. "I've been to parties like this since I was ten. I'll make my rounds, make sure everyone in the room gets an eyeful of me and my beautiful entourage, then we find Mr. Raymond. I'm sure his son will be nearby. Was I close?"

Olivia's mouth tightened. "Try not to fall in the punch bowl."

Miyuki whispered to Olivia, "What will you be doing?"

"I'll look around for Bertrand. If he's here, I'll capture him. You and Nadia keep your phones handy if I need help."

"If you find him, let me know too," Emma said.

"You worry about charming the Raymonds, love. I know it'll be a heavy burden for you."

"Hey."

Olivia retreated without a word and melted into the crowd.

"Why is she saying that? What did I do?" Emma asked.

Nadia showed her a grin. "She's only jealous. We're all jealous. Look how beautiful you are."

"Every girl in this room will hate you," Miyuki said. "Own it like a rock star."

"You'll stay close, right?" Emma asked. "I need at least two girls to like me."

Nadia and Miyuki followed Emma as she made her first large circle around the gala. Eyes turned. People whispered. Emma held her head up with a confident smile, stopping to chat with groups of people. Strangers laughed. Men stared. Wives emptied their wineglasses. One old man rested his hand on Emma's behind, wanting to take her on his yacht down in Florida. Emma was about to look for help when Miyuki pulled the old man's arm and pinned it to his lower back. Surprised and in discomfort, the old man allowed Miyuki to move him far away from Emma.

Completing her circle, Emma placed herself near a railing that overlooked the floor of the gala. A place where everyone could see her. And a place the Gems could keep a watch on everyone else.

"By everyone's reaction, I'd say you're making a good impression," Nadia said.

"That was the whole point, right?" Emma asked.

"I don't see Mr. Raymond anywhere." Miyuki took out her phone and pulled up some pictures of a short, bald man who was oversized in the belly department.

Emma glanced at the image. "Hard man to miss. Doesn't look like the Steve Jobs of food, does he?"

"If Steve Jobs ate all the food, yes."

"That's a terrible thing to say," Nadia said.

Miyuki frowned. "Sorry. You would think a billionaire could afford a gym and a diet coach."

A new problem came to Emma. "Do you think his son looks like him?"

Both girls shrugged.

Emma prepared herself. She might have to give her best actress of the year performance tonight. Would she have to kiss him? Touch him? Emma's stomach turned sour. All she could imagine was a fat, sweaty teenage boy who didn't put on enough deodorant or bother to brush his teeth.

Her night didn't look too promising.

"Guess who's her." Miyuki pointed downstairs.

Emma leaned over the railing and found Jacqueline poised with a glass of champagne. Her dress was cream white and tight-fitting to her body, which she was obviously showing off. She sipped her champagne as her personal assistant, Pierre, talked to her. There was also a much younger guy with them. Emma couldn't make out his facial features from this far away, but she could make out two things. One, he was around her age. Two, he looked really damn cute.

"Who's that hottie?" Miyuki asked.

"You spotted him too, huh?"

"He's very nice," Nadia added. "What is he doing with Jacqueline?"

The crowd below started clapping. A short, fat man came into view, showing off a well-fitting-for-his-size tuxedo. Mr. Raymond held up his hand to acknowledge the crowd. The older man's face was still attractive. His forehead, nose, and cheeks formed gentle angles. His hair was becoming gray on the sides but not on top. He had a cute dimple on his chin. But that was where it ended. His body was more like a bowling ball. Still, people wanted to talk to him as he greeted his guests.

Mr. Raymond glanced up at Emma. She straightened her back and stood against the railing with the confidence of a powerful queen. Mr. Raymond took her in for a moment before returning his attention to his guests. He greeted a fat teenage boy with a fatherly hug. They looked similar in the face. The boy then followed Mr. Raymond through the crowd.

Emma sighed. It was just as she feared.

"That must be Ryan," Nadia said.

"I guess so."

"Good luck," Miyuki said in her positive voice.

Emma took her time walking down the stairs, step by step,

slow and deliberate so people could watch. Emma did another half circle of the crowd while Nadia and Miyuki stayed farther back, but close enough for support if Emma needed them. Soon she came within a few feet of the Raymonds, but Emma didn't make an effort to approach them. She knew this game too well.

Mr. Raymond came right up to her and introduced himself. "You're Emma, Kenneth Rothchild's girl. Is that right?"

"Yes, a pleasure to meet you, Mr. Raymond."

The man softened. "I'm sorry to hear about your father. I admired him. A great business leader. And your father's companies always did top-notch work for me." Mr. Raymond paused. "How's your family coping with all this?"

"As well as they can, under the circumstances."

"Of course. Of course. It's a difficult time for any family, I'm sure."

The boy next to Mr. Raymond had the largest goofiest smile ever. Emma forced herself to smile. "Hello, I'm Emma." She gently squeezed his arm. "Are you Ryan?"

The boy lost his smile. Mr. Raymond laughed and wrapped his arm around the boy's neck. "Nah, this is my nephew Derek from St. Louis."

Emma removed her hand. "Oh, I'm sorry."

"I would be Ryan," a male voice said.

Emma spun around and peered into the deepest blue eyes ever. They were like vivid paintings of an ocean, colors deep enough to draw you in. Emma refocused her eyes on the face. Same facial features as his father. But...his hair was dark. His chin strong with a gorgeous dimple in the middle. A strong neck that sat on top of a thick frame that had no fat on it whatsoever. The boy was dressed in a sharp tux that concealed his body like a present just begging to be opened.

Emma shook off that last thought, then realized this was the boy she'd noticed earlier with Jacqueline.

The hottie.

"You're turning red," Ryan said. "Are you all right, Miss...? Was it Rothchild?"

"Emma."

"That's a lovely name."

Emma thought Ryan was quite lovely too. Maybe her

assignment was turning around after all.

Ryan held her eyes without blinking. There was a confidence behind the boy that Emma thought was hot. He touched her hand. "Are you sure you're okay? Looks like you could use some water."

"Water?"

"Yes, it's this liquid that comes from the sky. Very popular with the humans these days."

Emma caught herself giggling. She was totally losing it.

"I think this girl needs a refreshment," Mr. Raymond said. "Be a good host and take care of her, son."

Ryan touched Emma on the square of her bare back and her legs moved instantly. They would follow this boy anywhere. Ryan led Emma over to the bar, where he asked for two Cokes. The bartender popped open two bottles and placed them on the table. Ryan offered one to Emma. She sipped a little and forced herself to watch the gala. She wanted him to talk first.

Ryan let a moment or two pass. He was in no hurry. "How do you know my father?"

"One of my dad's companies did business with Raymond Foods," Emma said.

"And where is your dad? Shouldn't he be protecting you from boys like me?"

She felt a sharp pain that reminded Emma why she was here. "He's dead."

Ryan's confident posture disappeared as he stared at the floor. "That made me sound like a total jerk." He peeked up at her. "Forgive my insensitivity?"

Emma liked how his bangs hung over his eyes. It created this mysterious aura around him. "I kinda dropped that on you without warning. Not exactly fair."

"Did he die recently?"

"Actually, it's the reason I'm here. My father was murdered." Emma told Ryan about the plane crash. The sabotage involved. How she wanted to find out who was responsible. But she was also the heiress to her father's estate, and since Emma would own Rothchild Industries when she turned eighteen, she wanted to learn more about who her father did business with.

"What a load to carry," Ryan said. "Is running your father's empire something you want to do?"

Emma paused. No one had ever asked her that. "I wanted to be a doctor…or a vet. Most likely a vet."

"But now you can't?"

"Who says I can't? I could sell all the companies, I guess. I don't care."

"Why wait until you're eighteen? If it's in a trust, you could set up an agreement with the trustee to sell it all off to the highest bidder. Then you'd have this huge pile of money waiting for you on your eighteenth birthday. You wouldn't have to go to college. Heck, you wouldn't have to do anything. I'd love to be in your situation." Ryan took a swig of cola.

"I don't want to be one of those rich, bratty girls who do nothing with their life except spend money like it's leaves on a tree. No, I want my life to mean something. I want to do something that helps people." Emma tried to stop herself, but couldn't. "But my father built Rothchild Industries from the ground up and I feel like…I'm supposed to protect what he built. Not sell it off. To be honest, I feel trapped."

Ryan examined his bottle. "Did you get along well with your dad?"

Her emotions pushed Emma hard. A good cry would relieve it, but she didn't want to embarrass Ryan.

"We got along really well. He was my everything." She forced out a smile. "What about your dad? Does he have your life all planned?"

"Planning my life out would require him to pay attention to it," Ryan leaned against the bar. "My dad is obsessed with his company. Twenty-four seven. That's all he cares about. He works eighty hours a week. No joke."

"Eighty hours? That's crazy."

"Work is a religion to him," Ryan scoffed. "He missed my Little League world series game. We were a kick-ass team. Won all-city. Went to state. Won that. And then we were invited to play in the world series against this other Little League team from Japan. The game was on television all over the world. It was a huge thing. And I wasn't in the dugout either. I played first base. I led the team in home runs." Ryan took another sip of cola. "Do you think my dad cared? Do you think my dad could trouble himself to go to one of my games? Even with his son playing in a major game like that?" Ryan stepped away from the bar. "I'm boring you."

"Not at all." Emma touched his arm to prevent him from leaving. "My dad missed a piano recital when I was ten. It wasn't as big as a world series, but I was still upset. I understand more than you know."

Ryan gazed at Emma for a long moment. "Would you like to dance with me?"

She eyed the room. "There's no one dancing."

"Maybe these people can't hear our music."

Emma cocked her head to the side. "What music?"

Ryan took Emma's hands and swayed in place. "You don't hear it? I do." The boy gently swung her hands back and forth to the invisible beat. "It's old school. The Beatles. 'Sgt. Pepper Lonely Hearts Club Band.'" Ryan's lips moved as he whispered the lyrics.

Emma found this to be kinda weird, but she went with it because it was kinda cute too.

"I never listened to their music before."

"Seriously?" Ryan faked a shocked look. "How can you dance with me if you don't know the music?" Ryan tapped his chin as if he was thinking. "I have an answer to your problem." His hand slid down into his tuxedo pocket. Out came his digital music player and a set of earbuds. He held up one to Emma. "Would you be so kind?"

Emma smiled and placed it inside her ear. Ryan came in close to her face, as he placed the other bud inside his ear. Emma didn't smell garlic or Cheetos on Ryan's breath. It was mint. A delightful mint.

Ryan fiddled with his player before selecting a song and tapping play.

The music tickled her ear. "Is he singing about a walrus?" Emma asked.

"Crap. Wrong song," Ryan tapped a few more buttons. "Let's start at the beginning."

The opening beats of "Sgt. Pepper" started and Ryan was in the groove immediately, thumping his head to the music. Emma found her body mimicking Ryan's without her brain making any conscious effort. Soon they danced in place as their bodies synchronized with the song. The next was "Lucy in the Sky with Diamonds," which drifted in with strange swirling sounds of psychedelic beats that made Emma feel like she was on drugs. She said something about it to Ryan.

"John Lennon was experimenting with LSD when he wrote this song. Not that you could tell, right?" Ryan added with a dash of sarcasm.

Emma thought it was still fun to try to dance to the song. Before long, they brushed against each other numerous times, thanks to the short-length earbuds gluing them together. Neither one of them complained.

Ryan skipped the player ahead. "Strawberry Fields Forever" caressed their ears like silk. Emma shut her eyes and let the music take over her body. She and Ryan moved perfectly together. As the song's tempo increased, Ryan and Emma moved with it, orbiting each other like the earth and the moon. One in sync with the other. Then Emma noticed Mr. Raymond and Jacqueline Boyay watching them.

She stopped dancing and yanked out her earbud. Ryan followed her glance.

"Look at you two kids gyrating all over the place," Mr. Raymond said. "Are you already bored at my gala?"

"Not at all, Mr. Raymond," Emma said. "Ryan was talking about this new song he liked and I wanted to hear it, so—sorry if we embarrassed you."

Mr. Raymond waited for Ryan to say something.

But his son didn't open his mouth.

"Music is a luxury for the young," Mr. Raymond said. "Emma, I do believe you've met Jacqueline?"

Emma presented a smile. "Yes, she gave me an informative tour of your AgEurope facilities in Paris. Most impressive. How are you?"

Jacqueline raised her eyebrow. "Excellent, Miss Rothchild. I see you're alive and well."

Emma wondered what that was supposed to mean, but she blew it off.

"You must be proud of your new office building. It looks tall."

"Looks tall?" Mr. Raymond looked hurt. "Miss Rothchild, this building is the state of the art in architecture. It's strong enough to take a direct hit from an EF-five tornado and the foundation can survive a nine-point-zero earthquake. The security system is only a few steps below the Pentagon and Strategic Air Command. It's one of the best corporate headquarters ever constructed."

"And I thought you were only excited about food," Emma said.

Mr. Raymond stiffened and held his stomach in while his hand subconsciously touched his gut.

Emma wanted to kick herself. She'd just insulted a fat guy about his weight.

Ryan smirked.

Emma had to save herself. "Your passion and dedication for the advancement of food science is remarkable. The underground farms and seed vaults I visited were amazing. I'm thrilled that my dad's company was able to contribute to such a scientifically valuable project." Emma straightened. She thought that sounded mature and hoped it was flattering enough.

Mr. Raymond melted. "Young lady, your incredible intelligence outshines your incredible beauty."

Emma's cheeks warmed.

"She's too good for you, son. Which means you'll have to try harder to win her." Mr. Raymond's eyes settled on Emma. "Do you love hunting, Miss Rothchild?"

Emma instantly thought of a deer with a target on its head. A gunshot. There was no freaking way she was going hunting. It was barbaric and cruel and…Miyuki and Nadia nodded at Emma with enthusiasm. Did they want her to…?

A lump caught in Emma's throat. She didn't want to say it… but she did.

"I love hunting."

"I knew you were my kinda girl," Mr. Raymond said. "You should come up to the estate and be our guest for the weekend. I'm sure Ryan will find more music to entertain you with."

CHAPTER 18

Mr. Raymond's estate, Willow Run, was located one hour outside of Kansas City. The large front gate was guarded by a man in a suit. After checking with someone on the phone, the guard allowed Nadia to drive through. Olivia noted the man had a gun under his jacket. The private drive Nadia followed went along a portion of the stone perimeter fence of the property. Piles of barb-wire looped the top of the fence, leaving no doubt that Mr. Raymond took his personal security seriously. The private drive curved around the back side of a wooded hill. Soon the trees opened up to reveal a large western ranch-style mansion. It was three stories tall with a giant front porch capable of holding a backyard party all on its own. Nadia drove up the wide circular drive and let the other girls out in front before parking their rented BMW.

Inside, a butler greeted the Gems and showed them to their rooms upstairs. Climbing up the master staircase, the girls took in the mansion's interior. Small lamps with cowhide colored shades hung on the walls, and some cowboy-themed art stood on top of tables. The stairs, the walls, the ceilings—all of it made of polished oak. Emma could smell the strong sent of lemon varnish. By the look inside, this mansion must have had about thirty rooms.

Reaching the third floor, the Gems were met by a giant grizzly bear. It was at the top of the staircase, looming above it like a demon from hell. The stuffed bear stood on its hind legs with its jaws wide open as if frozen in mid-roar.

Emma wanted to vomit. It was disgusting to see a poor animal being presented like a piece of fine artwork.

The butler opened up a large suite. "Mr. Raymond is anxious

to speak with you, ladies," he said. "Please join him downstairs in front of the residence in fifteen minutes."

The Gems thanked him and waited until he shut the door.

"Why is he so anxious to—?"

Emma stopped when Olivia flashed a finger over her mouth for quiet. She gestured to a complimentary pen and pad of paper sitting near the mirror. Olivia scribbled *This room is bugged.*

Emma took the pen from her. *How do you know?*

Olivia showed Emma her phone. A red warning flashed across the screen. *Surveillance equipment detected.*

"Wish my phone had that app," Emma said.

Miyuki opened up a sliding door that emptied outside to a balcony. She swept her arm out like it was a new car they'd just won on a game show. Olivia nodded her approval and shot a knowing glance at Nadia, who got out her phone and worked on something.

"How about some fresh air?" Olivia asked Emma, who followed her and Miyuki outside to the balcony.

Nadia joined them.

"Want some gum?" Miyuki asked.

Olivia and Nadia declined. But Emma accepted and popped the piece in her mouth. It was grape. Grape bubble gum? Emma didn't like it, but she chewed it anyway.

"I didn't like seeing Jacqueline at the party," Olivia said. "She could be here warning Mr. Raymond or setting up a surprise for us."

"What about that dude with the goatee?" Miyuki blew a huge purple bubble that popped.

"I didn't see him last night. But keep your eyes open. Bertrand could show up if he and Jacqueline are mates."

Miyuki sucked in her bubble. "And if he shows, we take him and convince him to talk."

"I'll force him to talk. I'll keep kicking him in the head until he screams for me to stop," Emma said, not joking one syllable.

The three girls shot Emma a long look.

"What?"

Olivia folded her arms together. "If we capture Bertrand, we don't hurt him. We want information. Not revenge."

Emma leaned on the balcony and glared at the sky.

"Here's the plan for the day," Olivia continued. "Emma and I will find a way to distract Mr. Raymond and company while you two have a look around the mansion."

Nadia smiled. "And if I see a computer, have a peek?"

"Exactly, love," Olivia said. "Now, let's see what game Mr. Raymond wants to play today."

Minutes later, the girls went downstairs and out through the main doors to see three full-size ATVs parked on the main drive. Each had four seats and were decorated in hunter's camouflage. Seven men carried hunting rifles as they talked to Mr. Raymond, whose belly shook when he laughed at a joke.

Mr. Raymond noticed the girls and excused himself from his friends. "Welcome to Willow Run, Miss Rothchild. Did you settle in all right?"

"I think so. Thank you."

"Great. You're just in time. My friends and I are going on a hunt before lunch. Would you like to join us?"

CHAPTER 19

The caravan of ATVs hummed their way along a wide dirt trail that ran the circumference of a huge private lake. Emma and Olivia rode with Mr. Raymond and one of his Raymond Foods executives.

Mr. Raymond turned around in the passenger's seat and yelled above the noisy motor, "Your friends didn't wanna join us?"

Emma raised her voice too. "Sorry. They don't approve of hunting animals, so they're going sunbathing instead." The ATV rumbled along. "Will Ryan be joining us later?"

"He's still sleeping. Ryan's not what one would call the outdoor type anyway." Mr. Raymond leaned forward. "So…this business with your father. You're saying that someone killed him?"

"Yes. And I want to find out who. Do you know anyone who had a problem with my father? A grudge maybe?"

"I can't think of anyone offhand, but let me think on it."

The ATV caravan stopped about fifty yards short of a forest near the lake. The men climbed out of their machines and began loading their weapons.

Mr. Raymond picked a rifle from the back of his ATV and gave it to Emma. "This one has a smaller caliber. Easier to handle and learn."

Emma cradled the foreign object in her arms. She had seen guns in the movies, and people acted like it was no big deal to pick up one and start shooting. But Emma knew that was probably all crap.

Mr. Raymond went over to his other guests.

"Unbelievable," Olivia said. "He's like, *Here's a deadly*

weapon, love. Have at it." Olivia took the rifle from Emma. "My father was in the Royal Marines during the Falklands War. He taught me everything about firearms. Let's go over some basics, shall we? One, always treat firearms as if they're loaded, even when you think they're not. Two, never point the muzzle of a firearm at anything you're not willing to blow the piss out of. Three, keep your finger off the trigger until your sights are on target and you are ready to shoot. Four, know your target and what's beyond your target." Olivia gave her the rifle back.

"I don't want to do this," Emma said. "I can't hurt an animal. Could you shoot a fawn? Or a cute little rabbit?"

"If I was lost and starving in the wilderness for a month while facing my own death? Yeah, I'd shoot the cute thing and eat him. He would understand."

"Do you think Mr. Raymond would care if I bail?"

"You can't. He sounds like the type of bloke who'd be impressed by a girl who could hunt. Yet one thing to remember…just because you're aiming at a target it doesn't mean you have to hit the target. See what I'm saying?"

Emma thought about it. "Miss on purpose?"

"Yeah. It's your first gun, right? Your aim will be crap."

"But what if I accidentally hit the animal?"

"Everyone ready?" Mr. Raymond announced. "Let's get to the kill."

Emma floated Olivia a look of unease before carrying her rifle and following the hunters into the dense forest.

Olivia stopped her and pushed down the rifle. "Don't let the barrel come up like that. Keep it pointed at the ground in case it goes off."

"I got it. I got it," Emma said. "Did Mr. Raymond say what we're hunting?"

"Deer, Miss Rothchild," Mr. Raymond said. "Although, once in a while we're lucky enough to find some elk. Let's spread out. Why don't you girls take that far left side and step quietly. There's a hidden meadow through here a quarter mile. The deer love to hide there."

The group splintered off as it disappeared into the woods, leaving Olivia and Emma alone.

Olivia still spouted safety rules. "Everyone is wearing orange, so remember that before you pull the trigger."

"Relax," Emma said. "There's no one watching, so I don't have to shoot anything."

After ducking around trees for a few minutes, Olivia and Emma emerged from the woods and caught the edge of a hidden meadow. Just as Mr. Raymond predicted, a dozen or so deer were grazing out in the open. None of the creatures had a care in the world.

"Aw…" Emma knelt down and watched them.

Olivia did the same.

"They look so peaceful," Emma whispered.

The mother stepped up to the baby and nudged her, causing the baby to cling nearer to mama.

"Reminds me of Africa," Olivia whispered. "My father was stationed in Zambia for a brief time. We lived way out in the boonies. Every morning I would step on the porch and see a herd of gazelle just standing in our meadow. Hundreds of the buggers roamed freely around the area. For some reason they loved starting their day in our meadow. They were beautiful."

"That sounds amazing. I would love to go to Africa and see that someday."

Olivia sighed. "You know what? I can't blame you, love. I couldn't shoot at those gazelles either."

"What does your father do?"

"Works for the diplomatic service. Usually as an assistant to the ambassador. He and my mum move around a lot."

"Do your parents know about The Auth—"

"Not here," Olivia interrupted. "Ask me again some other time."

Trees rustled to their right. Someone or something was approaching them.

Emma took a few steps back. Olivia didn't move.

Finally, Mr. Raymond emerged from the brush. "Ah, you've found them. Lovely specimens too," he whispered.

Mr. Raymond aimed his rifle at the deer.

Adjusted the gun sight on his rifle.

Emma closed her eyes. She didn't want to watch.

"Range is fifty yards. Quite an easy shot. Why are your eyes closed?"

Emma opened them and faked a yawn. "I didn't get much sleep last night, sorry."

"No worries." Mr. Raymond laughed. "You should have first dibs."

"Oh no, it's your property. You should shoot first."

"I insist. Ladies first."

Emma glanced at Olivia.

"Just watch your aim," Olivia reminded her.

Emma thought that was great advice. She didn't have to hit anything. One loud shot from her rifle and those deer would scamper away.

"You should lie on your stomach," Mr. Raymond whispered. "It will steady your aim."

Emma placed her rifle down on the ground and lowered herself flat. Once she found a comfortable position to lie in, Emma pulled the rifle back to her and balanced her hands and arms while pointing the rifle towards the meadow. She peered through the gun sight. A sharp X hovered over something out of focus.

"I can't see through this thing."

"There's a knob on the side for adjustments," Olivia said.

Emma found the small knob and turned it one way and then the other. Soon the meadow came into focus. The X was centered on the fawn's little head. Emma took her finger off the trigger and coaxed the rifle farther left, putting the X near a faraway tree. She hoped the tree would forgive her. Emma's hands trembled. She feared this would cause her to shoot the fawn on accident.

"Don't be shy, Emma. You can drop the momma deer. She's a big target," Mr. Raymond whispered.

Emma ignored him. She wasn't about to kill a little girl's momma. Emma took a deep breath and tried to settle her hands. If she jerked at the wrong time, her shot could kill the momma or the baby. Emma took the safety off the rifle, relaxed, then placed her finger on the trigger. She double-checked her shot. Right at the trunk of the tree. *You can do it,* she told herself. She began squeezing the trigger just as the fawn hopped into her shot.

Emma froze and released the trigger again. Relieved the gun didn't go off, she nudged the muzzle over another few feet to the left. Emma aimed at another tree.

Not wanting to give the fawn time to move again, Emma swallowed and squeezed—

"Stop!" Olivia yelled.

The deer flipped their heads at the sound and bolted. Gunfire came from the woods as the hunters unleashed their weapons on now moving targets.

Mr. Raymond raised his gun, but cursed before bringing it down. "Can't get a clear shot."

The deer quickly scattered into the woods.

"Stupid girl. Why did you yell? You scared them off," Mr. Raymond said.

Emma stood up with her rifle.

Olivia immediately took the weapon from her. She put the safety back on and took out the magazine, then ejected the live round from the chamber. "This rifle is defective. See the chamber? That piece of metal is separated from the stock and blocking the barrel. If Miss Rothchild fired this weapon, it would blow back into her face."

Mr. Raymond examined the defect. "My God you're right. There's also a piece of loose metal sticking out of the side here. Excellent observation. Emma, your assistant knows her guns. You're a lucky girl."

Emma glanced at Olivia. Both girls had the same thought.

Emma wasn't lucky. Someone had tried to kill her.

CHAPTER 20

When Mr. Raymond offered a different rifle to Emma, she declined, finally stating her heart wasn't into hunting as much as she thought, so Olivia offered to take her place. Mr. Raymond acted like he understood. An hour later, one of Mr. Raymond's executives shot a mother deer while Mr. Raymond found a wild buck and took it down with one shot. They dragged both animals back to their ATVs. Emma couldn't look at their slain bodies. She knew that one peek would make her lose control and bawl like a baby. Instead of the carnage, Emma concentrated on the shimmering private lake, its soothing and gentle currents breaking against a large tree half-submerged in the waters.

"Hey, I looked all over for you guys. Nobody woke me up," Ryan said, his face pissed.

"There he is," Mr. Raymond said to everyone in the group. "Jesus, it's about one o'clock, son. I know you like sleeping in, but...that's just plain lazy." He looked for approval from his friends, who all chuckled in agreement. "Well, you missed the hunt and slept through welcoming our guests." Mr. Raymond gestured towards Emma.

Ryan frowned. "Someone should have woken me."

"You're not six anymore, kid."

"I was working late on a school project. It's due Monday."

"Discipline is an important attribute. You need to learn it." Mr. Raymond addressed his men, "Who's hungry for some barbecue and cold beer?"

The men replied back with enthusiasm as they tied the deer carcasses to their ATVs.

Mr. Raymond climbed into the ATV. "You coming, Emma?"

Olivia began walking over to Mr. Raymond.

Emma lingered near Ryan.

"You should go ahead," he said. "You're probably hungry."

Emma took one step, but hesitated. She noted another two-seater ATV, which was blue. Ryan must have taken that, which meant...

"Can you take me back to the house?" Emma asked.

Ryan drove the two-seater ATV behind the caravan heading back to the house. This ATV wasn't as smooth as the bigger ones. It took the bumps and jolts of the rocky trail harder, making Emma and Ryan jump in their seats.

Emma yelled above the motor, "I got up late this morning too and made us late getting here. And I didn't have a good reason, other than honoring my motto of sleeping is awesome and I love doing it as much as I can."

"So you're not mad I wasn't there to greet you?" Ryan asked.

"I wasn't mad. Maybe a tiny bit disappointed."

"Disappointed? I can't have that on my conscience. What can I do to make it up to you?"

"Let's see. Your punishment is to show me this family estate of yours."

"Do you want the nickel tour or the full top-dog one?"

Emma took a moment to answer. "Do I look like a nickel-tour type of girl?"

Ryan grinned. "More like a girl who wants everything out of life and will stop at nothing to get it."

An electric spark ran up her back. This boy knew how to say all the right things.

"I lost my mom. Now my dad. I've learned that life is too short. Too precious. Why settle for something you don't really want?"

"I like how you think." Ryan steered the ATV around the final turn, which would lead them up to the mansion. "Hope you're not a vegetarian because my father doesn't believe in vegetables as a food group."

Emma didn't look forward to hearing Mr. Raymond talk about shooting animals during lunch, plus that would take her away from spending time with Ryan.

"I'm not hungry," Emma said.

Ryan shrugged. "Me neither."

"Why don't we skip lunch and do that tour now?"

"Let me clear my schedule first." Ryan looked forward, almost like he was in a trance. Then he blinked. "Done. Let's go."

Emma laughed.

The boy yanked the wheel hard and Emma gripped the roll bars as the ATV spun a 180. Ryan drove the vehicle down the trail and out of sight of the mansion. He continued down the trail until he turned on to a tiny walking trail and followed it. The ground was rocky and uneven here, bouncing the ATV up and down. Ryan parked it near a large tree and killed the engine. He pointed above them towards an ancient tree house, where only a rotted wood-plank floor and one standing wall remained.

"Welcome to tour stop number one. My tree house...or what was my tree house. It had four walls and I would drag my small telescope out here to do some sky watching. The city lights don't reach out this far, so you can see plenty of stars."

"It does look like a peaceful kind of place to contemplate the meaning of the universe," Emma said.

"I also loved watching the lake. There's a good view from up there."

"Do you like viewing nature?"

"Yeah, there's plenty of nice views here. Some are naturally beautiful." Ryan met her eyes. "Others are just beautiful."

Emma's cheeks burned. She couldn't keep from smiling.

Ryan grinned and looked off into the forest. "We should continue the tour. Wanna drive?"

"Oh, I've never driven one of these before."

"I'm always up for a dose of fleeting danger."

Ryan didn't know how true Emma would make his statement. They swapped seats. Emma turned on the machine and hit the pedal. The ATV bumped and jolted back up the walking trail to the main trail. She then pulled a hard right, lifting two of the four wheels off the ground. The ATV plopped back down on the trail and Emma sped off, throwing dust and dirt into the air. Emma followed the trail as it snaked around the lake, tracing the path she took with Mr. Raymond. But this time Emma was behind the wheel and enjoying the drive with her handsome passenger. She noted another small trail branching downhill from the main one.

"What's down here?" Emma yanked the wheel and took the small trail before Ryan could answer. The ATV raced down the hill.

"This is a walking trail. I wouldn't take this down—" Ryan jumped about two feet, but the seatbelt held him down as the ATV bounced over a series of large rocks. "You're going kind of fast."

The ATV jumped and shimmied and bounced all over the place. Emma loved navigating her way through it. She reached the bottom and raced the ATV back up the other side because it was fun. They hit more rocks and kept bouncing. Emma pressed the pedal as far down as it would go, and the ATV picked up speed as it climbed up to the edge of the ridge.

"Ease up. There's a drop—"

Too late. The ATV jumped into the air as the land dropped away from under its wheels.

Emma and Ryan dropped into their seats in unison as the vehicle hit the ground again. She laughed and hit the brakes, causing the ATV to spin out to a stop.

Ryan shook his head. "Are you like a stunt girl for the movies? You drive like a complete maniac."

"Did I actually scare you?"

"No, it was awesome. Like a hillbilly roller coaster."

Emma gripped the wheel. This wonderful tingling sensation came all over her. Emma realized it was the first time she'd been this happy since her dad had passed and she didn't want it to end. "Do you know where we are?"

"Go ahead and cut through this clearing here. It'll take us back to the lake."

Emma hit the gas and spun out the tires.

"Here we go again," Ryan said.

Emma laughed and guided the bouncing ATV through the clearing as fast as she could. She then drove the ATV back to the main trail. Ryan directed her back to the lake and had her park near a small beach. By California standards it wasn't much. There was no sand to speak of; it was more like gritty rocks covered with mud. Ryan climbed out of the ATV, so Emma killed the engine and joined him.

"There's a place right over here." Ryan stepped on a series of large, chalky rocks that jutted out into the lake. He jumped over the water to reach a flat boulder just big enough for two. Ryan offered Emma his hand. She took it and jumped over too.

Ryan sat on the edge of the rock, allowing his legs to dangle and his shoes to touch the lake. The view was awesome here. Emma could see Mr. Raymond's large ranch-style mansion in the distance, a small pier that could be accessed from the house and patches of forest. A small island rested in the middle of the lake, not much bigger than a house. The water appeared clear and cool. Emma removed her shoes and sat next to Ryan, letting her toes dip into the water. The slight chill racing up her legs was exhilarating.

"I was going to take off my shoes, but..." Ryan stopped.

"But what?"

He chuckled. "It's too embarrassing."

Emma nudged his shoulder. "Now you have to tell me."

Ryan gazed at the lake and smiled. "I didn't want to gross you out if my feet smelled."

Emma laughed. "Go ahead. I'm tougher than I look. But if I pass out from the smell, you better jump in the water and save me."

Ryan stood on the rock and ditched his shoes. He plunged his feet in the water. "Ahh, good and cold. This lake never gets warm. But that's what I like about it."

"Do you swim here a lot?"

"My dad prefers the swimming pool, but...yeah, I like swimming in the lake. Feels more natural. What about you?"

"Not really. Back in New York we had a few beaches. Either I went to Coney Island or some of the beaches on Long Island, but I did more tanning there than I did swimming."

"New York, huh? We don't travel much," Ryan said. "Well, Dad travels all over the world on business, but not me. New York City would be on my list."

"Your list of what?"

"Places I want to see. Like Japan, New Zealand, England... oh, and the Egyptian pyramids. I've always wanted to see those."

"So your dad never took you anywhere? No family vacations to Disney World or the Grand Canyon? No offense, but I get the impression your family could afford it."

"My dad doesn't exactly do family things. Not since my parents divorced. My mom lives in Wichita. Some weekends I'll drive down there to visit her."

"It's great to have a mom to visit."

Ryan shifted his body on the rock. "Damn. I didn't mean to make you feel bad."

Emma touched Ryan's arm. "You didn't. I just think it's awesome that you visit your mom."

Ryan's eyes drifted towards the cool water.

Emma's did the same. Underwater, she noticed a fish wiggling along on its merry way. It had whiskers like a catfish.

There was another fish she thought was a bass.

The wind picked up, blowing tiny ripples across the water.

"For a girl you don't talk much," Ryan said.

"Sometimes I like peace and quiet," Emma said. "When you live in a big city, a place like this is hard to find."

"My ex-girlfriend would ramble on about all kinds of problems she was having. And when I would try to help her solve them, she got all upset. What is that about?"

"Maybe she just wanted you to listen."

"Guess I didn't do it enough."

"Did she dump you?"

"She wanted to be just friends. So yeah." Ryan sighed. "You seeing anyone?"

Emma grinned at the water. "That's not the right question. Do I need to see anyone in my life? That's more accurate."

"All girls need a boyfriend."

"Oh, do they?" Emma squinted at him. "I don't think so. Some girls need to find themselves first, and a boyfriend won't help them with that."

"Depends if they find the right boy."

Emma knew Ryan was putting on the full-court press to charm her, and according to Emma's mission, she needed to "surrender" to him.

This wouldn't be difficult.

Emma drifted her foot over to his, allowing them to touch underwater. "Do you have any suggestions? Any boys I should be checking out?"

"No need to look around because the best one is talking to you right now."

Emma loved his confidence. She scooped up a dead leaf with her toes. "You can't be my boyfriend yet because you haven't asked me on a date."

"What, this isn't a date?"

"It's a social outing with your family. You don't get to cheat me out of a real date."

"So you're a traditionalist, huh?"

"Dinner, something fun to do after. Yeah, I want all that."

"It's hard to do that when I don't live in California," Ryan said.

"True." Emma gazed over the water.

Ryan watched her a moment.

Emma didn't react on purpose.

"So I should make the most of this opportunity, huh?"

Emma shrugged. She knew Ryan was into her. And acting like this just reeled him in.

Ryan took out his digital music player and two headsets. He then attached an extension that allowed both headphones to plug into the same player. "Would you like to hear more Beatles?"

Ryan came prepared and Emma liked that. She nodded and slipped on one of the headphones. Ryan did the same with the other pair.

"Let's start with *Revolver*. Next to *Sgt. Pepper* it's one of my favs," he said. "Ready for John Lennon to blow your mind?"

"Please," Emma said.

Ryan pressed play. Heavy drumbeats started; then crazy-sounding laughs swirled around them as John Lennon told them to relax and let their thoughts flow down a stream. Emma let the music carry her above the lake. Above the ground. Above the sky. Above the world.

The music was beautiful.

Haunting.

Strange.

Wonderful.

Ryan and Emma swayed in unison.

Tapped their feet in the water in unison.

Began to dance on the rock in unison.

During "Eleanor Rigby," Ryan squeezed Emma's hand when Paul McCartney sang about a world of lonely people.

The sun fell from the sky.

And the music kept playing.

They went from *Meet the Beatles!* all the way to *Abbey Road.* And they didn't talk. They didn't need to talk.

Because they got each other.

CHAPTER 21

The moon reached in to the large guest room, casting ominous shadows across the wood-paneled walls and furniture. Olivia and Nadia slept in their makeshift bedding on the floor, while Miyuki mumbled in her sleep as she shared the large bed with Emma, who couldn't sleep. She watched the shadows on the ceiling and kept thinking about Ryan.

There was something…familiar about him. The way he talked about his dad. The way they both grew up as rich kids who isolated themselves instead of becoming celebrities on TMZ. Emma understood the guy. She could see the dark flaw in him because the same flaw was in her. This was the one boy who could understand her. But the huge question for Emma was where did Ryan fit into this conspiracy?

When they came back from the lake, Olivia told Emma that Miyuki and Nadia had found nothing during their search of the mansion. Nadia had even gained access to Mr. Raymond's computer and found nothing that linked him with Venomous or the man Bertrand Petit. The only link was that Raymond Foods owned AgEurope and Mr. Raymond placed Jacqueline in charge of it five years ago. Olivia asked Emma about Ryan. She wanted to know what he knew. Emma explained about Ryan's relationship with his dad and how they'd listened to music the entire day.

Olivia wasn't happy.

"This isn't a romance novel. Use those acting skills of yours to manipulate Ryan. Compromise his mouth so he'll talk. That's your job on this team." Nevertheless, Olivia wanted Emma to stay close to Ryan and see if she could gain closer access to Mr. Raymond. But she also gave Emma a warning. "Keep an eye on your back, love. Next time Mr. Raymond might give you something more dangerous than a defective rifle."

Emma remembered her finger on the cold trigger. Her nervousness of firing the rifle. She'd almost pulled it. Emma could imagine a loud bang and shards of jagged metal spinning at her face, turning her head into—she paused.

Did that shadow on the ceiling move?

No. It was still for the moment.

Did Emma need to see an eye doctor? Maybe her eyes were just acting weird.

But the shadow moved again.

All right, Emma tried to make sense of it. Was it a tree branch moving with the breeze?

No, the shadow looked solid. It moved down the ceiling and inched towards the window.

Emma was still. It wasn't a tree. Could it be an animal? A curious squirrel?

She rolled to her side and peeked around the corner of her bed for a better look at the window.

The shadow covered the glass. It had a long object in its right hand. A pistol?

No, pistols weren't that long. Then Emma remembered that silencer Mrs. B had screwed on to the end of her pistol. It had made the weapon appear long. Just like the shadow's.

The large window creaked open.

Emma cursed at herself. She was looking out the window earlier and forgot to lock it. Now this man was coming inside to kill them.

Emma slipped out of bed and hid beside the baseboard. Her heart pounded. A sense of panic came over her body, making it stiff and paralyzed.

It was too dark to see his face. But the dark outline of the man easing himself down from the window was unmistakable. He was quiet and patient as a cat.

He hesitated, looking at each of the three girls in the room. Olivia had insisted that all the girls sleep together in one room. For once, Olivia's paranoid mind was sound.

Emma pushed against her fear. None of the girls were awake. If she didn't do something soon—Emma tightened her fists, resting her thumbs on top of her fingers. She remembered her karate punches. Her first two knuckles would take the brunt of every blow. Once Emma attacked, the girl had to bring on the hurt. Punch this man relentlessly and without holding back. If she hesitated at all, Emma knew she might freeze up and the man would kill her.

The shadow lifted the long pistol and took aim at Olivia snoozing on the floor.

Emma screamed as she launched herself at the man. He stumbled back in confusion as Emma threw a series of karate punches to his gut, backing the man up against the wall. She punched and punched. The girl couldn't see exactly what part of his body she was hitting, but they felt soft and vulnerable.

The man struck Emma in the mouth. Her chin screamed in pain as the force of the blow knocked her to the floor.

The shadow aimed the long pistol at Emma.

She braced for the shock.

But another leg swung in, and a foot struck the man's wrist hard against the wall. Emma heard something metallic drop to the floor as the man turned on his new attacker. Emma could see long dark hair flying in the air and knew it was Miyuki as she unleashed a circle kick that connected to the man's cheek, throwing him against the wall.

The lights came on. It was the man with the goatee, Bertrand Petit. Both him and Miyuki squinted from the sudden light.

Emma saw the gun on the floor and jumped for it.

Bertrand tried to reach for it too, but tripped over Emma. He then stumbled towards the window on all fours like a dazed cat.

Olivia and Nadia flew past Emma and tried to grab Bertrand. He came to his senses and shoved Olivia into Nadia. Both of the girls crashed into the dresser, which toppled to the floor.

Bertrand unsheathed something near his waist. The moonlight flashed on the long, jagged blade of a serious hunting knife.

Olivia and Nadia jumped up from the floor.

Bertrand pointed the knife at them and backed up to the window.

The girls hesitated.

Bertrand slipped out the window and down the roof.

Miyuki was halfway out the window when Olivia grabbed

her.

"Put on your shoes first and we'll hunt that little twit."

Nadia threw a robe over her T-shirt and shorts. Miyuki and Olivia didn't bother but put on their shoes.

Emma stared at the gun in her hands. If the man with the goatee had stayed for another two seconds…

"Emma, put on your shoes." Olivia finished tying hers and slipped through the open window. Miyuki followed her and both girls slid down the roof.

Emma stuffed the gun in a deep pocket of her sweatpants and quickly slipped her running shoes on as Nadia waited by the window, tying off the waist of her robe while watching the other girls running in pursuit. Emma joined her, and Nadia climbed out of the window.

Nadia slid down the roof as Emma emerged from the open window. Down below she could see Nadia scrambling to her feet as the entire area was flooded with light as alarm bells clanged all over the estate.

Emma pushed off and slid down the roof. Her butt scraped against the wooden shingles, as her sweatpants offered no protection from the splinters that jabbed her butt. When the roof ran out, Emma tumbled forward as she hit the grass. A pop and a spark came from Emma's sweatpants leg. Emma blinked and checked her sweatpants for something hot burning her leg. She removed the gun from her pocket. The silencer portion was hot and she could smell gunpowder.

Emma panicked. Did she just shoot her leg off?

She did a closer inspection of her sweatpants, which now featured a large smoldering hole in the fabric. Emma could see her bare skin right through it. Luckily, her skin was only a tiny bit red from the heat. She then noticed her big right toe sticking out. There was a large hole torn across the side of her running shoe. So that was where the bullet went. Emma cursed at herself for being so careless. Didn't guns have a safety switch?

Emma found the safety switch, flipped it, and stumbled to her feet. She could barely make out Nadia ahead of her. The girl ran out to the edge of where the floodlights reached. Emma ran as fast as she could to catch up, holding on to the gun so it wouldn't drag her sweatpants down to her knees. She reached the edge of the floodlights and noticed a forest, the trees still visible thanks to the full moon. Voices carried through the forest as Olivia screamed orders from the left side while Miyuki answered from the right side. She then yelled something in Japanese.

Nadia stood on this side of the forest and watched the trees for movement.

"What's going on?" Emma asked.

"We've trapped him. He's in this area," Nadia said.

Olivia's voice called out to the woods, "Me and the girls here only want to have a chat with you. Make it easy on yourself, Mr. Petit. Drop the knife and come out."

The trees didn't answer.

"We know you're in here, you twit. Don't make us come in and get you," Olivia yelled, losing her composure. "See anything, Miyuki?"

"No."

"Nadia?"

"Not at all."

"I know you think we're just a bunch of girls," Olivia yelled, "but we'll sit here all flipping night if we have to, and then you'll have to fight all four of us at daybreak. Just remember, you caught us half-asleep tonight and we still chased you out of our bedroom. Imagine how pissed we'll be if you make us wait all night." Olivia's silhouette walked a few feet "You think girls are monsters on their period, love? Try keeping us from our morning coffee."

Once again, silence echoed from the trees.

Then something ruffled the bushes near Nadia and Emma.

Nadia prepared herself. Emma remembered the gun and flipped off the safety, aiming it at the bushes, keeping her finger off the trigger until she had a target.

Something was moving. They could see a dark form moving from tree to tree, hiding behind the trunks. It moved to the tree nearest to Nadia.

Miyuki's voice yelled, "Hey! He's heading for—"

Bertrand lunged out of the forest, the sharp end of the knife leading the way as he charged.

Nadia swung her leg out for a strike, but Bertrand veered away and her leg missed.

Bertrand headed for Emma.

She pointed the gun and placed her finger on the trigger.

Bertrand stopped with the knife still in his hand. There was fear in his eyes.

Olivia and Miyuki ran up to them.

Bertrand lowered the knife and kept his left hand up in the air, a gesture of surrender.

"Drop the knife," Olivia said, her voice all business.

Bertrand tossed it to the side and Nadia secured it. He brought both hands up to surrender.

"Well done, Emma," Miyuki said.

Emma's finger tightened on the cold trigger. The man who killed her dad and all those men. The man who tried to kill Emma and her friends...twice. He was right here. Right now. One squeeze of her finger and she could issue the justice her dad so rightly deserved.

"Said you wanted to talk, *oui*?" Bertrand asked. "I'm open to that."

"Now that you've lost your knife?" Olivia said.

The man shrugged. "Give me a good deal and I'll tell you what you want to know."

"Did you kill Kenneth Rothchild?" Emma demanded.

"Look, I know you girls are working for someone. Depending on what they offer me, I could answer all your questions."

"You'd be willing to do that?" Olivia asked.

"Here's my offer," Emma said. "Answer my questions or I'll shoot you."

"Emma, chill a second. This could be important."

"Olivia, stay out of this."

"He's offering us information."

"Did you kill my dad?" Emma screamed. She was through being calm.

Bertrand glanced at Olivia and then the other two girls.

"Answer me!" Emma yelled.

"Yes."

A relief came over Emma. She needed to hear him say it. She needed to be sure.

"Thank you."

Olivia stepped in front of the gun. "Put that flipping thing down, you twit."

"Get away from him."

"I'm not going to let you shoot him. We need him alive."

"He killed my dad."

"And he'll face the consequences. Mrs. B will make sure of that."

"This will be the consequence. Right here. Right now."

Olivia swallowed and moved cautiously toward Emma. "Why don't you shoot both of us, then? I know you're not too fond of me either."

"What?"

"Go ahead. It'll make you feel better, right? Funny how you can't shoot a fawn, but you love the idea of shooting people."

"Please step away." Emma heard her voice crack and waver. She was losing it.

Another hand touched her arm. "This not you, Emma. You're not a killer." Miyuki's calming voice took Emma down a notch.

She could feel her resolve breaking into pieces.

Emma lowered the gun and Miyuki removed it from her hand and gave it to Olivia.

Miyuki brushed Emma's cheek; only then did Emma realize she was crying.

CHAPTER 22

Bertrand Petit's flashlight made circular patterns of light against the bushes and the tree trunks as the Gems made the Frenchman walk deeper into the dark forest. Emma still had two hair scrunchies in her back pocket, so Olivia used them to bind Bertrand Petit's hands and legs together so the gun wouldn't be necessary. They needed to contact Mrs. B, but their phones were back at Mr. Raymond's mansion, so Emma volunteered to go back to get them.

"Fetch the car keys too," Nadia said, "in case we need to relocate our new friend."

Leaving the flashlight behind with the girls, Emma trekked through the dark forest, heading in the direction they came from and following the faint glow of the floodlights coming from Mr. Raymond's mansion. When Emma broke out of the forest and into the clearing, she noticed a group of people standing in the floodlights next to the mansion: Mr. Raymond, Ryan, Jacqueline, and a trio of men holding guns.

"What happened?" Mr. Raymond asked. "Why are you wandering the grounds alone?"

Emma hesitated. This needed to be good. "A coyote chased this poor Siamese kitty up on to the roof, and they were creating a heck of a noise, yowling at each other. Well, the kitty lost its balance and tumbled off the roof, where the coyote could get at the poor thing. So we yelled out the window and tried to scare the coyote off. Before you know it, we're all climbing out the window and creating this huge commotion to drive the coyote away. Then we ended up jumping off the roof and chasing it into the forest. The Siamese kitty ran off too, poor thing was so scared, but the girls found him and coaxed him out. We're

160

thinking about taking the kitty back with us."

Jacqueline scoffed. "This is all over a stupid feline?"

Mr. Raymond chuckled to himself. "Silly girls. You triggered the burglar alarms." He glanced at his men. "Stand down." The men nodded and holstered their weapons. "Please tell your friends to hurry up. My men can't reset the alarms until they're back." Mr. Raymond headed back inside.

Jacqueline watched Emma for a long moment.

Emma grinned.

Jacqueline didn't respond as she withdrew back inside also.

"A cat?" Ryan yawned.

"A Siamese kitty cat. Yes," Emma said with her brow raised.

"Did the cat try to eat your shoe?"

Emma looked down at her shoe with the bullet hole. Hmm. How could she explain that?

"The coyote did that. I was trying to keep him away from the kitty."

"Did you get bit?" Ryan asked, quite concerned. "Those coyotes could have rabies, you know."

"Nope, and I still have all my toes," Emma said. "Why don't you go back to bed? I'll give you the full play-by-play in the morning."

Ryan nodded and his sleepy eyes blinked as Emma followed him inside the mansion and up the stairs.

Emma parted ways from him at the scary stuffed Grizzly bear and went up to the girls' room. She grabbed all their phones and the keys to the car before slipping back outside. One of the guards told Emma to be back with her friends in no less than ten minutes or they would drag them back. Emma nodded before rushing back into the forest. She found the girls again and gave Olivia her phone. She called Mrs. B on a scrambled satellite line. They woke her up, but the woman didn't mind when Olivia told her the reason.

Olivia activated the speaker mode and held the phone up to Bertrand, whose hands were immobilized.

"What information do you offer?" Mrs. B's voice asked through Olivia's phone. "Why shouldn't we throw you in a dark cell and let you rot in it?"

"The FBI can't do that. You must follow rules, *oui*?"

Bertrand replied with attitude.

"I'm afraid we don't answer to the FBI or any other organization. We make our own rules. No one has to hear from you ever again, if that is what we wish, Mr. Petit."

Bertrand pondered that for a second. "Are you MI6?"

"You know who we are. Unless you're not that bright. Judging by your performance over the last few days, I would vote for the second possibility."

The girls smiled.

Bertrand frowned and then thought about it. "The Authority?"

"You're a genius," Olivia said.

Bertrand struggled against his bonds. "If I wasn't tied up..."

"Please spare my girls your macho attitude. It's quite pointless. Let's get back on point. What can you offer us?" Mrs. B asked again, sounding impatient.

"You've heard of Venomous, *oui*? The group."

"The organization you are no doubt a part of, yes."

"I have information about the group. Code names. Plans. Could be valuable to you."

"Possibly. Tell us some information and we'll see how much it's worth."

"Not yet. I want a deal in place first."

Mrs. B paused on the phone. "If you say that you want a million dollars and a private island, I'll have these girls string you up and play hit the piñata until you bust wide open."

"You look like a bunch of nice girls. You wouldn't do that."

Olivia smirked. "Black Opal here wanted to use you as target practice. Maybe she'd like another go at it?" Olivia held out the pistol.

Emma reached for it.

"Don't be so hasty," the man said. "How about I join you? Be one of those consultants? I know a lot. I could be valuable."

"Joining our organization as an equal is quite out of the question," Mrs. B said over the phone. "But we could relocate you to somewhere pleasant. You would, of course, have to earn such a privilege. How about answering a few questions first?"

"I've got one," Olivia said. "Is Jacqueline giving the orders? Is she a Venomous plant?"

"She's one of our agents. High up on the chain. The sixty-ninth of the order, to be exact."

"And who else?" Olivia asked.

"What about Mr. Raymond?" Mrs. B asked. "Is he a part of all this, or is he a Venomous pawn?"

"When you say somewhere pleasant, are we hinting at Tahiti? I would enjoy Tahiti."

"So far you've only earned West Texas," Mrs. B said through the phone. "Keep talking and we'll see."

"You posed as an AirTech engineer," Nadia said. "You worked on the new climate control systems for all those facilities owned by Raymond Foods. Were you responsible for the special modifications to them?"

"Yes. And I also worked on the projects at Ovechkin-Komstat in Ukraine. Kyo-Shun in China. The Lester-Sumner Company in Australia. Ganchi Farms in Mumbai."

"What was the purpose of all these modifications?" Mrs. B asked. "What is Venomous planning?"

"You know what? I'd also want a car. How about a Maserati? I would enjoy one of those in Tahiti."

"Answer the question," Mrs. B said, sharp as a knife.

Olivia cocked the hammer back on the pistol, but didn't aim it. "Answer the lady's question, Mr. Petit."

"No Maserati? I'll take a Lexus then. Surely The Authority could afford—" Bertrand slumped over and stopped talking.

Olivia shook him. "Hey! Oy! Can you hear me?"

Emma's eyes widened. There was the end of a large arrow stuck in the man's chest.

"What is that?" Nadia asked.

"Over there!" Miyuki pointed at a figure running from a tree with a crossbow in his hand.

Miyuki broke out into a run and chased after him. Emma and Nadia ran after her while Olivia knelt down to check on Bertrand.

He was dead.

The assassin weaved through the trees of the forest. But Miyuki picked up speed and closed in on him. The girl was like an Olympic athlete in the gold medal race. Emma was amazed at how in-shape she was. Miyuki chased the assassin down a hill, then up and over another hill until there was a county road at the bottom, where a car waited.

The assassin reached the road and swung around. Reaching behind him, the hooded figure pulled out an arrow. He inserted it into the crossbow and pulled back the string, locking it in place. The figure took aim.

The arrow swooshed over Miyuki's head as she dropped to the ground. The arrow thumped against a tree right next to Emma, making her freeze in her tracks.

The assassin slid behind the wheel and the car roared to life.

Miyuki jumped to her feet and ran to the road.

The car gunned forward. Its headlights shone against Miyuki's body. She tumbled out of the way just as the car sped off down the road.

"Are you all right?" Nadia called out.

Miyuki flashed her a thumbs-up.

Nadia watched the car for a moment and then swiveled to Emma. "We can still catch him." Nadia ran off, heading back towards the forest.

"We can? How? Where are you going?" Emma asked before whistling to Miyuki and signaling for her to follow.

The three girls ran back the way they came, zipping past Olivia heading in the opposite direction. The confused girl stopped and threw out her arms.

"What the hell is going on?"

The other girls didn't answer, as they were too busy running.

Olivia cursed to herself and ran after them.

The girls made it all the way to Mr. Raymond's mansion. Nadia headed for their rented BMW in the driveway. Emma felt almost out of breath, but she pushed herself harder and jumped into the passenger seat without thinking. Nadia fired up the engine and Miyuki slipped in back. Nadia swung the car around, throwing gravel everywhere as she accelerated.

"Wait a flipping second," Olivia yelled as she ran after the car.

Nadia braked hard and Miyuki opened the door.

Olivia jumped in headfirst as Nadia gunned the car forward.

"What's going on? Where's the assassin? Why are you girls running around the forest like a bunch of psychotic chipmunks?" Olivia sounded like she was on the verge of freaking out.

"How can you find him?" Emma asked.

Nadia swung the BMW into a perfect ninety-degree right turn and put in just enough input on the wheel to keep the car from fishtailing. "The assassin's still trapped inside the compound. That service road he's on circles around the back and empties out right here near the main gate."

Nadia guided the BMW up the gravel drive and they soon reached the main gate. The iron gates sat wide open with damage to both ends. One of the guards was on his phone, most likely calling it in.

"Monkey balls! He's already been here," Miyuki said.

Nadia gunned the engine and flew through the busted gate. "He can't be too far ahead."

The speedometer climbed as Nadia pushed the BMW to its performance limits. Emma checked her seat belt and hoped Nadia was a much better driver than she was. Nadia braked for a turn and accelerated into it, keeping the BMW in complete control as the tires squealed in protest. When she reached the top of a hill, Nadia kept calm as the car went slightly airborne. The girl wasn't all over the road either. Her moves on the steering wheel were precise and had purpose. When they cleared another fast turn, a set of red taillights pierced the night.

Nadia sped up. It didn't take long for the BMW to close the distance. The car came into focus. Emma didn't know much about cars. Was that the same one? The darkness didn't help.

"Is that him?" Olivia asked.

"A gold Kia. That's him. He almost ran me down," Miyuki said.

"Think you can run him off the road, Nadia?"

She smiled. "Please put on your seat belts first."

CHAPTER 23

The gold Kia accelerated down the dark, two-lane road as it realized the four teenage girls in the black BMW were chasing it. But the Kia's four-banger engine was no match for the V-8 as the BMW closed.

"Don't go crazy," Olivia said. "Knock him off into a ditch or something."

"Love tap!" Miyuki said.

Nadia floored the BMW and the front end smacked into the Kia with a jolt. Miyuki clapped her hands together with delight while Olivia looked like a concerned soccer mom. Emma just hoped Nadia knew what she was doing.

Nadia turned hard into the next turn. She accelerated out of it and rammed the Kia again.

Emma's heart jumped in her chest. That was more than a love tap. The lights of the BMW exposed the Kia's back bumper. The car's taillights were broken and mangled. Pieces of the Korean car were falling off.

"Hit him again!" Miyuki squealed, treating this like some kind of game.

"PIT him, for flipping sake," Olivia said. "Don't take us out with him."

"Pit him?" Emma asked, not familiar with the term.

"The police use the PIT maneuver to push a fleeing felon's car into a spin so they can end a chase," Nadia said in her calm and quiet way as she drove a car over ninety miles per hour. "I've only done it once, during evasive driving training."

"Sounds dangerous," Emma said.

"Don't worry. I'll be gentle." Nadia concentrated as she swung out to the left lane and sped up. She tried to make the right front fender of the BMW line up next to the left rear of the Kia's.

"Big truck!" Olivia pointed.

In one quick move, Nadia tapped the brakes and tucked the BMW behind the Kia. The semi roared past, blasting its air horn.

The two cars weaved through more turns before Nadia swung out to the left lane and gunned the BMW once again.

"You can do it!" Miyuki said.

This time the two cars were side by side when the Kia decided to smash into the side of the BMW.

Emma yelped as their car shook from the impact. Nadia fought with the wheel.

The Kia smashed into the side of the BMW again.

Nadia struggled to keep the car on the road. The car's headlights showed rows of trees on the left-hand side of the road. If they veered off the road, those tree trunks would pound the BMW like mallets.

"Is this part of the maneuver?" Emma asked.

The desperate little Kia swerved into them a third time and Emma's window exploded, throwing glass everywhere and making her scream. This was all getting too real.

Nadia braked and tried to clip the left rear of the Kia. But the little car avoided the BMW by swerving to the far right of the road.

Nadia backed off the chase. "Are you all right, Emma?"

"I think so. It was only my window."

"Maybe we should let him go," Olivia said.

"Are you coconuts?" Miyuki asked.

"Bananas," Emma corrected.

"It's too dangerous, love. It's not worth all our lives," Olivia said. "Let him go. We'll catch up with him again."

Nadia eased off the gas and the Kia quickly raced into the distance.

"Sorry, guys," Olivia said. "But we have to see the big—" A huge jolt flung all four girls against their seat belts.

Emma glanced in her side mirror as new headlights blinded her eyes. "Looks like he called some of his friends."

A giant Hummer bore down on the smaller BMW as it rammed them again from the back and bullied the car forward towards a turn.

Nadia hit the brakes and the rubber tires burned. But the Hummer shoved the BMW forward anyway. The next turn had a big drop-off past the guardrail. If they smashed through it, they would roll the BMW for sure.

Nadia gripped the wheel and mashed the gas pedal. The BMW scrambled off the front of the Hummer and accelerated towards the drop-off turn. The speedometer needle climbed.

Emma stopped breathing. Could Nadia make the curve going that fast? Wouldn't they fly off into the trees?

Nadia waited.

And waited…

Then slammed the brake pedal. The girls braced as Nadia hit the gas again and flung the car into the right turn. The BMW slid across the double yellow lines. The tires screamed. The left side of the car skidded towards the far end of the pavement, almost kissing the guardrail. But the BMW somehow cleared the turn.

Behind them, a loud crash of trees hitting metal. The headlights of the Hummer tumbled down the embankment as the large vehicle took out trees left and right.

Nadia braked the car to a stop.

All the Gems sighed at once as calmness finally descended inside the car.

Emma turned to Nadia. "Can I say that you're, like, a rock star behind the wheel of a car?"

Nadia smiled in her shy way.

The night air felt cold as the girls went down the dirt embankment to the overturned Hummer resting on broken trees. Olivia peeked inside it. No one was there.

"They must have gone into the forest," Olivia said.

A cold breeze blew under the oversized T-shirt Emma wore, chilling her to the bone. "Do we have to do this again? We're not properly dressed for all these outdoor activities."

Miyuki and Nadia hugged their chests. They could feel the breeze too.

"But they might know something," Olivia said.

"They also might have guns."

"Emma's right. We should leave," Nadia said.

"Mr. Raymond's goons are expecting us back any minute," Emma said. "They could be out looking for us right now."

Olivia didn't like giving up, that much was clear as the girl watched the forest. But Olivia let out a curse and led the girls back up the embankment to the BMW. Nadia turned over the engine and got the heater running as she drove the Gems back the way they had come.

"What will we do about Mr. Raymond?" Miyuki asked.

"Yes. We must find out what role he plays in all this," Nadia said.

Emma thought about Ryan. How genuine he felt to her. "I don't think Mr. Raymond knows. I mean, when I talked to Ryan, he told me how much his father loved his company. More so than his own son, and a man like that—why would he destroy something he worked his whole life to build? My dad had the same mind-set. He loved his company too and it wouldn't make sense for him to do something to hurt it. Honestly, I think Mr. Raymond is innocent. Jacqueline could be using his company as a secret base of operations."

"A good possibility," Nadia said. "He might not know what's going on."

"But he gave Emma that bad rifle," Miyuki said.

"Bertrand could have easily switched out those rifles before the hunt," Emma said. "Remember that I was the only one who needed the spare gun."

Olivia thought about it. "There's only one way to find out for sure. We should tell Mr. Raymond about Jacqueline and see what the man does."

CHAPTER 24

The next morning, the Gems were woken up by a knock at their door. The butler informed them that Mr. Raymond was expecting them for breakfast at 8 a.m. Hit by grogginess, the girls reluctantly said yes and rushed to put on clothes, brush their hair, and look halfway human. They went down the three flights of stairs and met the butler, who escorted them outside to a lovely wooden deck with a table set for breakfast. The deck faced the lake and the small dock, where Mr. Raymond's speedboat lazily bumped against its moorings.

Ryan stood up from the table to welcome them, while Mr. Raymond had his face buried inside the *Wall Street Journal*. There was no sign of Jacqueline or any of Mr. Raymond's hunting buddies. But a fly buzzed around a pat of butter.

"Long night?" Mr. Raymond asked through the paper, as if he knew the answer already.

"It was." Emma flicked a look at Ryan and smiled. "Morning."

"You look great for a Siamese cat wrangler," Ryan said. "How's the cat doing?"

"It's dead," Olivia said, without feeling.

Emma shot her a look. Why did their story have to end like that? They could have dropped it off at a shelter.

"Yeah, we couldn't save the poor thing," Emma said instead.

Mr. Raymond folded his paper. "Sorry to hear your efforts were in vain. Juice? Coffee?"

The girls found seats around the table as a servant saw to their requests.

Mr. Raymond picked a half-cut grapefruit from a tray and placed it in his bowl. "Hope you all love pancakes as much as I do, because that's what we're eating."

Olivia sipped her orange juice, glanced at the Gems, and focused on Mr. Raymond. "We should be honest with you, sir."

"Honest? About what?" Mr. Raymond rammed a spoon down into the grapefruit, causing it to squirt.

Olivia paused. "I don't work for Mr. Gooden or AirTech. And these two girls are not Emma's best friends. We're here to investigate Raymond Foods."

Mr. Raymond paused and then ate the piece of grapefruit on his spoon. "Investigate my company? Why?"

"Because Jacqueline Boyay is a spy for a criminal organization known as Venomous. We caught one of her operatives last night...the cat we were trying to save. We gathered some information from the man, but not all of it. An assassin put an arrow into him before we could finish."

Mr. Raymond didn't look up, but he stopped eating his grapefruit.

Emma spoke. "Jacqueline had this man sabotage my dad's jet because the engineers he was transporting were suspicious about some special modifications he made to your newly installed climate control systems."

Olivia took over. "We think Jacqueline was working with Venomous to disrupt or destroy your food production plants and distribution network to cause some type of worldwide famine."

Mr. Raymond sat back in his chair with a dumbfounded look.

Ryan stared at Emma, his face also surprised. "Whoa. Reset. So you girls are what? Spies?"

"They are." Emma referenced the other girls. "Well, I'm kinda one too, but I still need more training."

"So that's why you were so nice." Ryan fired a look at Emma.

She froze. Oh crap, but that didn't mean—her mind tried devising a way to get around the truth and failing.

Ryan eyes dropped to the empty plate.

"It wasn't—okay, at first, yes, I was trying to find out things, but then I got to know you and..." Emma's voiced trailed off as she noticed Ryan ignoring her.

"Teen spies? How absurd," Mr. Raymond said. "Is this a joke? Did one of my friends pay you girls to do this?"

"This isn't a joke," Olivia said.

"Well, you'll forgive me if I don't believe a word you're saying."

Nadia turned on a tablet and pushed it across to Mr. Raymond. "This shows the schematics of one of your AgEurope food storage facilities in Germany." Nadia went on to explain how the system was not set up for temperature control, but to introduce some type of liquid or substance to the seeds and food stuffs that was not water. She went on to show schematics of other Raymond Foods facilities in Europe, Africa, and North America. "Two common elements are that Bertrand Petit made these modifications and Jacqueline signed off on each and every work order."

"Did you know about that?" Olivia asked.

Mr. Raymond looked over the tablet with concern, rolling his finger as he checked the schematics and the emails.

He sat back. "My God."

To Emma, it was clear the man didn't know what was going on right under his nose.

"Do you believe us now?" Olivia asked.

Mr. Raymond nodded. "Why would Jacqueline do this? She's been my top executive for years. I don't understand."

"She needed a way in to your company to build the foundation for Venomous's plan."

Mr. Raymond's eyes drifted over to Emma. "And they killed your father?"

"Yes," she said.

Mr. Raymond took in the information with new eyes. "What organization do you girls work for?"

Olivia folded her hands on the table, all business. "Let's just say we're the good guys, and whatever Jacqueline and Venomous are planning, we want to stop it. Do you know where she is now?"

"After the alarms woke us last night, Jacqueline said she couldn't sleep and decided to go back to our offices in the city to get some work done." Mr. Raymond rose to his feet. "I'll order my security to detain her. Do you mind skipping breakfast and accompanying me? I want to hear what Jacqueline says before I turn her over to the police."

Mr. Raymond's corporate helicopter landed a few minutes later on a cement heliport pad near the mansion. The Gems climbed aboard while Ryan argued with his dad, who wanted him to stay at the house. Ryan insisted and won. He stepped inside the helicopter's large and luxurious passenger cabin. Emma slid over to make room next to her. Ryan looked at Emma, but chose the opposite side of the cabin to sit.

The helicopter climbed from its pad and twisted around, heading for the tall buildings just over the horizon.

It took twenty minutes for the helicopter to reach Kansas City. The craft gently descended and landed on another heliport pad on top of the new Raymond Foods headquarters skyscraper. Mr. Raymond, the Gems, and Ryan left the noisy helicopter and entered the building through a door on the roof.

Once inside, a flight of stairs led the party down to the top floor of the building. That was where three armed security guards met up with Mr. Raymond.

"Is Miss Boyay in custody?" Mr. Raymond asked. The guards confirmed she was. "Good. Take us there."

The cavernous executive floor had new carpet and new walls. Emma could smell the dried adhesives and fresh paint all over the place. Boxes of office desks, furnishings, and plastic-covered couches were grouped together in various rooms, waiting to be unpacked. The guards escorted the group to a large boardroom, its walls made of clear glass. Inside, Jacqueline waited at the head of a forty-chair meeting table made of dark oak. Ten armed security guards stood around the perimeter of the room.

"What's the meaning of this, Ron?" Jacqueline's voice was sharp and pissed. "Why are these trained monkeys making me sit here?"

Mr. Raymond made his way to the opposite edge of the table. The Gems walked into the boardroom, followed by Ryan.

Mr. Raymond pressed his fists into the table, almost if bracing himself. "I have some questions for you. And I expect truthful answers."

"Is that all? I don't see why we need to make such a production out of it. Ask me anything you wish."

"Did you sign off on unauthorized modifications to the

AirTech climate control systems? The new ones installed in all of our food production plants and seed storage facilities?"

Jacqueline didn't flinch. "Yes."

Olivia flashed the other girls a confused look.

Emma agreed. That was too easy.

Mr. Raymond continued. "What modifications did you have your associate Bertrand Petit make?"

"First we modified the new AirTech system so that it was possible to reverse the air removal process. Instead of a vacuum-tight sealed vault, we could trick the system into flooding the vaults with oxygen. Second, we put in a secondary sprinkler system throughout all the buildings, in tandem with the AirTech fire-suppression system. This sprinkler system was specifically designed to carry fuel."

"Why would you put in a system to spray fuel throughout the buildings?" Mr. Raymond asked, dumbfounded.

Jacqueline shrugged. "To incinerate the contents inside the buildings, of course."

Olivia stepped away from the wall and joined Mr. Raymond. "And if you pump the seed vaults full of oxygen…one spark and those airtight compartments go up in a flash."

Jacqueline smiled. "That's the general idea, yes."

"What happens after you torch all the food-production facilities?" Olivia asked. "No, wait. Venomous wants to threaten the destruction of those facilities, right? For what? A huge pile of extortion money?"

Jacqueline crossed her legs. "I knew Emma was who she said she was. But it was difficult to find out any information about you three girls." Jacqueline sat back in her chair. "I didn't know The Authority recruited young ladies for their glorious cause. I must make note of that to my superiors."

Olivia approached Jacqueline. "You're not telling anyone about us. You're going to jail."

The woman didn't flinch. "Am I?" She glanced over at Mr. Raymond. "Will you turn me over to the police?"

He smiled. "Now why would I do that?" Mr. Raymond stepped away from the table. "Guards…if the young girls move, shoot them."

The security men pulled out their weapons and pointed them

at the Gems.

"What are you doing?" Olivia asked.

A guard pulled Emma away from Ryan and guided her over to join Miyuki and Nadia.

Olivia backed away, ready for a fight.

Jacqueline took out her own pistol and aimed it right at Olivia. "Move over there with the rest of them."

Olivia hesitated and then complied.

"Dad? What's going on?" Ryan asked.

"Search them," Mr. Raymond said. "We're done with surprises today."

The guards lined the Gems up against the wall at gunpoint.

"Dad?"

"I'll explain later."

"I want to know now."

Mr. Raymond scoffed. "I didn't want you here at all. You don't need to be involved in this."

"Involved with what? Why are you treating them like this?"

"Ryan, shut up."

"Screw you. I'll say whatever I—"

Mr. Raymond struck Ryan across the face, knocking him to the ground. The man bent down. "You're still such a child, unable to see the bigger picture, even when the clues are right in front of your face."

Ryan rolled on the ground, his eyes red and watering. Emma's heart reached out to him. How could a father treat his son like that?

"This is the most ambitious plan I've ever created. It will triple our family's wealth. It's brilliant. Ingenious." Mr. Raymond paused, absorbed in his own thoughts and words, feeding off them like a crack addict. "A series of accidents will result in the loss of our critical food production plants and storage facilities across the world. The price of food will skyrocket since our company produces up to eighty percent of the food in some of those markets." Mr. Raymond approached Olivia, her cheek glued against the wall. "Yes, there will be food shortages. Demand for emergency food rations to combat the threat will increase, especially among the poorer countries in Africa."

Mr. Raymond shook with this sick glee. "And then my new E-Food division will come to the rescue with untouched warehouses full of emergency food packs designed for large-scale disasters such as this one. Countries will be desperate to pay me any price to feed their starving people. Even after rebuilding my destroyed facilities, I project a five-year profit of more than three hundred percent. It's staggering."

Mr. Raymond approached Emma. He reached up and combed her blond hair back with his fingers. Emma quivered from how weird it felt. "The best part of it all? The blame for this entire food crisis will fall on AirTech and Rothchild Industries. They put in the faulty climate control system responsible for creating the largest humanitarian disaster the world has ever seen since the Black Plague."

Anger flared up inside Emma. First, this man's crazy delusions got her dad killed. Second, the man would destroy everything her dad worked so hard to build.

Emma spit on his face.

Mr. Raymond laughed and wiped his chin before moving back to Ryan, who was still on the floor. "There is no secret organization behind this. It was all planned out by me."

Ryan slowly crawled to his feet. "Won't thousands of people die?"

"Hundreds of thousands, most likely. Africans, Arabs, and Chinese people mostly. And who honestly cares about them?"

Nadia pushed against the man holding her to the wall and glared at Mr. Raymond. "You're a sadistic man and a mass-murder."

"Killing for a profit is even more cocked up," Olivia added.

"Young lady, my competitors market and feed sugary sweets to obese children, giving them early diabetes and high blood pressure when they become young adults. All for profit and high stock prices. Now, who has the moral high ground in this scenario?"

Jacqueline pulled Mr. Raymond closer to her. "Please stop boring us with your plans. We have much work to do. First, we must dispose of our guests."

"You're right, of course. How should we proceed?"

Jacqueline's eyes took in the Gems. "I see a horrible traffic accident involving four teen girls trapped inside their burning car."

Mr. Raymond sighed. "Texting while driving. Such a tragedy indeed, Miss Boyay."

CHAPTER 25

Jacqueline and the guards led the Gems back up to the skyscraper's roof at gunpoint. The Raymond Foods corporate helicopter was waiting on the helicopter pad. Jacqueline motioned with her gun, warning the girls to stay away from the helicopter and climb up more metal stairs leading up towards the giant air-conditioning units on the roof, their AirTech company logos still fresh and new. Below the metal-grated platform they were walking on, Emma could see four shadowed silhouettes moving against the concrete roof. Four young souls who would never see their eighteenth birthdays.

"Line them up here," Jacqueline ordered.

"Change your mind about burning us to death?" Miyuki asked.

Jacqueline grinned. "After we shoot you, of course. You should thank me for not burning you four alive."

The guards lined up the Gems against the large air-conditioning units, then stood next to Jacqueline.

Emma caught Nadia looking down at what they were standing on, a concrete slab that supported the heavy air-conditioning units behind them. Jacqueline and the guards were still standing on the metal grating.

Jacqueline checked her pistol.

Nadia went down to one knee, her hand feeling around for something behind her. Emma wondered what she was doing. But Ryan's voice made her look away...

"You should stop this craziness now, Dad. You haven't done anything wrong yet."

"Wait in the helicopter," Mr. Raymond said.

Ryan didn't move.

"Boy, you better run over there or I'll toss you off this building, so help me God." Mr. Raymond glared, very serious.

Ryan's resolve disappeared as he headed back down the stairs towards the helicopter.

Emma checked on Nadia again. The girl had the access door open on the air conditioner behind her. What was Nadia doing?

"Arab girl. You. Stand up." Jacqueline gestured with her gun.

Nadia came up slowly, her right hand clutching a tiny bundle of wires bound together in a rubber cable.

"Whatever that is you're holding, drop it," Jacqueline commanded.

Nadia did.

Right on top of the grating.

The live wires of the bundle sparked as they made contact with the metal. Jacqueline, the guards, and Mr. Raymond shook as electric current made contact with their bodies, instantly dropping them to the floor of the grating.

"Wait," Nadia yelled before she picked up the rubber cable and placed it safely on the concrete slab.

"Are they dead?" Olivia asked.

"Not enough volts. These cables are to the accent lights for the air conditioners," Nadia said. "But they did receive a decent shock."

The guards shook their heads, trying to recover. Jacqueline struggled to get back on her feet.

Miyuki was on her in a flash with a down arm strike that knocked the gun out of her hand.

Olivia and Nadia ran forward, kicking the guns out of the guards' reach. One grabbed Olivia's ankle. She lifted her free leg and brought her heel down on his shoulder, causing him to release her with a shriek.

Emma looked around, seeing if she could help. One guard propped himself up using the railing. He aimed his gun at Nadia.

Emma ran at him and threw a strike at his neck which took him by surprise as the guard stumbled back, still holding the gun. Emma didn't have time to think. She spun herself around, like Lioness had taught her, and launched her foot at his head. It struck him on target. The large man fell to the ground and was knocked out cold.

Emma couldn't believe it. Did she really do that?

Someone grabbed her from behind and squeezed her neck. Emma gasped for breath. She kicked and kicked and kicked at the guard's shins. But it wasn't working. The man was determined to kill her. Emma tried to scream for help, but nothing came out of her mouth. She flailed her arms around like a crazy bird, hoping to get someone's attention.

Miyuki ran to the rescue with a kick to the man's side, breaking his hold on Emma. Miyuki then jumped into a handstand and kicked her legs forward for two strikes to the man's face. The guard shook it off and threw a punch, just missing Miyuki.

Emma recovered and kicked the guard square in the back. The force dropped him to the ground and knocked the wind out of him. The man stayed down.

From the platform, Emma watched Olivia and Nadia chase Mr. Raymond down the steps as he headed for the helicopter. Miyuki jumped clear over the railing that separated the two levels and landed right in front of Mr. Raymond.

Now trapped, he took out a gun.

Miyuki dropped and rolled as Mr. Raymond fired. He then pointed the gun at Olivia and Nadia now frozen on the stairway. They were too far to engage him.

Mr. Raymond kept the gun leveled in their direction as he ran towards the helicopter, its blades rotating. He was getting away and the Gems couldn't do a thing about it.

Emma examined the platform. All ten guards were down and out. But there was no sign of Jacqueline. She wasn't with Mr. Raymond, so…where did the woman go?

To check the other side, Emma jogged around the massive air-conditioning units and searched the other part of the roof. There wasn't much here. Only the roof's edge, where jumping off from a hundred-floor building would mean certain death. But there was nowhere else Jacqueline could have…

Then Emma saw the fire escape hiding around a corner. The red door was open to stairs leading back down into the building.

Emma scanned behind her. There was no one else to help.

So Emma gathered her courage and plunged through the door in pursuit.

CHAPTER 26

The fire escape was dark. Only the dim glow from a few overhead lights supplied any vision to Emma at all. She leaped down the concrete steps in twos, just like when she was eight years old, using the railing to support her. Emma descended the staircase as it looped around and around and around. She wasn't sure if Jacqueline was down here. The woman could have found a place to hide, like on top of one of the massive air-conditioning units on the roof. Emma could kick herself. Why didn't she think of that earlier? That was probably where Jacqueline was.

Emma slowed her pace. How many flights of stairs did she—

A gunshot ricocheted off the railing.

Emma tripped on a step and fell forward, rolling across the landing and smacking into the door. Pain shot up her back and arm. Emma checked herself for a wound, but couldn't find anything. At least she knew where Jacqueline was. But that woman had a gun and Emma didn't.

A clatter echoed below her, signaling Jacqueline was on the move again.

Emma picked up her sore body and ran down the next flight of stairs.

Reaching the landing of the eighty-first floor, Emma noticed the door closing. Its hinges must be sticky because it took its sweet time closing. She opened the door and stepped onto an office floor. The place should be quiet because it was Sunday. But Emma noticed about a dozen people pacing around in another glass-walled meeting room like the one they were in earlier. All these office workers were dressed casually, but still had their laptops and files all over the large table. Emma guessed they were Raymond Food employees who had already moved into their new offices.

Thanks to her fall, Emma limped down the wide hallway, with her head on a swivel, trying to find any sign of Jacqueline.

"We were just talking about you, Miss Boyay," a man announced. "Our department would love to have a sit-down to see how we can help AgEurope improve their market share. How long are you in town?"

Emma stopped. Her eyes followed the voice to a man standing near the bathrooms. He'd spoken to a disheveled woman who didn't want to be there. Jacqueline.

Emma limped toward her.

Jacqueline glued on a smile. "Sounds like a great idea, Donald. But Mr. Raymond needs me back in Europe Tuesday."

The woman tried to leave, but the male executive followed.

"That's a shame. Say, what are you doing right now?" He motioned towards the conference room. "Today I had to drag in my staff to meet a deadline. But we can change gears and show you some concepts we've been working on."

"Wish I had the time."

The encounter gave Emma enough time to reach Jacqueline. But now she wondered what to do. Should Emma throw a karate strike right in front of all these people? Spies were supposed to be discreet, right?

Jacqueline noticed Emma. The two stared each other down, both waiting to see what the other would do.

The executive stared at Emma too. "Well, this is a surprise. Miss Rothchild? You might not remember me, but we met at the opening gala Friday night."

Emma didn't remember. "Of course, I remember you. Donald…?"

"Hendricks. Raymond Foods vice president of marketing." Donald balked. "Oh, I didn't realize you're giving Miss Rothchild a tour of the new building. No wonder you're busy, Miss Boyay."

Jacqueline smiled. "I hope you understand."

"No need to explain."

Jacqueline grabbed Emma's arm and forced her to stand in front of her. Emma was about to twist around when she felt an object poking her back.

Emma reasoned it must be her gun.

Donald the executive withdrew into the meeting room, leaving Emma and Jacqueline alone.

Jacqueline pressed the muzzle of the gun into her back. "Walk to the elevator."

Emma bit her lip and did as she was told.

"Push the down button."

Emma complied. The doors of the elevator slid open.

"Move."

Emma stepped inside the large box. Jacqueline forced her to face the back wall at gunpoint while fishing for something inside her own coat pocket. Jacqueline came up with a key and inserted it into a hole near one row of floor buttons. She turned it and pressed the lobby button. The elevator doors closed.

"Executive key. Bypasses all the other floors," Jacqueline said. "You and I don't need any more visitors." The woman relaxed slightly, but kept the gun pointed at Emma's back. "For a daddy's little rich girl, you have remarkably thick skin. I would say The Authority has trained you well."

Emma didn't answer.

"Your friends are quite impressive. Most likely they've captured Mr. Raymond by now. Oh well. I'll have to leave without him."

"What will you do with me?" Emma asked, trying to sound confident, but her voice wavered.

"Kill you. Eventually. But you might have information in that blond-headed brain of yours that could be of interest to my superiors. The location of your headquarters. Lists of operatives. The real names of your friends. Or we could use you as bait to lure them into a trap and kill them. So many options."

"I won't tell you anything."

"We hire the best in the world. Men who invented the art of torture. I'm afraid you'll coo like a dove, Emma."

A sense of dread settled in Emma's stomach. A new hopelessness that told her this was it. The idea of being tortured didn't sit well with Emma. Or the idea of being left alone in a room with some sick man who enjoyed doing awful things to girls. If Emma had a choice, she would rather kill herself.

Emma took in a deep breath.

Or she would rather risk getting killed.

Emma pressed her palms against the cold back wall of the elevator and pushed off. She spun around and shoved Jacqueline into the opposite corner, holding the woman's arms down to prevent her from using the gun. Emma held the woman there with all her might. But Jacqueline was strong too. She managed to peel herself off the wall.

Both women strained against the other.

Each trying to gain the advantage.

Jacqueline managed to shove Emma off with her leg, causing the girl to fall to the floor. Jacqueline then aimed the gun. "I changed my mind. You're far too dangerous to be left alive."

A fury overtook Emma, that survival instinct that turned nice girls into animals. Emma launched her leg upward into Jacqueline's arm, smacking it against the elevator doors. The gun fired, splitting their eardrums. Next, Emma struck Jacqueline's shin with her heel. The woman went down with a thud.

Emma scrambled to her feet and noticed the gun had dropped to the floor.

"You little bitch." Jacqueline pushed against the opposite wall, using it to pull herself back up. The woman stopped when Emma pointed the gun at her.

Emma touched the cold, metal trigger and secured the weapon with both her hands. Jacqueline was so close; there was no way Emma would miss. She didn't have to be an expert about guns to know that.

Jacqueline slid back down to the floor and flashed a crazy smile, the type of smile that made normal people nervous. "Do you have what it takes to kill, Emma?"

"Don't try me."

"I'm not so sure. You could have shot my operative in the forest. But you hesitated."

Emma paused. "You were the assassin with the crossbow?"

"Asset Twenty-One was weak-minded. He became sloppy and unreliable. Twice he failed to kill you. Venomous doesn't accept failure well. Besides, the man was going to turn, wasn't he? We couldn't allow that."

"Did you give the order to kill my father?"

That sick smile returned to Jacqueline's face and Emma wanted to blast it off.

"Ah, yes. Revenge. You might kill to revenge your father. I understand you better now. You didn't partner with The Authority to save the world or to be a good public citizen. You wanted blood." Jacqueline observed her for a moment. "We have more in common than I thought. Venomous could use a smart girl like you. Would you consider switching sides?"

"Answer my question."

"You know the answer…must I say it?"

Emma tightened her grip on the weapon. She could feel the power coming from it, seducing her into pulling the trigger.

Jacqueline glared and lowered her chin. "Our venom flows through the veins of the animal. Its death is certain."

Emma paused. What the hell did Jacqueline mean by that?

"Time is ticking. What's the verdict?"

"Stop talking."

An unbalanced laughter bubbled up from the woman. "Tick-tock. Tick-tock. Tick-tock."

The elevator dinged. The door opened, unleashing sunlight into the box. Jacqueline crawled towards the light. Emma followed her with the gun, but couldn't pull the trigger. Something was stopping her and she didn't know what.

Outside the elevator, Jacqueline noticed something out of Emma's vision. The woman turned hysterical. "Oh my God. Please don't kill me! She's crazy! That young woman is crazy!" Jacqueline stumbled to her feet. "Help me! She's crazy."

Emma lowered the gun.

"Hey!" A lobby guard appeared, saw Emma's gun and reached for his holster.

Emma retreated back into the elevator and pressed a button for a higher floor. She hid behind the panel as the elevator doors shut. The gears and the sounds of the elevator dominated Emma's hearing as it went back up. Emma backed up against the rear wall and let gravity take her down to the floor. And that was where she wept.

CHAPTER 27

Her bedroom lacked any comfort. The light from her ceiling fan cast a harsh light against her soft skin, emphasizing the spots of acne trying to form on the surface. Emma stared past the image of herself in the mirror as her mind drifted a thousand miles away. It was still inside that cramped elevator. Still holding a gun on Jacqueline. Still wanting to kill her, but didn't.

So why didn't I? Emma wondered. Did she question her right to kill another person? Was she just scared?

Yes. Emma was scared...of herself. She'd felt real power holding that gun, as if something inside Emma wanted to pull that trigger and obliterate that person in front of the muzzle. Realizing that fact...shocked the hell out of her. When she'd hit Snoopy with her car, Emma felt evil inside. Taking a life, which was so precious. What right did she have to do such a thing? Only evil people killed defenseless creatures.

Well, Jacqueline didn't have the gun. Emma did. If she'd pulled the trigger...wasn't that murder? Wouldn't she be as evil as Jacqueline? Or Bertrand?

Emma didn't have a clear answer to the question and that bothered her.

But there was plenty of good she did help with. Through their network of US contacts, Mrs. B and The Authority leaked Mr. Raymond's conspiracy to the FBI, Interpol, and other intelligence agencies overseas. Raymond Foods subsidiaries around the world were raided and evidence gathered. The FBI then "discovered" Mr. Raymond hiding out in a truck stop near Amarillo, Texas and arrested him. It was all clean and tidy. Something The Authority specialized in according to Olivia.

They were still looking for Jacqueline, but thanks to her

Venomous contacts she had effectively disappeared from the face of the earth. Emma hoped she would stay that way.

Before the Gems left Kansas City, Emma gave Ryan her number. Last week, he'd called her to apologize for his dad. The boy sounded distressed and sad. So much so that Emma wanted to reach into the phone and give him a big hug. Ryan told her he was packing his car and driving to his mother's house in Wichita. There he wanted to chill and think things through.

"That's a great idea," Emma said. "I can't imagine the craziness this has caused you and your entire family."

"Yeah, tell me about it," Ryan said, hesitating. "Next time I'm in San Francisco, could we hang out?"

Emma's mind grabbed on to that scenario and ran with it. She saw images of her driving Ryan over the Golden Gate Bridge. Showing him Fisherman's Wharf. Taking him to her favorite places to eat. Seeing the boy grip his car door handle in terror as Emma drove on the expressway.

Maybe she should let Ryan drive her car.

"I would love that," Emma told him before they said their goodbyes.

Her phone rang.

Emma noted her reflection still gazing at her from the bedroom mirror and shook off her daydream.

Wait. Could that be Ryan?

Emma ran over to the dresser and checked the phone. Crap. It was her grandma.

"I'm almost ready. Promise."

"Good," Grandma said over the phone. "Ben and his family are here, so step on it."

Emma checked her outfit and makeup one more time. Snoopy waddled into the room and looked up at Emma.

"I know. I know." She knelt down to scoop up the dog and carried him downstairs.

Grandma's backyard flickered with light from a series of lit tiki torches placed strategically throughout her garden. The stone fire pit at the center of the garden burned at full strength while people lounged around in chairs or stood watching the soothing dancing flames. A large grill sizzled with food. A quartet of street musicians played a Celtic-sounding tune with fiddle and guitar for the patrons.

Grandma swayed with the music. Her two pigtails of white hair were decorated with flowers. Grandma's friend Phil and his husband, Daryl, talked as they supervised the grill, flipping over burgers, beef and chicken kabobs, and grilled veggies. They waved at Emma and she waved back. Emma put Snoopy down on the grass. The dog took off at a waddle to explore the party. Emma joined her grandmother, who brushed a piece of Emma's hair back.

"You okay, young one? Been quiet since you got back."

Emma flashed a grin. "I know. Just thinking."

"Emma!" two little girls shouted and ran across the garden, almost tackling her.

Emma hugged them tight. "How are you guys?"

"Will you come to New York with us?" the first girl asked.

"She just moved out here, dummy," the second girl said.

The two little girls started arguing.

"Stop it," Emma said. "Or I won't show you a magic trick later."

"Wicked," the first girl said. "Which one will you do?"

The second girl scoffed. "Can you do one where my sister disappears?"

Ben Gooden and his wife approached the girls. "I'll make you both disappear if you don't cool it," his wife said.

"Told you they missed their babysitter," Ben said.

The Goodens talked to Grandma and Emma about their plans for a house in New York. They mentioned finding something in Brooklyn or way out in Long Island.

"Thank you both for recommending me," Ben said. "I know it wasn't an easy decision."

Emma brightened. "For me it was the only choice. My dad would've wanted you to succeed him."

"When Emma brought up the idea, I thought it was a good one," Grandma said.

"Even though you had to force it down the board of directors' throats?" Ben asked.

"I couldn't let those power-hungry capitalists take over and ruin Ken's vision for Rothchild Industries. They would've taken advantage of Emma's situation and have her pushed out as soon as she officially inherited ownership. It's Emma's company and she should have a say on how it should be run."

"And I want you to run it, Ben," Emma said.

"Thank you again and I hope to earn that trust you both have placed in me."

Emma noticed a new group of guests entering the garden. Olivia, Miyuki, Nadia, and Mrs. B wore casual clothing. Aardvark wore a pink Hawaiian shirt over his gargantuan build.

"Would you please excuse me?"

Emma slipped away from the Goodens to greet her friends.

"Apologies for crashing your party," Mrs. B said, "but I need to speak with your grandmother."

Emma peeked over her shoulder. Grandmother glared at Mrs. B from a distance. "I don't know if that's such a good idea."

"Why don't you girls find something to eat from the grill." Mrs. B walked forward using her cane; she rested her hand on Emma's back. "Let's have a talk, my dear." Mrs. B guided Emma away from the group while Aardvark trailed them. "How would you feel if the Gems stayed here? With you and your grandmother?"

"Seriously?" Emma asked.

"I promised the girls' families that we would provide ongoing education while they were in our service. I could have the girls stay in Napa, but it's not practical to ferry them back and forth to the city for their education. And since your grandmother refuses to let us tutor you…the only alternative I see is allowing them to go to school with you here in Berkeley, with your grandmother's blessing, of course."

"There's no way she'll go for that," Emma said.

Mrs. B raised her chin. "She will if you sell it, my dear."

Emma managed to sweet-talk her grandmother into following her into the kitchen where Phil was preparing some fresh salmon for the outside grill. Emma waited for him to finished up his fillets and bring them out to the grill before closing the French doors behind him.

"What's on your mind, young one?" Grandma folded her arms. "Who were those teenage girls with Laura? Friends of yours?"

Emma nodded.

"Is there a reason she's here?"

"Well...yes."

"Whatever you did for Laura...is it over now? Are you done?"

"The mission is over, yes."

"Then you can quit. Laura doesn't need you anymore, so you can go on with your life. I'll help you get out, Emma. I'll explain everything to Laura and make her leave you alone for good."

Emma looked away. "I don't want to quit."

Grandma pulled out a stool from the kitchen island and sat.

Emma took her cue and pulled out another stool. Emma sat down and sighed, knowing she was about to poke the beehive again.

"Grandma Laura proposed this great idea. Something I think you'll like. She wants—"

"I don't give a damn what Laura wants," Grandma interrupted. She then tried to calm herself. "Did you know the CIA is obsessed with closing The Authority down? I know things, Emma. Thanks to your mother and father, I know more about The Authority than I should. I could hurt them. One phone call. One email. A secret trip out of the US to a CIA safe house overseas. I could tell them and they'll listen."

"Why? Why would you do that?" Emma asked.

"Because my life means nothing without you. If I lose you to Laura...I might as well become worm food in the cemetery."

"Please don't talk like that. I would never turn my back on you. That would never happen."

"It's either me or her. I'm sorry, but I can't let you stay under Laura's spell."

"You can't tell the CIA about The Authority. If Grandma Laura finds out about it..."

"She'll kill me, Emma. Make no mistake about that. Laura might lose sleep over it...but she'll order it if necessary."

"Why do you have to put her in that position?"

Grandma softened. "Love. Pure and simple."

Emma could feel the weight pushing her down to the floor tiles. "That's not fair."

"No, it's not. I'm being selfish, yes. But that's a

grandmother's choice when she loves her grandbaby as much as I do."

Emma said nothing as she slid off the stool. She took one last look at her grandmother before walking out of the kitchen.

Emma ran upstairs to her room, her mind swirling in thoughts and emotions. Grandma's ultimatum. Her new friends. Mrs. B wanting Emma to carry on her parents' mission. Emma even wondered if Mrs. B would ask the Gems to kill her grandma.

What a horrible thought.

It was too much. It was all just too much.

Closing the door behind her, Emma flopped onto her bed. She let the tears trickle down the creases of her eyes and onto the pillow. Something scratched at the door. A dog's snout then pried open the door as Snoopy let himself into her room. Emma must not have shut the door all the way. With effort, the small dog hopped on top of the bed. He looked Emma over and lay down beside her, as if he could read her sadness.

Emma rubbed his ears and the dog closed his eyes. What was she going to do?

She couldn't let Grandma go to the CIA. That sounded like the worst thing ever for everyone involved. That only left one option, telling Mrs. B she wanted out. Hopefully she would understand. They'd only needed Emma for that last mission anyway, right? Now that it was over, they could let her go. Besides, The Authority hadn't given her any real spy training yet. How could she be an official spy without proper training? That made sense. There was also another reason to quit. That girl inside the elevator. The one holding the gun. Emma wasn't sure she wanted to be that girl ever again.

Our venom flows through the veins of the animal. Its death is certain.

Jacqueline's words came back to Emma as she relived the moment.

It was haunting…

Strange…

Emma sat up straight. A new thought sliced through her emotional fog. That wasn't some strange poem Jacqueline pulled down from midair. She knew Mr. Raymond was about to be captured. She knew his master plan was already in jeopardy.

Our venom flows through the veins of the animal. Its death is certain.

Emma tumbled the words over and over in her mind. Why would Jacqueline say that? She was arrogant, almost as bad as Mr. Raymond. But had Jacqueline given Emma some sort of cryptic warning? Thinking Emma was too dumb to figure it out?

Our venom was obvious. *Flows through the veins of the animal* could mean…their plan was still in place.

Its death is certain.

Emma studied the phrase. Did that mean their plan was going forward still? But how? Without Raymond Foods, what damage could Venomous cause to the world's food supply?

Emma flopped back down on her pillow, her mind churning through all the information Bertrand Petit had given them in that forest before Jacqueline killed him. But she couldn't remember all of it.

Emma called Miyuki's phone and told the girls to come up to her room as soon as possible. The girls came inside and Olivia closed the door.

"Doggie!" Miyuki flocked to Snoopy, who got all excited by the new attention.

Emma told the girls her suspicions about Jacqueline and Venomous. "What did Bertrand tell us in the forest? Do you remember? There could be something we overlooked."

Nadia opened her small purse and took out her tablet. She accessed The Authority recording of the conversation Mrs. B had with Bertrand over the phone. They played it back and listened. Nothing raised a flag until they came to…

"I also worked on the projects at Ovechkin-Komstat in Ukraine. Kyo-Shun in China. The Lester-Sumner Company in Australia. Ganchi Farms in Mumbai."

Olivia tensed. "Those are all food-production companies, some of the biggest in the world."

"Bertrand must have modified all their systems," Miyuki said.

"Could he do all that work by himself?" Nadia asked.

"Doubt it," Olivia said. "But under Bertrand's direction, Venomous agents could have made those modifications on the other facilities as well. Many of them have AirTech systems installed, remember?"

"And because of that, those computer control systems can be networked together easily," Nadia said. "If Venomous still has the means to destroy that amount of food production...there would be a worldwide panic."

Olivia left the room. She brought up Mrs. B and Aardvark from downstairs and closed the door again. The girls briefed her on what they'd discovered.

Mrs. B sat down on Emma's bed, her mind evaluating the info as quickly as a computer. "There's one missing key to all this. Venomous is quite thorough. They don't conduct operations like this half-cocked. To disrupt the world's food supply, they would need to be in control of all of it."

"If they still have a way to sabotage Raymond Foods and all those other companies...what else would they need?" Olivia asked.

Nadia gasped. "The global seed storage vaults in Norway."

"Precisely," Mrs. B said.

"What's that?" Emma asked.

"A giant underground facility carved under a mountain," Nadia said. "It's administrated by the Norwegian government, but most of the world keeps their seeds there as a backup. That way if there were some kind of man-made or ecological catastrophe that destroyed their crops and seeds, a country wouldn't lose their native plants. I read an online article about it last year."

"Controlling that facility would be key to any plan to disrupt the world's food supply," Mrs. B said. "Aardvark?"

The man held Snoopy in his large hands and the dog licked his face as the man quietly giggled in a rare moment of enjoyment.

"Aardvark?"

The man finally heard Mrs. B and put down the dog.

"Please contact Mr. O and tell him I have a job for his section. If you're done making out with Emma's terrier, that is."

CHAPTER 28

A half hour after Aardvark sent the information to The Authority headquarters, Mrs. B discreetly led the Gems outside to the front of Grandma's house. Aardvark stood near a stretch-limo parked on a side street and held open the back door for them.

Once inside the limo, Mrs. B called out to Aardvark. "Cone of silence mode, if you please."

He nodded and activated something on the dash. A low hum radiated around the vehicle, something Emma remembered from the first time they'd used this device. Mrs. B touched her fingers to a tiny square on the roof pillar, which exposed a hidden panel inside the limo. Mrs. B took out a tablet attached by USB cable and tapped in a code. The monitor just behind the driver's compartment flickered to life. *Begin Signal Scramble Mode* flashed on screen. Then *Transmission Link Established.*

An older Indian man flashed on the screen.

Mrs. B addressed him. "Aardvark informs me your section has news, Mr. O."

"Indeed," the man called Mr. O replied. "Code one satellite sweep of the global seed vault facility is complete. Nothing is out of the ordinary. No alerts from the Norwegian security forces regarding the facility. We also analyzed all communications from the facility in the last month. Again, nothing out of the ordinary. We checked all Norwegian security forces computer servers for any recent officer assignments to that facility. No new assignments. We even checked for emails referencing the facility in general. Again, nothing out of the ordinary. I will continue the satellite surveillance and alert you with any new details."

Mrs. B nodded. "Excellent job from your section, Mr. O."

She switched off the screen and held her cane closer to her. "Well, that is that. Is it possible that Jacqueline's obscure and cryptic blathering could be only a generalization, Emma?"

"She's a nut job," Miyuki said.

"*Our venom flows through the veins of the animal. Its death is certain,*" Olivia repeated as she crossed her arms. "Sounds like a motto they say at their flipping secret meetings. Did the woman look like she was just messing with your head?"

"No. She looked confident," Emma said. "She played off Mr. Raymond's capture like it was nothing, like whatever we uncovered didn't faze her. That's what makes me think Venomous has something bigger going on."

Mrs. B examined Emma as her mind sorted through the information. "I'm sorry, but we have no evidence to support your hypothesis. It's possible that the plot at Raymond Foods could have been the first phase of a larger plan. The second phase might have been the other food companies Bertrand mentioned that he visited. He could have been preparing those sites for a future operation."

Emma frowned. But she was so sure.

"I think it's safe to say that the plot at Raymond Foods has been rooted out, thanks to you young ladies."

"Can we go to Norway to have a look anyway?" Olivia asked. "Just in case?"

"I'm not sending you girls to the Arctic circle to prove a hunch. We pride ourselves on collecting data. Facts. We only act on facts, not hunches. Hunches need to be proved. You don't risk people's lives on them."

"How are we risking our lives?" Miyuki asked. "We just hide in bushes and observe."

"Ladies, this Norwegian facility is located at the base of a mountain. The only road in is heavily monitored and patrolled. Therefore, you would have to hike through the forest in subzero temperatures and survive in that climate for hours to properly observe the facility in question. You might even be forced to climb up the mountain and rappel down it in order to observe it. You girls are not trained to take on a mission like that." Mrs. B checked her watch. "It's getting a bit late for my taste. Did you have a chance to speak with your grandmother, Emma?"

Emma balked. If she said the wrong thing to Mrs. B, her grandmother could be in danger.

"I'll need more time. She's...stubborn."

Mrs. B gripped the top of her cane. "That, your grandmother is. All right, I'll have Aardvark drive me back now. Then I'll send him back to collect all of you when you're ready to leave. I'm sure you girls would like to stay and socialize. Please enjoy yourselves. You girls deserve it."

The Gems emptied out of the limo. Aardvark nodded to them as he guided the long vehicle down the street.

Miyuki and Nadia walked across the street to Grandma's house and stopped when they realized Emma and Olivia weren't with them.

"What do you think?" Emma asked Olivia.

"I don't like it. It feels wrong. Call me paranoid, fine. But it was way too easy to nab Mr. Raymond. All of it felt false to me. When you told us your theory...it then made perfect sense. A woman like Jacqueline wouldn't give up that easy. She's still up to something."

"Maybe the Norwegian place isn't the target. Maybe it's something else."

"And yet...nothing else makes sense. Nadia's right. Bertrand must have set up some kind of remote network to control all those systems since Venomous doesn't have enough people to be at all those places at once. So their operation would need to have a command and control center."

Emma thought about it. "Somewhere that's protected. Somewhere safe. Secure. Like a castle or a fort."

"Or a global seed vault built inside a mountain?" Miyuki asked, joining them.

Olivia crossed her arms. "I have this eerie feeling we'll catch those Venomous twits in Norway with their hands in the cookie jar."

"Why does it matter?" Nadia asked as she approached the group. "We're not permitted to go."

Emma ignored her. "I could buy us plane tickets with my credit card. But where do we get equipment?"

"We buy our climbing gear in Norway," Miyuki said, excitement bubbling in her words. "And our winter clothing!"

Olivia nodded. "Should be easy to find that in Norway."

"We can't go without Mrs. B's permission." Nadia glanced at Olivia. "Please tell me you're not considering this idea, are you?"

"Mrs. B didn't exactly order us not to take a look. She just thought it was dangerous."

Nadia looked panicked. "It sounded dangerous to me too. How do we get climbing equipment? Steal it? Mrs. B took away your special credit card, didn't she?"

"I have my Visa gold card," Emma said. "The tickets, clothing, equipment, I got it."

"But we can't do this without orders." Nadia looked totally stressed out. "We'll be in so much trouble."

Miyuki smiled. "I say we go have a lookie."

"Of course you would," Nadia snapped. "You're the craziest girl I've ever met in my life. You have, like, this death wish."

"Hey, chill out," Emma said.

"And why do you pretend to know everything?" Nadia fumed. "You're a good actress, but you don't fool me. I'm not risking my life on your half-baked theories. You're not even a part of our group. You were our cover for the mission. That's it. Now, the mission is over and you can walk away to your rich and ultra-extravagant lifestyle while the rest of us try to struggle to live a clean and healthy life in poverty." Nadia stormed off into the house.

Emma shook her head in total disbelief. "I always thought Nadia liked me."

"It's not you, love. She's been stressing about this mission for a long time now," Olivia said.

"Stressing?" Emma shot her a look. "How can you tell?"

"She's always so quiet," Miyuki added.

"And quiet girls hold it all inside until they burst open like the Hindenburg." Olivia took out her phone and filled out a text. "Give me a moment and I'll go talk her into it."

"Are you texting Mrs. B?" Miyuki asked.

"Don't be daft. I'm shooting Aardvark a message. I want him to pick me up a few things from EQ division on his way back here. He's such a sweetheart."

* * *

The Gems took an overnight flight to New York, then hopped on a second plane that flew them to Oslo, Norway. From there, a regional flight landed them in Narvik where Rothchild Industries helped Emma rent a big four-wheel-drive Range Rover. Emma then bought all the Gems brand-new winter clothing and climbing equipment. Finally, stowed in back of the Rover was a gift Aardvark had brought the girls from EQ division.

Olivia drove the girls into the mountains that ran along the western coast of Norway. The wind blew snow across the windshield as the Rover navigated the two-lane road. The weather itself was clear, only a strong north wind was kicking up the snow that had fallen yesterday. The late afternoon sun tried its best to pierce through the blowing snow.

"I still don't like this," Nadia said from the backseat. Her arms crossed. Her eyes burning into the window.

Emma scoffed in the front seat. "Unbelievable."

"You could've stayed behind, love," Olivia said.

"And be interrogated by Mrs. B when she finds you three gone? That's not a real choice, thank you."

"So you couldn't bring yourself to rat on your true friends," Miyuki said with a bounce in her voice.

"True friends wouldn't put me in this position."

"Can we leave her in the car?" Emma asked.

"You're so rude. I—"

"I'll ditch you both with the flipping car if you don't shut it," Olivia said. "This is serious. We need to focus, alright?"

Olivia followed the directions from her satellite phone's sophisticated GPS system, which had her turn off the main road and take another road that bordered a large perimeter fence.

"I thought Mrs. B said this road was monitored?" Emma asked.

"Right, but we should give the easy way a try first. You never know." Olivia turned the wheel and the Rover came across a checkpoint of some type. A heavy metal gate supported by heavy concrete posts blocked the road. A sign announced *This is a Norwegian Government Facility. NO Trespassing.*

"If I give the word," Olivia said, "rush these guys and take them."

"What if they're real Norwegian army guards?" Emma asked.

"Let me worry about that. Just be ready."

Olivia pulled the Range Rover up to the closed gate. Two soldiers with Norwegian flags on their shoulders emerged from the building. One soldier approached Olivia's side of the vehicle while the other did a check around the vehicle. The first soldier tapped on Olivia's window and she flicked a switch to bring it down. The soldier asked her something in Norwegian.

"Sorry. Can't speak the native lingo. Do you speak English, love?"

"Why are you here?" the soldier asked in broken English with a distinct Norwegian accent.

Olivia pointed ahead. "Is that the way to the ski lodge? We turned way back there and I think I got us bloody lost."

"No ski area here. The one you want is forty-three kilometers south of here."

"What's up there? That's a lovely mountain for skiing."

"Government facility. No trespassing. No visitors. Back up your vehicle and head back to the public road."

"Is there a place to eat around here? We've been driving for ages. Do they have something hot to drink up at that facility of yours?"

Emma poked her head over Olivia's lap. "I could use some hot chocolate or coffee. Do you have any of that?"

"This is a government facility. There is no hot chocolate, no coffee, and no skiing. Turn your vehicle around."

The second guard acted more nervous, handling his machine gun clumsily for someone whose main job was holding a gun. And Emma noticed his skin was darker.

"It'll be nightfall before we get to our lodge," Olivia said. "I hate to get lost again, especially in a foreign country. Mind if we park just over there and camp for the night? We won't be a bother."

"Go back to the road or we will arrest you for trespassing." The guard pulled back the charging handle on his machine gun, making his point clear.

"Right. We'll clear off then," Olivia said.

She put the Range Rover in reverse, then turned it around and headed away from the checkpoint.

"That second soldier was Latino or Spanish," Emma said.

"He tried to hide his face too," Miyuki added.

"But that bloke I spoke with was real," Olivia said. "We need to get a bird's-eye view while there's still light."

Olivia pulled the Rover to the side of the road and popped open the cargo door. Together, the Gems took out a box and opened it. They pulled out a small drone and snapped its four propellers into place.

Inside the Rover, Nadia opened her new laptop and accessed the drone's piloting software. The little drone hummed into life as its propellers spun. Nadia then handed a video game controller to Olivia, who studied the laptop screen. Emma and Miyuki looked like giants through the drone's wide-angle lens as they stood over it.

"Clear," Olivia shouted as her thumb pushed on the little stick for power.

On the screen, the giant images of Miyuki and Emma dropped away as the drone shot up into the air and hovered. Olivia manipulated the controller like a pro as she commanded the drone to fly towards the facility.

Nadia peeked over Olivia's shoulder. "I'm having the laptop record the drone's video output just in case."

Emma and Miyuki jumped into the Rover and shook off the cold.

"That looks like fun," Miyuki said.

Olivia hovered the drone above the Norwegian facility. They could see the front gate where they had talked to the soldiers. The outer buildings of the facility stuck out from the mountain they were built into. A couple of army trucks were parked to the side.

"There's a hiking trail up the mountain," Olivia said. "See how there's a line crisscrossing through the trees and rounding the base of the mountain above those buildings? It must be just outside the fence perimeter. Could be a way to drop in."

"Yes. But everything is peaceful. Like in those satellite photos," Miyuki said.

Olivia swung the drone over to the other side of the compound for another angle. There was no activity at all.

"Looks like Emma's theory was completely wrong. I'm not surprised." Nadia threw her a look that made Emma want to smack her.

Olivia's thumbs worked the joysticks. She brought the drone a few feet above the ground as she buzzed near one of the outer buildings. The camera found a window and zoomed into a blur. Then the auto-focus took over to reveal a hallway. There were two men with rifles standing guard by a door.

"Those blokes are not in Norwegian army uniforms," Olivia said.

"Black military fatigues," Miyuki said. "Different uniforms than the guards we encountered had."

"Let's see what they're guarding." Olivia nudged her controls and the drone silently drifted over to the next window and peeked inside the room. Through the glass, there were around fifty men in Norwegian military uniforms, all of them tied up on the floor. "Oh that's brilliant. Must be the facility's real garrison. Venomous has control of this place all right."

"We should free the soldiers," Miyuki said.

"We should first contact Mrs. B and let her know what's going on," Nadia said.

"I'll call her," Olivia said.

"Think she'll be pissed that we're here and using this equipment without permission?" Emma asked.

The three girls flashed Emma a collective look. *What do you think?*

Olivia placed the call.

"Why are you in Norway?" Mrs. B's voice was sharp over the satellite phone, the speaker amplifying her anger.

"It's my fault, Mrs. B," Emma said. "I wanted to see for myself and I dragged—"

"Emma, we all came voluntarily," Olivia said. "You should be cross with all of us. Not just Emma."

Nadia rolled her eyes and tossed her angry stare out the window of the Rover.

"You should have told me what you were up to. I do not appreciate being lied to," Mrs. B said.

"I understand, ma'am. But what's important is that Venomous has taken over the facility," Olivia said. "We found the garrison tied up under guard and—"

"Yes. Yes. We know about all that," Mrs. B said.

"You do?"

"Venomous just released a demand to the United Nations. Either the world pays them fifty billion dollars or they'll incinerate the world's food supply."

CHAPTER 29

The Norwegian mountain looked down upon the parked Range Rover. Exposed by the cold weather, a trail of exhaust curled up from its tailpipe. The wind kicked up a few flecks of snow from the ground, tossing them into the air like confetti. Inside the vehicle, the Gems listened as Mrs. B continued on speakerphone.

"Because of the takeover, the Norwegians are sending army units to surround the facility and we've picked up signs that NATO is sending in special forces. I want you girls to leave the area at once and fly back to America. There's nothing more you can do there. Are those instructions clear?"

"Yes, ma'am," Olivia said.

"Recite them back to me, please."

"Leave the area at once and fly back to America," Olivia repeated and paused. "Ma'am, we have an X-1 class drone with us. It's given us visual intelligence those special forces could use if they make an assault. May we send you that data?"

Mrs. B paused on the line. "Coordinate with Mr. O and upload all the video you have. We'll make sure the Norwegians get it. Who gave you permission to take out a drone?"

Emma bit her lip. Aardvark had been so kind, and throwing him in front of the train for helping them was wrong. Olivia must have felt the same way because she didn't answer the question.

"I see. All right, we'll all sit down and hash this out in my office, ladies. Contact me when you're on the plane home."

The phone went dead.

"I knew we shouldn't have come," Nadia said.

"We were right to come," Miyuki said. "We were only too late."

"Let's get the drone back up and collect some up-to-date

video before we totally lose the sun. Do the X-1 drones have audio capability, Nadia?"

Five minutes later, the drone was back in the air with Olivia guiding it towards the facility. She did another flyby, recording in high-definition video the surrounding area. Olivia then went closer again to the buildings and shot through the windows. Some of the Venomous terrorists walked in and out of the hallways. Olivia then maneuvered the drone closer to the large glass window showing the two men in the hallway, guarding the captured Norwegian soldiers.

Olivia pressed a button, releasing the special shotgun microphone from the drone's underbelly. She aimed the microphone right at the men standing guard. She increased the gain, and the whirl of the drone's blades disappeared as the interior noise of the hallway came on full. New boot steps echoed down the hallway as Pierre, Jacqueline's assistant, rounded a corner and approached the guards.

Miyuki shook Nadia's shoulder. "It's that guy!"

"Why is he here?" Olivia asked.

On the video, the two men on guard duty straightened their stance.

"Any problems?" Pierre asked in English.

The guards shook their heads.

"Good. We've changed our minds about the prisoners. They're more of a risk if we keep them alive, so kill them all." Pierre waited for both guards to acknowledge the order before leaving them alone.

Back inside the Rover, there was an eerie silence between the girls.

"We can't let them kill those soldiers," Emma said.

"Mrs. B was quite clear. We don't interfere," Nadia said. "Besides, we can't reach them in time without putting the whole place on alert; then they'll incinerate everything."

Voices from the microphone echoed inside the SUV.

"Have you ever executed someone?" the older guard asked the younger one.

The younger guard shook his head.

The older guard wiped his mouth, unsure. "Do they have alcohol in this place? I might need a drink before we—what about you?"

The younger guard nodded and followed the first guard down the corridor.

"Sounds like they're off to get sloshed first," Olivia said.

"We should go now," Miyuki said. "Hike up mountain trail and rappel down to the buildings. Be ready for guards when they come back."

"I agree," Emma said.

Olivia made a face, as if she hated the idea. "Mrs. B will kill us all...oh, piss on it all...grab the climbing equipment and weapons and head up the trail quick as you can. Take out the guards and have the soldiers crawl out the window. Have them use your ropes to climb back up to the trail. That way we don't alert Venomous. I'll stay here and use the drone to keep an eye out for you. Get in and get out. Don't do anything else."

Ten minutes later, the sun fell behind the mountain. It was cold and the temperature dropped like a stone. Emma could feel it on her face as cloudy breaths puffed out of her mouth. The full winter parkas she'd bought in Narvik were quite comfy and should have been fine for the Arctic Circle. But Olivia insisted they buy more clothes and layer those under their parkas. Now Emma felt like an overstuffed pizza roll about to pop.

Miyuki, Nadia, and Emma headed straight north through the trees to intercept the old hiking trail that would take them up the mountain. As soon as they broke out of the trees, the girls came across the trail, which was now harder to see because of the fading sun. But Olivia guided them right to it using the drone's infrared camera.

Olivia's voice came over the girls' satellite phones, now switched to two-way radio mode. "Did you bring a flashlight? Or do you need me to guide you straight in?"

Miyuki switched on a flashlight, which lit the darkening trail ahead. Nadia pressed the transmit button on her phone. "We'll approach with the flashlight, but we'll need your help when we rappel down to the roof."

"Roger."

Miyuki picked up her pace as the trail climbed in elevation. Nadia kept up behind her. But Emma's legs screamed for her to stop.

"Can we take a five-minute break?" Emma asked.

"Sorry, it's not convenient. We have no time to spare," Miyuki said.

"Those guards will be back soon," Nadia added.

And those poor soldiers would be killed. Emma bit her lip and pushed herself forward, ignoring the pain.

After twenty minutes, the girls reached a blind curve in the trail that snaked around the mountain. Miyuki peeked over the edge. The buildings of the facility were below them. She turned off her flashlight.

Nadia hit the transmit button on her phone again. "We're in position. What's the situation now?"

Emma could see their drone, a small dark mass hovering below them. It slowly rotated around the ground near the building.

"The guards haven't returned yet," Olivia said over the radio. "Let's do this, ladies."

Miyuki took out a rock hammer and pounded three holding pins into the rocks just below the trail as Nadia tied rope lines to each pin. Emma wished she could do something to help them, but she barely knew how to tie her shoes let alone tie a rope knot that was strong enough to hold her own weight. Curious, Emma peeked over the exposed edge. There was at least a five-hundred-foot drop to the solid concrete roof of the building.

Now Emma wished she hadn't looked.

The girls finished securing the lines. Miyuki pulled her rope tight and rappelled down first. She hopped from rock to rock, confident in every move she made. Her boots dislodged rocks and lose dirt that tumbled down on the roof. Soon Miyuki made a final hop and her boots landed on the roof.

Miyuki made it look easy.

Emma became more confident. She could do this too.

"Go ahead. I'll follow you down," Nadia said.

Emma gripped the middle rope. Cold air swept into her lungs as she prepared herself. Emma slowly leaned out over the drop. This felt wrong to her body, like it was wondering what the hell her brain was thinking. But Emma felt the security of the rope holding her tight and this made her nervous stomach relax. She could do this.

Emma did a hop and descended a few feet. Not too bad. She did another hop and lowered herself down a little farther, landing on another outcropping.

Miyuki's voice came over her earbuds. "Good job, Emma! You're halfway there."

The encouragement helped Emma's confidence soar. She jumped and swung over to the left, aiming her boots at another outcropping. When Emma put her full weight on it, the outcropping broke into pieces. Her body dropped like a lead block. The shock made Emma lose her grip on the rope and it flung around like an angry water hose at full blast. She couldn't grab the damn thing as the side of the mountain rushed past her.

A scream escaped her lips.

Emma knew this was it. She was going to die.

CHAPTER 30

The mountain was mostly in shadow as a young girl's terrified scream echoed through the cold Norwegian air.

Emma flailed like a baby. Free-falling. Plummeting. Hurtling towards the solid concrete roof of the building. Once she hit it, her body would break apart like a bag of ice.

Emma shut her eyes.

This was going to hurt.

Then something yanked Emma's body to a dead stop.

She opened her eyes in just enough time to see her body's momentum swinging Emma towards the rocky side of the mountain.

She hit it and yelped as a sharp pain went through her cheek. But at least she wasn't falling anymore. Emma noticed the rings on her climbing equipment were straining against the rope that still hung tight to her body. They must have snapped into action the moment she lost her balance.

"Emma? Are you all right?" Miyuki asked from below, searching the cliff with her flashlight. Soon Miyuki's beam discovered Emma hanging in midair. "Don't move. We'll come get you."

Fear drowned Emma's senses as all her prior confidence was flushed away. Tears streamed down Emma's cheek, which now stung from the rocks. It didn't matter. She was convinced this was still the end. The cold weather soaked right through her heavy coat, causing Emma to shiver. Or did fear strip away the warmth from her body? Emma wasn't sure.

A glove rested on her shoulder. Emma turned and saw Miyuki hanging on to her first line. The girl had climbed up that rope so fast. Like she was part monkey.

"Are you hurt?" Miyuki asked. "You have a nasty bruise on your cheek."

"Think I hit a rock," Emma said, her words flooded in sobs. She couldn't help herself.

Miyuki maneuvered herself closer to Emma and wrapped an arm around her. "Don't worry. Your rope line still strong."

Nadia dropped down on Emma's right side. "How is she?"

"She'll be all right. Let's help her down," Miyuki said.

The two girls each laid a hand on Emma's opposite shoulder while balancing their other hands on their ropes. This made Emma feel better.

"Ready to go down?" Miyuki asked Emma in the sweetest voice ever.

Emma nodded.

All three girls rappelled down in smaller increments, always staying close to Emma in case they needed to help her. When her boots made a solid thump on the roof, Emma was relieved. Miyuki and Nadia freed themselves from the rope lines and helped Emma out of hers. They checked in with Olivia.

"Guards are still not back. Pressing our luck though," Olivia said over the radio. "You three better be in the hallway to intercept them. How's Emma?"

Thanks to the drone's camera, Olivia must have seen her tumble.

"We're good," Miyuki transmitted. "Stand by and we'll contact you when prisoners are released."

"Roger."

One by one, the girls slipped off the roof and landed on the ground near the large window. Miyuki took a peek while Nadia and Emma stayed out of sight.

"I don't see the guards. But the door to the room is open now."

Emma was about five feet back from the other two girls. She peeked through the window that was above her, and it looked straight into the storage room. The two guards were inside. The youngest one took a large gulp from a glass bottle of liquid. They must have found some alcohol.

"They're already inside the room," Emma said.

The older guard braced himself and aimed his rifle at the

prisoners.

Emma cursed. She had to do something. Quick.

Hanging on the back of Nadia's pack was her rock hammer.

Emma pulled it off and swung the hammer hard against the glass. The window shattered.

"What are you doing?" Nadia asked.

More glass broke as Miyuki hammered the window near her and jumped inside the building.

Emma gawked at the shattered window, amazed at how easily she'd broken it.

The two guards were staring right at her.

Emma cursed again.

"Halt!" The guards stumbled forward and leveled their rifles at Emma.

She froze with the hammer still in her hand.

The older guard stepped to the windowsill and gestured with the butt of his AK-47. "Drop the hammer and climb through the window," he ordered, slurring his words.

Emma let go and the hammer thumped to the ground. She lifted her boot to climb into the window when the younger guard called out in alarm.

Coming hard through the door, Miyuki was on the young man in a second, sweeping her legs under his and knocking his butt to the floor.

The older guard swung his rifle in Miyuki's direction. She took two steps forward, swung her body around and launched her boot at the man's head with a strike that knocked the man to the floor. Nadia came through the door to assist. But the older guard was already out cold.

The young guard was still on the floor, terrified. Miyuki picked up his AK-47 while Nadia closed the door to the storage room. Emma carefully climbed through the broken window.

Miyuki kicked the young man's boot. "Stay quiet. Try to lift one butt cheek and I give it new hole."

Nadia was already wrapping the young guard up with rope. She looked at Emma. "Could you please untie the soldiers?"

Emma went over to the first soldier she saw, an older gentleman who wore stars and fancy things on his uniform. Emma guessed he was an officer. She removed the tape over his mouth and started on his other bindings.

The Norwegian officer coughed and looked dumbfounded, as if the girls just blew his mind. "Who are you?"

A thought popped into Emma's head and she went with it.

"The Girl Scouts. We're just passing through selling cookies, and noticed you guys needed some help." She finished removing the man's bindings and hopped over to the next soldier.

Miyuki stood guard by the closed door while Nadia tied up both guards and helped Emma with freeing the rest of the soldiers. Nadia then relayed their situation to Olivia.

"That's fantastic! There's no sign of an alert either," Olivia's voice crackled over the radio. "Have the soldiers evacuate using the ropes and the trail. Good job, ladies!"

The Norwegian officer rubbed his wrists where the bindings were. "We will not evacuate. Terrorists have control of our facility and it's our duty to take it back."

Nadia looked at Emma, then Miyuki.

"You have no weapons," Miyuki said.

"Incorrect. Thanks to the Girls Scouts, we now have two machine guns," the officer said. "It's enough to storm the armory and rearm my men for an assault on the vaults."

"They'll destroy the vaults if you do," Emma said.

"We'll risk that." The officer picked up the older guard's AK-47 and checked the chamber to see if it was loaded. He reached his hand out to Miyuki, wanting her to hand over the weapon. "It's time for the professionals to do their job."

Miyuki frowned, but gave the officer her weapon.

The officer gave it to a sergeant, who took Miyuki's place guarding the door. "You girls go back the way you came. Have the authorities been contacted about the situation?"

"NATO is sending special forces, and your army has units on the way," Miyuki said.

"Reaction Plan R must be in effect. Good. We know what to do. Thanks."

The officer faced his men. He gave some kind of heroic speech in Norwegian and the men cheered. The officer and his sergeant led the soldiers down the hall, leaving the three girls alone.

"Why do I have this feeling like we've been dumped by our

boyfriends?" Emma asked.

"Now what do we do?" Nadia asked before telling Olivia the news.

"Why'd they flipping do that?" Olivia asked over the phone. "Stupid blokes and their stupid balls. They'll mess everything up."

"We'll help them," Miyuki said. "What else can we do?"

"Don't forget we have no orders," Nadia said. "We freed the prisoners and they didn't want to escape. That isn't our fault. We should leave."

Emma didn't know much about guns. She wasn't a soldier. When facing actual death on the side of a mountain, she'd cried like a child. Emma didn't think she was brave at all. Sure, she knew some karate and a few moves that could take out a rapist. But this was combat, wasn't it? Why shouldn't they leave this to the soldiers who were trained to risk their lives in situations like this? What could three teen girls do that a squad of men couldn't?

Olivia's voice came over the speakerphone, "You're right. Come on back, girls. We're in enough trouble as it is."

"I'm not going back," Miyuki said. "Those soldiers need help whether they realize it or not."

Nadia put down the phone. "Didn't you hear Olivia? She said to—"

"Olivia's not here. We are. And we can help." Miyuki glanced at Emma. "Right?" Her eyes were steel, her petite body ready for a fight. If Miyuki unleashed those fighting skills Emma had witnessed at the training center in California, Venomous wouldn't know what hit them.

Emma knew these were the people who'd killed her father and his employees. The people who had tried to destroy her family's company. Now they wanted to risk starving people to death for money. This crisis was bigger than her. There was more at stake than Emma's future as a vet. Besides, if she abandoned Miyuki now and she died trying to help the soldiers, then Emma would hate herself forever.

"We could create a diversion. Something to help distract Venomous while the soldiers make their attack on the armory."

Miyuki brightened. "Good idea, Emma."

"I swear, Miyuki—how you aggravate me so. I don't like this idea," Nadia said.

"Hey, I'm not talking about going crazy," Emma said. "I'm talking about doing something small that occupies their attention."

Nadia paced the room. Her face scrunched in frustration as she thought it over.

Her phone beeped and Olivia's voice became audible. "Is everything okay, love? You three haven't left the building yet."

"We need you," Emma said. "Three kick-ass girls are better than two. Well, maybe it's two point five girls if you count me, but still."

Nadia flashed a look at Emma, then back at her phone. "Olivia will murder me." She pressed the transmit button and informed Olivia about what the three of them were about to do.

CHAPTER 31

The three girls found themselves deep inside the Norwegian Global Seed Vault complex. Emma sensed this portion of the facility was inside the mountain itself. First, there were no windows to look out of, and second, the regular building-like walls were gone and replaced by solid rock that had been chiseled back to make these passageways. They halted at a junction point that formed a T with another passageway. Miyuki gripped the long-bladed knife she'd taken from one of the guards and peeked around the corner.

Nadia checked their position on the vault complex diagram she had on her tablet. "This branch of passageways leads to the main seed vaults," she said. "If they send men to deal with the attack on the armory, they must pass through this junction."

"We put explosives here. Set them off to seal them in," Miyuki said.

"Yes, but that won't stop them from issuing commands through the online network to burn all the food facilities and seed vaults if they sense an attack," Nadia said.

"We need another way to distract them. Something they wouldn't see as a threat." Emma took her own peek around the corner, studying the floor of the passageway. "Do we have more climbing rope?"

"Yes. I believe so," Nadia said.

"Think you could disable some of those lights in the passageway so someone couldn't see the floor well?"

"I can do that," Miyuki said. "What are your plans?"

* * *

Carved out of solid rock, the four giant seed vaults were at least three stories high. Their massive square doors were the same ones used at NORAD headquarters to seal up their Wyoming mountain fortress during a full-scale nuclear attack by the Soviet Union back in the day. All four doors were cracked open. Cables ran out of each vault and were wired into a roll-away equipment rack. A laptop sat on top of the rack with a long Ethernet cable running from the laptop to the facility's master control center computers, which were built into permanent desks.

Men dressed in black military fatigues filled the control center. Some were technicians manning the computers and laptop. Other techs were slipping in and out of the vaults, checking the cables and charges. More men stood guard with AK-47 machine guns.

Jacqueline paced the floor. Her own black fatigues had a belt snugly fitted to her waist. The belt had a radio, gun holster, military knife, and even throwing stars attached to it. Jacqueline spoke into the radio. "Asset Sixty-Nine to Asset Eight-Three."

"Go ahead," another voice replied.

"Status of the prisoners in custody?"

"Gave orders for termination. Should have been carried out by now."

"Your guards haven't contacted us yet," Jacqueline said. "See what those idiots are doing and report back. Asset Sixty-Nine out."

"Oh, you don't have to worry about those soldiers anymore," Emma said in a loud voice, her acting skills masking the fear pressing against her chest. Maybe Emma couldn't stop herself from being scared, but she sure as hell could act like she was brave.

Jacqueline came to a dead stop. The radio slipped from her hand and fell to the ground.

Every man in the room stopped what they were doing and stared in amazement at the blond, teenage girl looking gorgeous in her manufactured fur coat, leaning against one side of the control room, with her arms crossed.

"Me and the girls freed the soldiers just so we could piss you off," Emma said. "Did it work?"

Jacqueline came to her senses. Her eyes burned. "Why you little—get her!"

Emma ran out of the control room and hauled her butt down the passageway. Boots thumped behind her. She looked back and could make out four armed men. Emma swung her attention forward. It was harder to see down the passageway since Miyuki had unscrewed a few of the light bulbs. The men yelled for her to stop or they would fire.

Emma hoped they were bluffing.

She ran as hard as she could towards the T-junction point. Instead of veering left towards the base of the T, Emma ran straight past it and did a bunny hop over the rope strung out over the floor.

The first two men tripped on the rope and did hard face-plants on the ground as their weapons clattered against the floor.

The second pair of men jumped over the rope.

And that was when Miyuki and Nadia launched themselves from behind the junction. Miyuki brought her man down with one kick. Nadia threw a karate strike at the fourth man to disarm him. She then swept his legs out from under him. Emma ran back for the assist with a roundhouse kick that knocked man number four out cold. Emma was still amazed she could actually do that.

Miyuki held up her hand for a high five. "Don't leave me hanging."

The two girls slapped it. Now they each had a rifle.

Emma searched one of the unconscious men and snatched his radio.

"What will you do with that?" Nadia asked.

Emma showed her a devious grin. "Start a catfight."

Miyuki grinned and let out a meow.

Nadia rolled her eyes.

Emma pressed the transmit button. She could hear the other radios of the unconscious men echo from the feedback. "Asset Six-Nine, come in," she said.

"Asset six-nine...who is this?"

"Hi, Jacqueline! It's Emma and the girls. Sorry, but...um... four wasn't enough. You'll need to send more guys."

Miyuki covered her mouth and giggled.

"Oh, Emma." Nadia shut her eyes and said a prayer in Arabic.

A loud woman's voice echoed down the passageway as it barked out orders. Jacqueline ran out of the control room, with a gun in her hand and several armed men behind her. She fired off a whole magazine of ammo down the hallway towards the T-junction.

Nadia and Emma dropped to the ground.

Hiding behind the T-junction, Miyuki fired her machine gun and sprayed the hallway with bullets.

Jacqueline and her men stopped running and took cover along the walls and floors of the passageway. They returned gunfire.

Nadia rolled her body like a hot dog towards Miyuki and took position behind the T-junction, crouching just under Miyuki. She added her machine gun to the firefight.

Both sides were pinned down as bullets pinged off the rock walls and whizzed all over the place.

Emma soon realized that being exposed on the ground like this was no place to be. She rolled her body toward the junction like Nadia did. Once Emma was behind both of her friends and the shielding offered by the junction, Emma stood up and pressed her right shoulder against the rocky wall of their passageway. The constant rattle from the gunfight hurt Emma's ears and made her heart race way too fast.

She gripped her rifle, but didn't have any training on how to use it or even a safe place to shoot from. Unless Emma jumped to the other side of the passageway and hoped she wouldn't get turned into Swiss cheese. Emma thought better of it. It was safer here, behind her friends.

Something then pressed in between Emma's shoulder blades, making her tense up. What was that?

"I don't wanna hurt you, Emma. So please put down your weapon."

The calm, young male's voice made Emma crane her neck.

Dressed in black military fatigues, Ryan stood behind her with a gun pressing at her back. Ten armed men stood behind him with their guns drawn.

The boy smiled. "We have more guys now."

CHAPTER 32

The four giant seed vaults towered over the three girls. Jacqueline had her men tie each girl to one of the main iron support beams that kept the ten-thousand-foot mountain from crushing the facility into a pancake. Emma noticed the explosive charges inside the control room and assumed the vaults were wired too. There was more activity around the computers and the roll-away equipment rack anchored with the network of cables leading out to the vaults.

Emma still wondered about the single laptop on top of the rack. Venomous must have brought it with them, since it didn't match anything else in the control center and had to be plugged in by a long extension cord. She wondered what the laptop controlled. Emma saw Nadia studying the same thing. If anyone knew how to use that laptop to shut all this down, she did. Emma then caught sight of Ryan. The traitor.

The boy watched her from across the room, like he did when they sat together on that rock by the lake. Blinking those cute eyes of his and trying to woo her with that dimpled chin. Emma would give anything for a shot at that chin with the heel of her boot.

Emma wondered why Ryan was helping Venomous. Did he lie to her about everything? Was Ryan secretly helping his dad while lying to her about it all? Too many questions and Emma didn't know if she would live long enough to get the answers.

Jacqueline paced the floor before she was back on the radio. "Asset Sixty-Nine to Asset Eighty-Eight. Have you found the soldiers yet? What is your situation?" The radio crackled, but no one answered. "*Merde*," Jacqueline yelled. She ran up to Nadia. "Where did the soldiers go after you released them?"

Nadia was silent.

Jacqueline struck her across the face. "Answer me, you Muslim rat."

Nadia's face hardened. She was a rock.

Jacqueline hit her face with another slap.

Nadia didn't look up again. But a tear formed in the corner of her eye.

Jacqueline moved over to Miyuki, who met the woman's eyes with an unnerving stare like the black eyes of a cobra all coiled up and ready to strike.

Jacqueline skipped her and stood in front of Emma. "Where did the soldiers go after you released them? You'll save those men's lives if you tell us. I don't want to kill prisoners. I only want them out of the way. If they surrender, then we won't have to hunt them down and risk hurting them."

Emma didn't believe her.

The radio crackled. "Asset Eighty-Three to Asset Sixty-Nine." Gunfire could be heard in the background. "The soldiers have taken over the armory. Five of my men are dead. Retreating back to the break room area. We'll make our stand there."

"Of course, the damn armory," Jacqueline said to herself before answering the radio. "Understood. I'll send you what I can." She pointed to one man. "Send your unit to the break room area."

The man nodded and ordered his men to follow him, taking away most of the armed men in master control. But Emma noted that some of the techs still had pistols in their holsters and most likely knew how to use them. Plus Emma was shackled to a metal support beam by people who knew how to secure someone. Emma wiggled around and found her handcuffs gave no slack whatsoever. Emma assumed Nadia and Miyuki were finding out the same thing. Emma just hoped that Olivia would find a way to save them in time.

Ryan eased his way over to Emma. She looked away, refusing to meet his eyes.

"Sorry about all this."

"Spare me your pity. I don't want it," Emma said.

"I'd never pity you. But I do want to explain."

"Like father, like son. What is there to explain?"

Ryan bristled at the comment. "I'm not like my father. He only cares about making money and showing off. He can't rise above that. I can."

"Alright, I think I'm putting it together now. You're doing all this to spite your dad. Taking some crazy plan he dreamed up and using it against him."

Ryan paused. "To be honest, Venomous wanted to expand my father's plan. They're more ambitious than he was, and I like that about them. Venomous is an organization with vision. They understand the true meaning of power."

"If Venomous is so above money, why do they want fifty billion dollars?"

"A criminal organization runs on money. Same as a major corporation. You need money in order to exercise power."

"I actually felt sorry for you," Emma said. "I thought we could talk to each other."

"You can always talk to me."

"I would tell you to talk to my middle finger, but it's tied up at the moment."

"I know you're upset, and I understand why you would be."

"Causing millions of people to starve to death would upset most people, Ryan."

"The United Nations will never let it go that far. They'll pay us soon."

"And what if they don't? Can you live with the consequences?" Emma asked.

"I'm not the one throwing the switch."

"Maybe not. But you're supplying electricity to the chair."

Ryan balked at that last comment and went silent for a moment.

Jacqueline's assistant Pierre jogged into the room.

"Why are you here, Eight-Three?" Jacqueline asked.

"Asset One sent me a message. He'll be transmitting soon," Pierre said.

"Excellent. Perhaps they've heard from the UN. What's your situation?"

"My men have held off the soldiers in the break area. Our evacuation route is still open."

"Excellent work."

"A transmission is coming in, Miss Boyay," a tech called out to the room.

"On screen."

Everyone turned their attention to the master control area, where a large monitor above flickered to life. A man wearing dark sunglasses with thick white frames appeared. He had extra-long blond hair which hung straight down each side. The man's square face contained no emotion.

Resting on the back of the man's chair was...

Was Emma hallucinating? No. Resting on the back of the man's chair was a beautiful black falcon. It stood proudly behind its owner.

Jacqueline straightened as Pierre stood by her side.

"Status of your operation, Six-Nine?" The man's voice was deep, rough, and filled one's bones with fear.

Jacqueline stepped forward. "The global seed vaults are rigged for incineration."

"Do we still have remote control...over the AirTech climate control systems?"

"Yes. The network is still strong. We can wipe out over four hundred facilities around the world from our location. It's enough to carry out our threat."

"Quite acceptable," white sunglasses man said.

"Have the United Nations given in to our demands?"

"They create excuses. Delays. Our patience...wears thin," white sunglasses man said. "Behind you..."

Jacqueline hesitated and then turned. "The seed vaults?"

"The girls. Who are they?"

"Oh...them," Jacqueline said. "The Authority is recruiting children against us. I'll have them killed at once."

"The Authority...they're aware of your plans?"

Emma noticed that this white sunglasses man had a strange way of speaking. He paused in the middle of his sentences, taking his time to speak as if each syllable had as much meaning as an entire book.

"A minor inconvenience, sir. They have been dealt with, as you can see."

"The soldiers...attacking your position...when they surrendered...why were they not killed?"

Jacqueline eyed Pierre, who betrayed nothing. "We have the Norwegians pinned down. They will not cause any disruption to our plans. You have nothing to worry about, sir."

The black falcon stretched, extending its large wings.

"On the contrary...since this operation began there have been...complications. We worry about complications."

"I've dealt with each complication and eradicated it," Jacqueline said.

"Your methods of dealing with complications...lead to more complications. This is unsatisfactory to us. First error...killing an ex-Authority member in a jet crash...ignoring that such an action...would attract their attention. Second error...the failure on numerous occasions...to kill these Authority 'children' as you say. Now these children have released your prisoners...who are now armed and threaten to disrupt your operation. And finally... the third error...trusting this operation to a man like—"

"May I speak?" Jacqueline interrupted.

The man with the white sunglasses leaned forward. "Do you feel...that is wise?"

Jacqueline lowered her head. "Forgive me."

White sunglasses man eased back into his chair. "And finally...trusting a man like Ron Raymond as a partner...in such an important operation. His capture...further jeopardized it." The man stopped and crossed his legs. The falcon walked down the man's arm and hopped on top of his leg, using it as a perch. "This organization prides itself...on efficiency. We despise sloppiness. We regret...your talents...will no longer be required, Six-Nine."

Terror gripped Jacqueline's face, her confidence gone. "But we're so close to the end. I promise you that this operation will succeed. I—"

Jacqueline clutched her chest as pain overwhelmed her face. Pain so intense, Jacqueline fell to her knees.

"This operation will succeed...if you are not leading it."

The woman cried out as she rolled to the floor, still clutching her chest.

"Asset of the eighty-third order?" White sunglasses man asked without emotion.

"Yes, Asset of the first order?" Pierre answered.

"Commence the incineration...evacuate the facility. You are now...in command. Asset of the ninety-fifth order?"

Ryan stepped forward. "Yes, sir?"

"Your contribution to this operation...has been noted. You will be second-in-command. Carry out the orders."

"Yes, sir."

The screen went black.

CHAPTER 33

On the cold floor of the control center, Jacqueline's body didn't move. Her eyes were still open and staring at nothing. Emma was sure she was dead. What did they do to her? Who was that weirdo with the falcon? What would happen to them? There was one person Emma could ask. The same person she never wanted to speak to again.

Emma forced her mouth to say it. "Ryan?"

The boy stood near Pierre, who was giving last minute orders to his men still left inside the control center. Ryan held up his hand, as if telling her to wait. He then came over. "Yes?"

"May I have a sip of water? My mouth is dry."

Ryan smiled. "Sure." He left for about five minutes and came back with a bottle of water. Ryan opened the plastic top and held it up for her, gently tilting it so she could have a good swig.

"More?"

Emma nodded.

Ryan tilted the bottle again and Emma took in more of the cool liquid.

"Thanks," she said.

"My pleasure."

"What happened to Jacqueline?"

Ryan glanced over at the woman's body. "Asset One had her chip activated. It triggered a heart attack."

"What do you mean chip? Like a computer chip inside her body?"

"We all have one surgically inserted." Ryan turned his left arm over, pulling back the armband of his watch to expose his wrist. There was a small incision, barely a scar. "Most of the time the chip only sends pain messages to the nervous system.

However, a message can be sent for the heart to stop beating."

"Why? What's the purpose of that?"

"Discipline. Order. Venomous operates on the principles of reward and punishment. You either succeed or you fail. Failure means pain. Success means reward. Honest and simple. Normally Jacqueline would have received a heavy shock not strong enough to kill her." Ryan looked back at Jacqueline. "But she made too many mistakes. Pierre and I were hoping Asset One would realize that. And he did."

"It all sounds brutal to me. Who is Asset One?"

"The man on top of the pyramid."

"He referred to you as Nine-Five," Emma said. "So that means Asset Nine-Five?"

"I'm on my way up in the organization. After this operation, I might get promoted into the eighties."

Emma sneaked a peek at Nadia and Miyuki. Both girls had the same look. Emma knew what they were thinking because she realized it too. They were helpless. Unless Pierre and Ryan took the girls with them, they would die in the inferno when this place went up.

Ryan touched her face. "Done with your water?"

"Yes. Thank you."

Ryan was still friendly to her. He still wanted Emma to think he was a good guy. Wanted her to believe in what he was doing. Maybe Emma could use that to her advantage. Maybe she could get Ryan to change his mind and go against Pierre and his operatives. It was worth a try at least.

Emma calmed herself and reached down deep inside her acting bag of tricks. Emotions began to float up to the surface. She felt a tear streaking down her face.

"What will happen to us?" Her voice quivered slightly. So slightly it sounded genuine.

Ryan knelt down and stroked her blond hair. "You'll be left here. Most likely."

"To burn to death?" Emma's voice shook just a tiny bit more. Damn, she was good.

Ryan's mouth softened. "What else can we do? If we let you go, your friends will disrupt the operation, maybe capture all of us. I wish you hadn't come. This would be easier. I never wanted to hurt you." Ryan's mouth went stiff. "But I gave an oath to Venomous, so I can't back out now." Ryan played with the ends of her hair, not wanting to let go. "Why did you have to come? You should never have gotten involved with any of this. You should be home in California, where I could've met you at some coffee shop and asked you out. I bet we would've fallen in love."

Emma went in for the kill. "It could still be like that. We could have a future."

"How? How could we do that?"

"I'll have to whisper it. I don't want the other girls to hear."

Ryan looked confused, but leaned over close. Very close.

"What if I joined?" Emma whispered.

Ryan searched her eyes. "Joined? You mean join Venomous?"

"I know a lot of things about The Authority. I could be valuable." She stared into his blue eyes. "And we would be together." Emma drifted her lips to his and kissed him. Ryan loosened up and kissed her back. This unleashed a series of light and tender kisses.

Ryan withdrew his lips; his breathing was fast and out of control. He opened the bottle of water and finished the rest of it.

Emma knew she had him. "Is there somewhere we could talk? Privately?" Emma referenced Miyuki and Nadia. Another hint she wanted to defect.

Ryan watched her a moment, no doubt trying to decide if he could trust her. "One moment."

The boy stood up and discussed something with two of the Venomous technicians. They came back with Ryan and unlocked the chains from Emma's hands and legs.

She stretched her limbs, trying to avoid them cramping up. "Thank you." Emma drew cold stares from Miyuki and Nadia, as if they felt something wasn't right. As if they expected Emma to selfishly save herself by any means necessary.

Ryan rested his hand on her back and guided Emma inside a small supply closet, switching the light on and closing the door. Emma sat on a box of printer paper while Ryan leaned against an empty shelf.

"How about some information first?" Ryan asked. "Tell me something we don't know."

"NATO is sending a special forces team here. They could be on the ground already. The Norwegians should be here with army units too; I wouldn't be surprised if they've reinforced the soldiers you're battling in the break room. Your situation is hopeless. You could destroy the seed, but you can't get out of here alive," Emma said.

"Don't worry about escape. We have a plan. Sounds like we need to leave immediately before our men are overwhelmed. Thank you, Emma."

She tilted forward and wrapped her arms around Ryan, placing another kiss on his lips. The boy responded by cradling her lower back with his arms. Emma allowed him this privilege as she pressed her fingers against the inside of his thigh. Ryan opened his legs, expecting something special from her.

And Ryan did get something special.

A karate strike to his walnuts.

Ryan's voice went up a few octaves as he shrieked. Emma then shoved him into the wall, brought her leg up and pressed her hiking boot against his neck, pinning the boy to the wall. Emma leaned on her heel, making the boy gasp for breath.

"Please drop the gun on the floor. I'm not playing."

Ryan didn't at first. But another shove of her boot made the boy comply as his mind starved for oxygen. He dropped the gun.

She removed her leg, and Ryan collapsed into the corner of the supply closet, still overwhelmed by the pain between his legs.

Emma picked up the gun and edged towards the door. The only thing she could do was somehow slip out of the closet and not be seen sneaking out of the control room. Then maybe Emma could make it into the passageway and gain some time to think about what to do next.

Emma calmed herself and opened the door for a peek. From what she could see, Emma had a straight shot across the room to the passageway. She might be able to make it over there undetected if she were quick and lucky.

Emma opened the door and prepared herself to launch forward when…a gun hammer clicked back.

Then another click.

Emma glanced around the door.

The two technicians Ryan had talked to earlier were aiming their guns at her face.

Emma dropped hers.

CHAPTER 34

Emma's gun was taken away as the control room technicians chained her back against the iron support beam near the four giant seed vaults. Right back where she started. Ryan waited for them to finish and return to their workstations before he knelt down in front of Emma. Ryan grimaced from the aftereffects of the girl's attack.

Emma smiled to herself.

"Well played," he said. "For a brief second, I believed you. So disappointing. You would have made an excellent partner."

"Screw you," Emma said in a calm voice. She didn't want to give the guy any satisfaction of seeing her getting emotional about the situation. If this was it for her…if her young life was about to come to an end, Emma wanted to face it like a young woman, not a child.

"You're an impressive girl. It's such a waste to leave you here."

"Ryan? Your compliments sink to the bottom of my stomach. In other words—spare me your pity."

Pierre came over to Ryan. "I've contacted the submarine. Begin the evacuation while I set the charges."

Ryan helped the technicians pack up their gear as they hustled out of the control room and down the passageway. Pierre radioed his men still fighting in the break room to pull back and evacuate. He then used the laptop on top of the roll-away equipment rack.

Ryan lingered around Emma.

Pierre finished his work and noticed Ryan. "Don't be gracious and shoot them. Let them burn along with the seeds. The enemies of Venomous deserve no mercy."

"Of course," Ryan said. "See you at the submarine. I'll help these last two men pack."

Pierre hurried out of the control center.

"A submarine?" Emma asked, her curiosity too strong to stay silent. "How will you pull that off?"

"One thing I must credit Jacqueline for...she was brilliant when it came to planning an operation. It's an ingenious escape plan. A small submarine through the ice. There's a flooded cave on one of the lower levels of the facility, where the water purification equipment for the facility's drinking water is located. Most of the water is frozen on the surface, but the cave itself empties into a fjord near here. The cave is just big enough for the submarine to pop in and out."

The last two technicians hustled out of the room.

Ryan kissed Emma on the forehead. He then produced a set of keys out of his pocket and moved behind her. Emma felt the keys being put inside her palm.

"A present for you," Ryan whispered. "You won't have enough time to stop the bomb or save your friends. But you might have time to save yourself. I hope you make that choice." Ryan brushed her blond hair back. "Goodbye, Emma."

Ryan grabbed his things and ran out of the room.

Emma couldn't believe he did that. But there they were, the smooth, cold keys in her hand.

She had to hurry.

Emma fumbled with the set of keys, trying to find the keyhole strictly by feel. There it was. She tried the first key. Didn't fit. She then tried the second one. Too big. The third key slipped into place and she turned it. Emma didn't hear a click. Did it work? Emma tried pulling her wrists apart and a metal clang echoed as the handcuffs dropped to the floor. Her wrists were free.

Nadia and Miyuki both heard the sound.

"Hurry! We don't have much time," Nadia said.

Emma used the set of keys to free the other locks and pulled the chains off her body and ankles. She stumbled over to Nadia with the keys and tried her locks.

None of the keys fit. It was just like Ryan had said.

"These keys won't unlock you."

"Try Miyuki's handcuffs," Nadia said.

Emma rushed over to Miyuki.

The keys wouldn't fit hers either.

"Damn it," Emma said.

Miyuki's dark eyes softened. "You should run...save yourself."

Emma knew she was right. But how could she leave her friends here to die? Maybe she could somehow stop the bombs from going off.

The laptop. Emma ran over to the roll-away equipment rack. "Can you hack into their system?"

"I can try," Nadia said.

Emma brought over the laptop with its long Ethernet cable connected to the other computers. It barely reached. Emma laid the computer on the floor.

Nadia squinted. "I can't see it down there."

Emma searched the room and found a chair. She brought it over and placed the laptop on top. "How's that?"

"Much better." Nadia studied the screen for a moment. "This program controls the AirTech climate control systems in all those facilities Jacqueline talked about. It's on a five-minute timer. Emma? Click on the next menu for me."

Emma double-clicked.

Nadia studied it closely. "These systems are programmed to spray fuel through the irrigation system and ignite it throughout all the food-production plants and storage facilities. Let's see if we can shut it down. Emma? I need you to be my hands. Click on the C drive." Nadia guided Emma through the laptop as she tried to make changes to the computer program. An error message flashed on the screen...

Changes require administrator password.

"I don't have enough time to hack their password." Nadia sighed.

"Can you kill the program?" Miyuki asked.

Nadia examined the screen and shook her head. "Not without triggering the backup programs inside the other computers. Venomous has them programmed to execute their commands automatically if they lose communication with this laptop."

"What? You mean there's no cancel button?" Emma asked.

"Once this program is activated, it won't stop until the countdown runs out."

"So pulling the Ethernet cable is no good either?" Miyuki asked.

Nadia shook her head.

"How much time is left?" Miyuki asked.

"About three minutes," Emma said, her voice wavering. "What can we do? There has to be something. Think."

"I don't have access to their network. That password is the only way to get in using this...laptop..." Nadia trailed off, her mind turning gears.

"Did you think of something?" Emma asked.

"The back door I put in still might be in the Raymond Foods mainframe. Open the Internet browser."

Emma's fingers hurried with clicks and swishes across the mouse pad. Nadia told her a web address to go to. She gave Emma the password and username to get in. The Internet page loaded. Graphics came up saying *Welcome, Nadia!* A bunny rabbit hopped over to bring flowers.

"Seriously?" Emma chuckled.

"Oh...just double-click on the bunny."

Emma did what Nadia asked. The webpage blinked a couple times and suddenly they had access to another program. The Raymond Foods logo was in the corner of the page.

"Yes!" Nadia became excited. "Through Jacqueline's work computer, I now have access to their network."

"Now what?" Emma asked. "Can we shut down the other computers?"

"Wait. Oh, that should work! All we need to do is give a command to all the network computers to reboot themselves using their last restore point. Hopefully that should bypass the Venomous program that was installed later."

"How much time do we have?" Miyuki asked.

"Two minutes," Emma said.

"Since we have access to the emergency systems, let's trigger the fire alarms to get people out of the buildings just in case." Nadia issued more instructions to Emma as she went in and out of various menus, each one controlling a different group of facilities under each company. The Lester-Sumner Food Corporation in Australia. Raymond Foods in America, Europe, and Africa. Kyo-Shun Foods in China. Ganchi Farms in Mumbai, India. And finally Ovechkin-Komstat in Ukraine.

A series of similar messages ran down the screen...

Rebooting system to last restore point.

"Go back to the countdown screen," Nadia said.

Emma clicked out of a few menus and brought up the event timer. The numbers counted down to forty-five seconds.

"Look!" Nadia pointed at the screen. "All the facilities are now grayed out. This computer can't send out any commands to the climate control systems."

"What about the explosives here?" Miyuki asked.

Nadia's happiness disappeared. "We saved the world. But not us. This laptop doesn't trigger the local explosives. It only starts the clock inside that equipment rack."

Emma cursed as she raced over to the rack. "What should I do? Is there some wire I can pull?"

"Rip open the box and look," Miyuki said. "See where the wires are all bunched up."

"Thirty seconds," Nadia said.

Emma felt around the box, looking for a way inside. Her fingers touched some metal clasps. She pulled up on the clasps and the panel popped out. She tossed it and searched inside the small equipment rack. A jumble of wires ran up through the bottom of the box into some kind of junction box.

Emma searched around for something to pry open the junction box with. She ran all over the control room like a crazy girl and found zilch.

"There's a screwdriver on that table!" Miyuki said, jerking her head towards it.

"Twenty seconds."

Emma flew over to the table, grabbed the screwdriver, and ran back to the rack. She jammed the end of the screwdriver around the edge of the metal panel protecting the junction box and tried to pry it off, using all her strength.

"Fifteen seconds."

The square panel popped off, exposing three skinny little wires.

"Is the red wire good or bad?" Emma asked.

"Red wires are bad," Nadia said.

"But that could be the one she needs to cut," Miyuki said.

"Blue? Is blue the one I should cut? Or how about this yellow one?"

Miyuki and Nadia looked at each other.

Emma realized they had no idea. She examined the three wires. Cutting the wrong one would splatter them across the rocks and bury them here for hundreds of years. Cutting the right one would...

The yellow wire. Emma always did like yellow.

"Five seconds!"

Emma pulled the yellow wire and braced for the explosion.

Nothing happened.

She glanced at Miyuki and Nadia.

They both smiled.

Emma flopped down on the ground in total relief. Her lungs drew in as much air as they could hold.

A loud clatter of footsteps echoed down the passageway as Olivia appeared around the corner with a gun in hand. She lowered it and smiled when Olivia saw her friends. But the girl tensed up at the sight of all the explosives rigged around the control center. "I need that flipping bomb squad up here now!"

A squad of Norwegian soldiers dressed in padded bomb gear ran around the corner and descended on the small equipment rack.

One of the bomb techs pushed Emma away. "We've got this, young lady."

"But I pulled the—"

The techs ignored Emma as they analyzed the bomb mechanism and wiring, talking among themselves in rushed, excited voices.

Soon, the leader of the squad ripped off a layer of padding on his clothes.

"Stand down," he said. "This bomb has already been disarmed."

Emma stood up and raised her chin with pride. "I was going to say…it was the yellow wire."

CHAPTER 35

Grandma's garden became chilly as the clouds rolled in from the bay and shut out the afternoon sun. The woman wrapped herself in a Navajo Indian blanket and relaxed on one of the canvas lawn chairs, reading Robert Frost as she burned more sage in a clay pot.

Emma watched Grandma through the French doors in the kitchen.

"Just go ask her, love," Olivia said.

"It's not as simple as that," Emma said. "My grandma despises everything about The Authority, and she doesn't trust Grandma Laura…I mean Mrs B."

"Grandma Laura?" Miyuki asked.

"You're related?" Nadia asked.

"Hold on," Olivia said. "You're messing with us, right?"

Emma hesitated. "You guys can't tell anyone. Seriously. I don't think Mrs. B wants you to know."

"You're flipping serious? You and Mrs. B are relatives?"

"Tell us everything!" Miyuki said.

"To be honest…even I don't know the whole story yet, so stay tuned for further updates." Emma turned her attention back to Grandma and scoffed. "I can't do this now."

On the other side of the glass, Snoopy ran up to the French doors and barked at Emma. His tail wagged with excitement.

"Puppy!" Miyuki said as she waved.

Outside, Grandma leaned forward in her chair to look. She smiled and slipped a bookmark into her novel.

Emma rolled her eyes. "Thanks, puppy." She opened the French doors and stepped out into the garden. The chill in the air made Emma wrap her arms around her midsection before making herself comfortable on a lawn chair next to Grandma.

"It's cool today," Grandma said. "You'll need a blanket if you want to stay out here."

"It's fine," Emma said. "Can I talk to you?"

Grandma placed her book on a side table and folded her arms across her chest. She raised her eyebrows to imply that she was ready.

"Think I understand now why my mother and dad joined The Authority. It felt…good to stop the bad guys. When Dad met Mom, didn't he believe in what The Authority was doing? If Dad was as high in the organization as Grandma Laura said he was, it must have meant very much to him, didn't it?"

Grandma hesitated. "It did…until your mother's death broke him. Like your death would break me."

Emma saw it in her eyes. Her grandmother's worst fear. "Life isn't a guarantee, is it? I could be driving to school one day. Flying on a plane. Standing at the wrong place at the wrong time. Death is everywhere. I can't let it stop me from doing what I want to be doing."

"You should be a vet like you wanted. A person who saves living creatures, not destroys them."

"I want to be a spy. Like Mom was."

Grandma's wrinkled hands played with the ends of the Navajo blanket. "Is this goodbye, young one?"

"What? No way. I'm staying here with you and going to public school, just like you wanted. I talked it over with Grandma Laura and she agreed." Emma got up from her chair and sat next to Grandma, wrapping herself inside the same blanket, leaning against her like she did when Emma was young. Grandma's hand brushed back Emma's hair as the two just sat there a moment, enjoying each other's company.

"Why are those girls here?" Grandma finally asked.

"Grandma Laura would like you to take them in."

Grandma chuckled. "Of course she does. What does she think this place is? A youth hostel?"

"These three girls are my friends and they're far away from their families. They need a home and we have plenty of room here. I think it's a great idea."

"Let me take a stab at this. If I don't take these girls in, Laura will insist on keeping you away from me?"

"Nope. It's a request, not a threat," Emma said. "And I'm making the request because they're awesome girls. Seriously, you would like them, Grandma."

"If I allow them to live here, then I would be contributing to Laura's fascist organization."

Emma rolled her eyes. "Oh my God. You're so stubborn. They're not fascists. You don't even know what you're talking about."

"I've never trusted them, Emma. Even when your father was a member. I never trusted them."

"Do you trust me?"

"You know the answer to that."

"So when it comes to my friends, you know I'm telling you the truth. This isn't for Grandma Laura. This is for me."

Grandma sighed and thought about it. "For you, huh?"

Emma flashed her the cutest little-girl-like smile ever. "Please?"

Grandma didn't answer.

"I can't do any of this without you."

"Well, I won't do it for Laura." Grandma combed her fingers through Emma's hair. "But...I'll do it for you. And only you." Grandma's face hardened. "If these girls live under my roof, then they'll have to follow my rules. Even if Laura disagrees with them."

"I think it's safe to say that Grandma Laura already anticipated your terms and will reluctantly accept them."

* * *

The school's auditorium stage was bathed in colors. White for the actors. Orange for the wooden set representing the faraway pyramids of Egypt. Blue to emphasize the painted sky backdrop above it all. It was the Sunday matinee and the last school performance of *The Spy Who Loathed Me.*

Emma stood on stage in her floor-length dress. Once again, she played Olga Tetrovich the Russian spy. And once again, M16 spy George Bond hid behind a fake tree, waiting for Olga to show him the location of the microfilm.

Emma picked up the clay model of the pyramids from a souvenir stand, smashed it against the table once again, and held up the microfilm for the audience to see. But this time Emma sneaked a peek at them.

Grandma's white hair with two ponytails was easy to pick out. But there were three other girls with her...Olivia, Nadia, and Miyuki, their eyes captivated by what was happening on stage, like they were totally into it. That was what fascinated Emma about live theater. The hold an actor could have on an audience. It was powerful. And so wonderful.

As Emma turned to face Bond, she noted a tall man standing in back of the auditorium. He was quiet and hovered near an older woman gripping a cane. Emma smiled to herself and went on with the scene without a second thought.

That afternoon's matinee performance went off without much of a hitch. Even Lewis pushed himself and turned in an awesome performance that earned him a few extra claps at the end. After their curtain call, Emma and the rest of the cast came out to the lobby to greet the audience, a custom their drama teacher encouraged.

Emma received a lot of attention, especially from the old ladies, who would hold her hand and say she had talent. Emma finally was able to break away from all the strangers and join Grandma and her friends. There was no sign of Mrs. B or Aardvark; perhaps she'd had to leave early to plan some future operation.

"Please quench my curiosity," Grandma said. "Is this play based on the James Bond movie or the Ian Fleming novel?"

"It's based on all the spy movies," Emma said. "The playwright mashed together scenes from the movies and created a storyline to match. It's more of a loving tribute to James Bond. That's why Bond is named George. It was a big hit on Broadway a couple of years ago."

"I see. Well, you elevated the material up to a point where it was entertaining."

"What's your costar's name again?" Olivia asked.

"Lewis. He was good tonight, wasn't he?"

"He's easy on the eyes."

Miyuki clapped her hands together. "You have a crush!"

"Just said the bloke was handsome. That's all."

Nadia poked Olivia's shoulder. "Tell him how much you liked his performance."

Olivia cocked her head and checked out the boy standing on the other side of the lobby...alone. "Maybe I will."

Olivia stuffed her hands in her jean pockets and nonchalantly moved in the boy's general direction. Lewis made eye contact with her and smiled. This caused Olivia to veer away from him and pretend to get a drink at the water fountain.

The girls all laughed.

"Emma?" It was Mrs. Tuttle, her drama teacher. She held a bouquet of twenty-four roses. "These were just delivered with your name on them."

"Thank you." Emma took the bouquet and marveled how beautiful and fresh the roses were, from a first-class florist for sure. She found a gold envelope and popped open the seal. Inside was a fancy card with crisp edges. Emma slipped it out. There was a note handwritten in ink...

Congratulations. You were so beautiful on stage that I couldn't keep my eyes off you. Glad I spared your life. Heading off to Egypt myself to see the real pyramids. I'll send you a picture.

Unless you'd like to join me?

Ryan

THANK YOU FOR READING!

Dear Awesome Reader,

I hope *Spies Like Me* met with your approval. This is the first book of The Gems spy thriller series and it was inspired by my obsession with James Bond movies. (Sean Connery is still the best!) I've been wanting to write a spy series for a long time and finally I was able to come up with a concept that I haven't seen in the world of young adult novels. I want this series to be fun, yet I still want to put the emphasis on the characters and the story instead of the gadgets. (Although, I'll put in just enough for the spy-gadget geeks like me out there)

I'm proud of the girls. I wanted them to come from different cultures, but not have those cultural differences define them as characters. I plan to use each girl's point of view in future books as a tool to help tell the story. Since there was so much to introduce in this first book, I didn't have time to explore Emma or the girls' lives at school. Believe me, this will be a constant problem for The Gems in future novels. Because how does a girl fit in spy missions, a social life, and school work on a weekly basis? I'm looking forward to seeing how the girls juggle both sides of their soon-to-be-hectic lives.

Book reviews are huge to authors! You don't have to give a full book report, a sentence or two is fine. But I would love an online review of this book if you have time. Love it or hate it. Doesn't matter. I would just enjoy the feedback.

What do you think of the new characters? What would you like to see in future novels? I'd love to hear from you! Please feel free to write me at dougthewriter@gmail.com or visit www.dougsolter.com for more options to stay in contact.

Want some free stuff? If you join my Readers' Group List you'll get free digital books plus other goodies! You'll also be the first to know when I have a new book out or have something awesome to give away. Don't worry, your details will never be shared and you can unsubscribe whenever you want.

Thank you again for reading *Spies Like Me*!

All the best,

Doug Solter

ACKNOWLEDGMENTS

Beta readers are critical in helping shape a novel. Without their feedback this novel wouldn't be half as good. Huge thanks to my key beta readers Kate Tilton and Laura Benedict. A big thanks to new beta reader Jorie from Jorie Loves a Story Book Blog. Jorie challenged me on many things in the book which I'm glad for since it made the manuscript clearer and stronger. Thanks, Jorie!

Travis Miles, for designing book covers like a Greek god. (If the ancient Greek gods actually designed book covers) His website: www.probookcovers.com

My editor Pauline Nolet, for working with me when I missed my deadline. She provided exceptional proofreading and editing as always. Her website: www.paulinenolet.com

Max Adams, for her writing classes and constant support of her students. I highly recommend her screenwriting classes. Her website: www.theafw.com

For their constant support: Jerry Bennett, Renee Bilyeau, H.M. Clarke, Joe Kinkade, Trevor and Talon Lane, Jennifer Latham, Valarie Lawson, Barbara Lowell, Erin McHenry, Anna Myers, James Morgan and his family, Helen Newton, Cheryl Rainfield, Shelby and Marlee, Courtney Summers, and Amy Tipton. All my friends at the Oklahoma chapter of SCBWI. All my screenwriting friends through Max Adams' AFW program. I appreciate you all!

Thank you to all my friends and family.

And another thank you to Dad for supporting my life.

ABOUT THE AUTHOR

Doug Solter began writing screenplays in 1998 and became a 2001 semi-finalist in the Academy of Motion Pictures Arts and Sciences' Nicholl Fellowships in Screenwriting. Doug made the switch to writing young adult novels in 2008. He is also a member of the Society of Children's Book Writers and Illustrators. Doug respects cats, loves the mountains, and one time walked the streets of Barcelona, Spain with a smile on his face.

ALSO BY DOUG SOLTER

ISBN-13: 978-1502412638

Only eight races left to turn it all around.

Only at the bottom does Samantha finally understand. She's pushed everyone away. A comeback? That's almost impossible. How can Samantha convince the team to believe in her again? And the competition on the track is fierce. Samantha needs an edge. But she has no idea where to look or anyone willing to help her find it.

It's difficult being on the same team with Samantha, so Manny distracts himself by working on his experimental transmission. It's revolutionary...but so far unreliable. Another welcome distraction is Hanna. She's willing to help her ex-boyfriend forget all about Samantha.

ISBN-13: 978-1502412638

Dad taught Samantha how to handle everything inside a racing car...except the world outside of one.

Racing in her second F1 season, Samantha wants to prove she's a future world champion. But what stands in her way? Her new teammate Emilio Ronaldo. Last season the man humiliated her. This season...it's payback.

Emilio once thought Samantha was a joke...he was wrong. Emilio now wants to be Samantha's mentor. But how? The angry young lady has shut him out. Patience is Emilio's gift. But will he run out of time before Emilio can fix things right?

Manny is in love. Samantha is...well, she's his everything. But during the season, Samantha changes. What the hell is going on? Manny doesn't know and Samantha can't tell him. If this keeps up...Manny will have to do something drastic.

ISBN-13: 978-1477432655

2013 Best Young Adult Indie Book Semi-finalist
- Kindle Book Review

Seventeen year old Samantha killed her father in a tragic accident. Her father's dreams for her will be fulfilled...even if it destroys her. Eighteen year old Manny is next in line to run his uncle's Formula One team. But he's not ready. It's hard to be confident when the crew still sees Manny as that shy kid they would tease in the garage.

When Samantha's driving talents put her inside Manny's world, even the crew feels the electricity between them. Samantha thinks she can face her fears. But she's wrong. First female world champion? Samantha won't stand a chance unless Manny can step-up and be her rock. When the dark clouds unleash their fury. When her hands quiver on the wheel. When the walls close in at over 230 miles per hour.

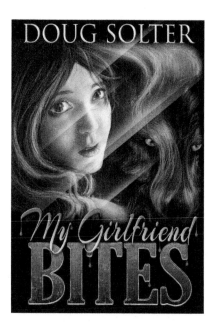

ISBN-13: 978-1491275337

**2014 Best Young Adult Indie Book Semi-finalist
- Kindle Book Review**

Sixteen-year-old Aiden wants a girlfriend, but struggles with depression. A girl falling in love with him? There's no way. Aiden tried to kill himself once. He might try it again.

Hiding inside a human city is lonely for a girl. But Bree can't make friends at her new school. They might find out what she really is.

A rainy-day brings them together. A dark night reveal makes Bree all too real. Aiden must accept her.All the fur. And all the fangs. Bree must teach Aiden to believe in himself before it's too late. Her enemies are coming. She'll need his help. They'll wipe out her parents just like they wiped out her pack. If no one stops them, they'll wipe out her species.